KATYA

Kathryn Mattingly

Winter Goose
PUBLISHING

Winter Goose Publishing
45 Lafayette Road #114
North Hampton, NH 03862

wintergoosepublishing.com
Contact Information: info@wintergoosepublishing.com

Katya

COPYRIGHT © 2022 by Kathryn Mattingly

Cover Design and Formatting by Winter Goose Publishing

ISBN: 978-1-952909-25-2

Published in the United States of America

For Hailey, Taryn, Maya, Alexandra, Paityn, Samantha, Raegan, and Kooper Kit
I hope all of you find true love, and I know some of you already have

A MOMENT IN TIME . . .

A cold shower slammed into my umbrella as I walked down Franklin Boulevard. It was large and black, and my father had insisted I pack it. Rainwater ran along the curb beside me and sloshed into my sneakers. There was nothing unusual about June rain in Oregon or students in hooded sweatshirts heading toward the university. I don't know why on that day, of all days, I didn't rush across the street to the Art building. Maybe it was the ominous cloud hovering over the campus that caused me to hesitate. An old Beatles tune floated on the breeze from a popular brewpub half a block away.

The song whirled faintly about my head while I stood there wet and shivering, despite my father's efforts to keep me dry beneath a large black umbrella. Eleanor Rigby floating on the breeze lured me toward the brew pub. When I reached the entrance part of me wanted to dash back down Franklin Boulevard and into my art history class, but then someone opened the heavy glass door. I slipped inside and found myself looking at a dark-haired stranger. I could only presume he was a fellow college student, judging by his approximate age.

"Did you skip class too?" I asked, immediately embarrassed for having accused him of such a thing, but then he smiled. We lingered awkwardly in the entryway until the dark-haired boy asked if he could buy me a beer. Right at that moment thunder clamored in the distance, startling us both. I took it as a sign.

"I'd love to have a beer with you." It was an uncharacteristic response for me. I was a reclusive art student. Having beer with a stranger wasn't what I normally did. Something about him enticed me. Admittedly he was appealing to look at, but it was more than that. His confidence perhaps, or his low, husky voice which I found quite sensual. Looking back, I believe more than anything it was how the light danced in his eyes.

He said his name was Parker and I told him I was Katya. We sat at the end of the bar where I couldn't help but marvel at what opposites we were. I was fair skinned and petite, with blond clouds of hair that moved about my head in the slightest breeze. Parker was tall with angular features and shiny raven hair. We discussed our college majors and future goals as the hours sped by and the rain stopped. He'd grown up in St. Helena, California, where his parents owned a winery. I shared about my childhood on a small ranch in Central Oregon.

At nearly dusk we left the bar and had a few more drinks at a house he rented with several other students. I became helplessly inebriated by my attraction to him. At midnight Parker and I stifled laughter over spilt beer, so as not to awaken his roommates. Together we wiped it up, with his hand and mine intertwined on the kitchen towel until our eyes met, and we froze. There was something sobering about Parker's hand on top of mine. I sensed we both felt it. He leaned forward to kiss me and when our lips touched it felt as if the room had begun to spin. Parker's hands were soon tangled in my hair and mine were holding his face, as if I feared letting him go, only to discover this was all a dream. If it was a dream, I didn't want to wake up. We still held each other when the kiss ended, and I could feel his breath tickle my cheek as he whispered *let me walk you home*. Without hesitation I whispered back *which room is yours?*

"Are you sure?"

"Quite sure."

Until that moment I'd never slept with anyone but Miles, who was an on-again-off-again boyfriend. Being with Miles did not compare to my night with Parker, who had awakened something in me I didn't know existed. It was as if, when our hands touched, a fire ignited that could never be put out. I like to believe our souls had fused together. We'd failed to exchange last names or phone numbers on that random night in my otherwise very ordered world. Maybe we would have, but I'd slipped into my jeans and sweater at first light of day and tiptoed out the door. I could still taste Parker on my lips while sprinting across campus to my dormitory. Hard as I tried, I couldn't push away my guilty thoughts for such impulsive behavior, nor could I regret it. The only thing I knew for certain was if there really is such a thing as destiny, we would meet again.

NAPA

I was temporarily held hostage by the soul-searching tune of a live jazz band two doors down. Every artful pluck of the strings on the bass guitar played with my emotions. Even sipping wine felt like a chore, as if life had stopped for a moment to let us all purge our regrets. I listened to the same jazz band every Sunday afternoon from the front porch of our Napa home, while enjoying a full-bodied cabernet. I swirled this nectar of the gods in Grandma Rose's antique stemware while watching tourists meander down First Street. My husband Miles was an attorney in St. Helena. He spent his Sunday afternoons fraternizing with clients in posh tasting rooms along the Silverado Trail. I preferred my front porch to the noisy crowds in the tasting rooms.

Historical Old Town, where my home sits, has a soft earthy scent floating on a sultry breeze energized by an invisible stimulant. Perhaps that electrical charge is in the sea air off the San Francisco Bay, which frequently traveled inland to kiss our cheek. Maybe the mystical energy in the air comes from the Napa River, which loops around Old Town and gives this Oxbow District its name. Whatever the source, it often seeped into my skin and caused hair to rise on the back of my neck.

My father's presence was still felt in the rooms of this Napa home, sparking memories of my childhood when visiting Grandma Rose. We'd come every summer from Central Oregon where my father had bought a small ranch. I loved helping him tend to the horses we boarded, when I wasn't sitting on the fence drawing them. Grandma Rose and my father were my two favorite people on earth, until meeting Parker.

The woeful jazz lulled me back to moonlit lovemaking and dead of night spooning with a dark-haired boy, long ago, before I married Miles. Memories of Parker will still be there when God takes me home. I was certain flashbacks of my time with Parker would persist until the last wisps of air left my lungs. If only I could relive that exquisite day, rather than leave this porch to climb a ladder I had dragged up from the basement.

Grandma Rose had willed Genevieve to me. That's what I named the one hundred and sixteen-year-old home, or rather her spirit within it. I couldn't really separate the two because the house had such an invisible energy, as if alive. Genevieve's long, narrow windows were flung open most of the year, letting in the early morning scent of bread baking at the Italian Grotto two doors down. Sweet fragrances from flower baskets hung on poles along First Street wafted in with the afternoon breeze. Miles and I married a few months after Grandma Rose passed and moved in shortly after. She had drifted away peacefully in her sleep with no morphine laced IVs or deathbed drama, just as we'd all like to do. Seven years had passed, and still I missed her terribly.

Begrudgingly I left the porch and entered the kitchen. The music had stopped, and my wine bottle was empty. It was time to complete my task before Miles returned from the tasting rooms. I stared up at my destination while brushing aside cobwebs between the ladder rungs. Until this moment I'd never had a reason to access the cabinets nearly touching the roofline. It was finally clear to me why someone might want to store things in a cupboard hung ridiculously high. Who would bother to look in them unless you needed what was there?

The generous kitchen was the heart of the home, set in the back of the house. I often envisioned my father eating breakfast at the table we'd kept when moving in. It was made of dark walnut, solid and square. Fruits and vegetables placed in baskets on the black marble counter were bathed in sunlight, which flooded through the open window. Green muslin curtains made by Grandma Rose still hung there and moved slightly in the breeze.

The ladder smudged with old paint colors and dirt looked completely out of place beside the white Victorian cabinets. I'd found it beneath the back porch stairwell. It had been shoved into the cellar, which I often called Genevieve's belly. Thinking about the belly of Genevieve reminded me of my own emptiness. I had truly believed I was with child, that Miles and I had finally conceived an infant. I'd never skipped two months before. It had been more than enough time to let me dare hope, but I couldn't allow myself to dwell on possibilities I'd dreamed about just yesterday.

Instead, I placed a pale-yellow onesie on top of the other onesies, making a nice stack of gender nonspecific clothes for a newborn. I stared at the tiny pastel pile of clothing longer than I wanted to, but it was hard not to relive that day when I purchased them. There had been so much hope on that day, so much anticipation. I'd spied them on an end aisle and couldn't resist reaching out, with a near trembling hand, to run my fingers along the neatly folded infant wear. I watched the saleslady place each one into a Macy's bag. It had been two months after all. Who skips two months unless they're pregnant?

It was important that Miles never know, which was why I needed to place them up in the cabinets accessible only with a ladder. That way he couldn't chide me for buying baby clothes on a whim, without any proof I was pregnant. It weighed heavily on me that Miles seemed less invested in starting a family with each of our seven wedding anniversaries. A mutual desire for children was what I'd liked most about Miles. Had he lied to me about wanting children? Or was he afraid to hope anymore?

I had an inexplicable desire to lavish all the love I never felt from my mother onto children of my own. Although my father adored me, he was a workaholic. Most of my childhood lacked any form of nurturing except for those cherished twenty minutes before bed when he would finally return from work and read me a bedtime story. Miles shared with me once how he wanted to be a hero to his children like my father had been to me. Maybe Miles no longer believed he'd ever have children. Maybe that's why we seemed to have drifted apart.

I shivered while looking up at the cabinets, despite the kitchen being stifling hot in the typical July heat. The steady Napa sun turned our house into an oven every afternoon about this time. Miles and I would feel like freshly baked lemon tarts if we ate dinner in Genevieve July through September, so instead we ate on the front porch, which is where we spent most of our time anyway, except in the dead of winter. I'd furnished the porch with a tropical theme. Our California coastline was not tropical of course, but on a warm summer day it felt like it. Bodega Bay was an hour west of Napa and often sent sultry breezes our way.

I had bright orange throw pillows on the loveseat and rattan chairs (one chair on each side of a rattan table with a glass top). The whole set had been quite a steal at the local furniture store that first summer we lived in Napa. Since then, I'd added a couple of potted palms in blue ceramic pots. A large colorful rug completed my tropical look. The cheery colors were uplifting whereas the palms were quite calming. It was a perfect place for people-watching, or to sit and think, or drink wine and laugh with a friend.

On a Sunday afternoon such as this, tourists were out in droves on First Street. Some would disappear into the trendy restaurants or quaint clothing shops. Others were headed to the wine bars or brew pubs. I wanted to disappear into a wine bar at this very moment, but instead I stared up at the ladder leaning against the wall by the impossibly high cabinets. Climbing one rung at a time, I balanced the onesies in my left hand while gripping the ladder with my right. When I came eye to eye with the cabinet door, I reached over and pulled on it. It didn't give way. I tried again, more forcefully, and it popped open nearly spilling me off the ladder and onto the stone floor.

Nothing at all was inside.

I'd envisioned all types of pleasant and unpleasant (mostly the latter) scenarios for what might be in the mysterious upper cabinet. It was disappointing to find nothing there, not so much as a frightened spider in a spindly web. I set the baby clothes on the bottom shelf and wondered what Grandma Rose had stored here. Surely it was something she might never need, like baby clothes were for me. Thinking about how I had no need for the infant wear caused warm tears to flow down my sweaty cheeks.

Once I had myself under control, at least for the moment, something unusual caught my eye at the back of the cabinet. I squinted and wondered if it could be a doorknob. Why would there be a doorknob at the back of a cabinet? I lifted myself up and hung on the edge of the shelf while trying to grab the brass handle. I'd nearly succeeded when a loud bang startled me. I fell back onto the ladder, almost knocking it over.

"Katya?"

It was Miles.

He'd slammed the front door as usual, instead of closing it softly as I'd often requested. Genevieve was quite an old lady. Slamming anything within the house was, in my opinion, ill advised. Soon he was standing in the kitchen staring up at me in disbelief. I quickly shut the cabinet door and turned to face him, smiling awkwardly as I stood there on the ladder.

"What are you doing and where did that old ladder come from?" he asked, looking perplexed to say the least. It wasn't an unusual look for him, regarding my behavior, which he often found perplexing.

"You're home early," I said, evading the issue.

"That's beside the point, Katya. You're lucky I didn't find you on the floor with a broken neck. Why are you trying to reach useless cabinets?"

"I had some extra linens to store." This lie came so easily it surprised me.

Miles rolled his eyes and stepped into the master bedroom, which was my cue to scramble off the ladder and return it to the cellar. By the time I reentered the house, Miles had changed out of his suit and was drinking a beer on the front porch. I heated up leftovers from the Italian Grotto and joined him.

Neither of us mentioned the ladder again.

CROW

I began weeding rows of raised beds on our small plot of land early the next morning. Working with my hands in the malleable earth was a daily ritual. I found it to be quite spiritual, with the warm sun on my back and rich soil between my fingers. Soon the heirloom tomatoes would be sold to the highest bidder among the restaurants in Old Town, along with my pole beans and Chinese eggplant.

When starting this venture, I wasn't sure I could count vegetable farming among my gifts. I had, in fact, no idea whether I could make anything at all grow, let alone make a decent wage from it. The idea had come to me early one morning while standing in our yard watching dewy grass glisten beneath a rising sun. Why not utilize this fertile land behind Genevieve? My grandmother grew roses here, but they'd eventually been choked out by weeds. Regardless of Miles believing the idea to be ridiculous, I read a few books and ordered some seeds, tools, and fertilizer. Our second summer in wine country I began planting coveted varieties of organic vegetables. It was hard to fathom why I was earning top dollar for backyard produce with nothing more than an art degree. I reasoned that raising delicate, hybrid plants somehow satisfied my need to nurture and fuss over something.

Nothing was more peaceful than working in my garden each morning as the sun rose to greet me and Crow watched from the fence where he sat. Crow was shiny and black, but he was not a bird. Feral kittens had birthed under the house after we moved in and only one survived. I named him Crow because I thought it was a baby black bird, tiny and wounded, and barely moving in the doorway to the cellar. I gave the kitty a bowl of milk every morning until one day I switched to canned tuna. He had grown enough to eat solid food. I put the canned tuna in a carrier when Crow was half grown and trapped him there, so we could visit the vet. He screamed at the top of his lungs the whole way. They neutered Crow, gave him vaccinations, and parasite meds. When he was ready to return to Genevieve, he screamed every bit as loud on the trip home. His meow sounded just like a crow's husky caw. I smiled, knowing I'd named him appropriately.

I never knew when Crow ate the one meal I left for him every morning, only that the food dish was always licked clean when I replaced it. Miles told me it was wrong to feed a wild cat because it would grow dependent on me and become too lazy to hunt. I knew this wasn't true because I'd seen Crow catch birds in the alleyway behind us, and Genevieve never had a mice problem like many of our neighbors.

This morning he sat on the fence as usual and watched as I harvested a crop of young zucchini, being mindful to keep their delicate flowers intact. I was carefully placing each plant in a produce box when Miles exited the back door with a briefcase in one hand and a Starbucks mug in the other. Crow and I stared at him, impeccably dressed in his Gucci suit. It hugged his muscular body nicely and reminded me of one reason I'd married him. Just like every weekday morning, Miles was headed for his law office in St. Helena.

"I won't be home until late, Katya. I have a dinner meeting tonight with a client." Miles shook his head as he skipped down the porch steps. "You're going to have a lot of back issues one day from all this gardening."

"It's micro farming, Miles. Not gardening."

"Well, whatever it is, it can't be good for your back." He climbed into his BMW and backed out of the open gate, which I closed behind him. I watched Miles drive down the alleyway and turn onto the side street, thinking I shouldn't have married him. Miles Harrington had wooed me into wedlock because any hope of fairytale love had passed me by. He would show up at my door with flowers for no reason at all and convince me to leave my tedious art projects for long hikes along the river. All the attention from Miles helped me heal from my father's abrupt death, and the recent passing of my Grandma Rose. Miles breathed life into me again. He gave me a reason to leave the house, and for that I was thankful, but nonetheless, I shouldn't have married a man I didn't love.

I had foolishly hoped I would grow to love Miles. I wanted to believe settling down and having children would expand my affection for him. Even now I couldn't bring myself to give up on us. Perhaps it was only because I ached for pink-cheeked children with skinny sun-browned legs. I longed to run my fingers through their tousled hair and feel their feathery kisses. I needed to lavish my adoration on them in all the ways I had never felt adored by my own mother. So, there I was, with the good earth to place rows of seed into, but my own seed would not take root and sprout.

Later that morning I delivered my zucchini through the back door of a Napa restaurant that regularly bought my produce. The smell of pastries baking in the ovens filled the air in the crowded kitchen, along with pots and pans clinking, and line chefs shouting across the room to one another. The French bistro wouldn't open for another hour, but there was always much to be done ahead of time at Angele.

Lorelei took my basket and admired the shiny green zucchini with their vibrant yellow flowers. "They're perfect, Katy! This will be on our menu tonight: fried zucchini blossoms with the specials, and sautéed zucchini with the sides. Maybe we'll drizzle a balsamic reduction on the zucchini and add some shaved Parmesan. I'll ask the chef what he thinks." She set the basket on the end of a long butcher-block counter and hugged me. "How are you, my sweet friend?"

"I'm fine," I said, and then I smiled as if to prove it.

She scrutinized my face with her ocean-blue eyes. I often wished I could jump into those sparkling pools and swim away. Lorelei was my one true friend in Napa. We'd bonded at first sight. Growing produce was an obsession with little down time. The few moments I had to myself were either spent with Lorelei or sitting in a vineyard sketching. It was a stress reliever for me. I could forget about clients anticipating delivery of my vegetables and how bearing children seemed less likely by the minute.

My peculiar need to sketch obsessively was something Lorelei had easily accepted. We'd spend hours on my front porch, sipping wine and crunching baguette slathered in creamy Brie, while I drew flower baskets hanging from light poles and Lorelei assessed everything happening along First Street. She'd been hired to manage Angele my second year in Napa. When I delivered produce that spring, Lorelei De Luca introduced herself. I could feel change in the air as soon as I entered the kitchen. Her creative genius permeated all the way through the hot, crowded kitchen and into the cozy front dining area. Even the spacious patio beside the Napa River had subtle changes after just one week. She had brought with her a frenzy of creative energy.

Whenever standing beside this tall, sumptuous woman I became aware of my delicate features and subtle curves. *Just a wisp of a child* Grandma Rose would say. A good wind could have sent me airborne. Lorelei had striking auburn hair, which I envied. She was assertive and outgoing, whereas I was quiet and reserved. It was her humor I especially adored. Despite working endless hours at the bistro, my Lorelei never failed to show up on Friday night with a bottle of wine. Sometimes she'd bring Pistou Linguine from the bistro, and we'd feast until midnight, while trying not to awaken Miles with our laughter. She knew I'd hoped to be pregnant. Sparkling water with a twist of lime had been my drink of choice lately while our conversations kept circling back to how I should take a pregnancy test. But I'd refused, and Lorelei never asked why. I think we both knew I didn't want to know. I needed to believe.

"Let's go out back and sit by the river. I'll bring us an iced coffee." Lorelei brushed a wisp of hair off my furrowed brow.

"I can't stay long," I answered. "I need to finish the sketch I'm working on."

"Go find a table in the shade. I'll be right there." She ushered me out onto the patio where I dutifully sat at a table shaded by an umbrella. Colorful kayaks paddled upstream in the Napa River, which curled around Old Town and eventually out to sea. It rose and fell with the tide, much like my whimsical moods of late. Lorelei soon slid in beside me and set down two tall glasses of iced coffee with a rich dollop of cream floating on top.

"What's making your eyes avoid mine this morning, Katy?" Lorelei took a sip of her decadent drink, licking a trace of cream from her upper lip.

"I'm not pregnant," I blurted out, nearly choking on my words. "I've known for a couple weeks now, but I haven't been able to face it."

She reached over the table and gently stroked my arm. "I'm so sorry."

"Me too." I sipped on the icy drink and willed myself not to cry.

"So, that's why you've been so distant and quiet. How devastating for you. It will happen, maybe when you least expect it."

"Maybe. Or maybe I'm just not meant to have children. Tears streamed down my face and soaked the cuffs of my white cotton shirt, which I had used to hide my face. Lorelei was in tears herself, from witnessing my misery.

"You can always adopt, Katy," she offered up. Her tone was optimistic and soothing, which was why I loved her. Lorelei had a heart of gold beneath her take-charge demeanor.

"Yes." I nodded in agreement, but I knew Miles had no intention of seeing fertility experts. He'd said if it didn't happen naturally it wasn't meant to be. I hadn't argued with him. I wasn't sure my excessive hunger to bear children was reasonable. Perhaps it was just another thing I needed to overcome, like my father's sudden death. We drank our coffee in silence for a while, watching the lazy river carry kayaks begrudgingly along. But then my sullen mood got the best of me. "I don't want to take up any more of your time, Lorelei. I need to sketch in the vineyard. Pencils are the only company I am good for right now."

Lorelei squeezed my hand. "I completely understand. Go sketch. One day your exquisite work will hang in the best galleries. I don't know why you won't frame some of it and approach our local art dealers."

"I don't have time to find an available gallery," I argued. Lorelei had been my biggest fan, frequently admiring the tedious etchings and translucent silk screens, which I created and kept in Genevieve's third bedroom. My vineyard sketches had inspired them, and truth be told, lately I'd rather draw on a hilltop than work in my studio.

"I think you should make time. It could cheer you up after this pregnancy thing." Lorelei gave me an exasperated look. It was one she often used on me when annoyed with my stubbornness. "And why do you keep returning to the same vineyard, Katy? It almost seems psychotic at this point. There are so many other places you could be exploring with your sketchpads and pencils."

I shrugged. "You know why the vineyard is special to me."

"Because a boy you knew back in college for one day and night described it to you? Because his family might own it?" Lorelei shook her head at me, and her eyes indicated a lack of comprehension.

"It does sound psychotic when you put it like that," I admitted. "There's more to it," I explained. "I've grown to love that vineyard. I could never run out of inspiration there. Weather, time of day, and changing seasons all make it continually new. Why should I go somewhere else? It feels like my second home."

"If you say so. I think you believe this boy will simply show up one day, and you can begin again where you left off. But then of course, there is Miles, and the fact that you're married. I'm not sure how you planned to get around that." She grinned, obviously amused by my fantasy.

"Make fun of me then. I don't care." I laughed, feeling more lighthearted than foolish.

"I'll be on your porch Friday night as usual." Lorelei hugged me tightly before I slipped past the patio gate and drove to St. Helena. I had shared with Lorelei (over a bottle of very good wine) about my afternoon with Parker in a brew pub near campus, and how our attraction was so strong I'd gone back to his room that night. I had relived that day and night too many times to count. Even now it was foremost in my mind as green hills sped past the car window. Everywhere I looked there were endless rows of grapevines against a clear blue sky.

I couldn't pinpoint what made me choose my specific hill to sketch on. It couldn't be consciously defined, and neither could my connection with that one boy, on that one rainy day, all those years ago. Ten to be precise, almost to this very hour, as I pulled into the parking lot.

VINEYARDS

Peering out over the ripe grapes from my Jeep Wrangler made my spirit soar. Vines ran straight as arrows far into the distance. I parked and climbed the hill, turning to view the valley when halfway up. It was quite warm by the time I arrived, as it should be by the first of August. I pulled off my ball cap and let my hair fall free. It was my nemesis. Lorelei likened it to spun gold. She claimed to love my hair, especially the untamed yet angelic look of it. I believed she was only being kind. While men were drawn to the wildness, or perhaps the blondness of it (which had not darkened with age), school friends pitied my inability to do anything at all with the soft, feathery curls, except tie them up in a confining knot or let them hover unrestrained.

It wasn't long until I reached the sprawling oak at the top of the hill, the one I always leaned against to draw. The ancient tree dwarfed me, as if I were a tiny ant beside a broken twig. I relished becoming an obscure part of the landscape while able to spy on the ripened grapes. It was almost time for the fruit to be harvested. Normally this would be my favorite season to sketch the vineyard, but not this year. I would have preferred to draw barren vines, dead and shriveled, leafless . . . lifeless . . . just like my womb and the nonexistent fetus I was mourning. Nonetheless, I soon became absorbed in my sketching, with only the buzz of an occasional bee to break the silence, until the distinctive voice of a man startled me.

"It's a beautiful view, isn't it?"

Quickly standing, I spilled my pencils from the box. Then I swung around to see his silhouette outlined against the sun. A chill ran up my spine. I would know that voice anywhere.

"I'm sorry. I didn't mean to frighten you," he added.

His face was still hidden in shadows, but I had no doubt who it was, which made my heart beat fast and hard. "Is this your property?" I asked, awkwardly, not knowing what else to say.

"It's my family's land." He took a step closer. "I'm Parker Mancini." Parker could clearly see me now, bathed in the afternoon sun. We stared at one another for a few seconds. "Katya. I can't believe it!" His eyes lit up with recognition.

Leaning against the tree for support, I hugged my sketchbook and said nothing. I didn't trust my legs not to buckle beneath me. We continued to stare at one another for longer than we should have, until finally I said just one word. "Parker."

"I see that your eyes are still stormy and gray." He smiled, but I didn't smile back. I could only gawk at him, realizing I had somehow correctly chosen the vineyard his family owned, Three Gates Winery. Part of me wanted to dash across the hill and down the slope or disappear somewhere in the fruit-laden vines, but my feet were as rooted to the earth as the ancient oak I leaned against. While I stood there speechless, Lorelei's words flooded my head. *I think you believe this boy will simply show up one day, and you can begin again where you left off.*

Parker was observing my panic-stricken moment. "I think your eyes are even stormier than I remembered." We were standing so close I could feel the warmth from his skin and see his forehead glisten in the hot sun. My heart continued to beat as if I *had* run down the hill. I couldn't seem to speak, so instead I studied his raven hair and dark eyes, which still held dancing specks of light. Was this God's little joke, bringing me face to face with the life I might have had? After our whirlwind day there had been no opportunity for a second. I didn't finish spring term that year at the University of Oregon because my father had died unexpectedly from a heart attack. Now here we were ten years later, nearly to the minute. I thought I'd spend the rest of my life blaming fate for my altered path. But somehow fate had redeemed itself, if not too late to matter.

Bursts of sunlight peeked through the leaves of the oak and for just an instant I believed we might kiss. But then Parker reached out and touched my face lightly with his fingertips. It warmed me all the way to my toes. I nearly dropped my sketchbook. "It's so odd to see you again, here in this vineyard of all places, Katya Rose. I remember you telling me your middle name was Rose, after your grandmother." Parker's gaze was so intense I had to look away. I stared into the blue sky behind us, my memory zooming light years back to that day in the pub. It was as if every day between then and now had vanished.

"You told me she had red hair and grew roses in the back of her Napa home."

"That's true. I'm surprised you remembered," I said, forcing myself to look at him again, which was almost painful. Parker was every bit a man now. The boy in him was gone. The years we'd spent apart were glaring at me as much as they didn't seem to exit.

"There isn't anything I've forgotten about that one day we had together, but then you were gone. Just like that. I couldn't find you anywhere, and often thought of you as an angel I had imagined." Parker gently touched my hair. "I see you still have gold dust framing your face." He slowly shook his head in disbelief. "The more I thought about you, the less sure I was you existed at all, and now here you are." Parker's eyes reflected the longing and regret I felt.

"I . . . left the next day," I explained. "It was a family emergency." I peered over his shoulder at the one lazy cloud rambling along in a sea of blue, feeling guilty. If he'd only known how often I daydreamed about being alone on this hill with him. I could see now that it was wrong of me to hope this might happen. "I didn't return until the next fall," I added, forcing myself to look at him, hoping the guilt wouldn't show in my eyes. Then I smiled, knowing that afternoon so long ago had haunted him, too. "What have you been up to all these years?" I asked, trying to ignore my rush of feelings for this man I could never have, or hold, again.

"There's not much to tell." Parker sighed rather sadly, as if wishing to dismiss everything that had happened after our one day and night together.

"Surely you're married?"

"Not anymore."

"Divorced then?"

"Yes." He didn't offer an explanation. "I see you're sketching." Parker looked at the small leather-bound book I was holding.

"I did get an art degree, but it isn't how I make my living," I confessed.

"I don't use my psychology degree either, except maybe to change my brother's stubborn mind." He reached over and took my hand, to study the modest diamond, which sparkled angrily in the bright sun. "I see you are married."

"Yes." I pulled my hand away. "Miles and I married a few years after we graduated, right after Grandma Rose died and left me her Napa house. Miles is an attorney at a law firm here, in St. Helena."

"I see." Parker studied the same stray cloud, that one flaw in a flawless sky. "Do you love him?" he asked.

I pondered that question, unsure of what to say. "Why would you ask that?"

"I apologize. It's just important to me that you be happy, that this man is worthy of you." He soon changed the subject since I'd chosen not to answer. "The reason I remembered your middle name is because you are so delicate, just like a rose. It suits you." We stared at one another silently again, and for some reason it wasn't at all awkward this time. "Perhaps you wouldn't mind if I called you Rose?" he added.

"That's what my father called me. I miss having someone call me Rose."

"Good. Then Rose it is. Let me show you the winery. I'd love to give you a tour, have you taste our blends. They are fantastic. The best wines in the valley."

I grinned at his confidence, his way of making you believe whatever he said. I had so admired this about him in the pub that afternoon. I didn't mention never having been in the tasting room. Part of me was afraid I'd see him there and be faced with the inappropriate feelings I was having at this very moment.

He winked at me. "Come on, let's do it."

"Let me put my pencils away," I managed to say, while thinking of all the reasons I shouldn't taste wine with Parker. He helped me scoop them up and stuff them in the pencil box, which I returned to my tote bag. Then we scrambled down the grassy hill and walked single file between two rows of vines oozing clumps of purple fruit. I wondered if I should be entering a tasting room in cut-off jeans, a white cotton shirt with tear-stained cuffs, and flip-flops. But Parker appeared casual as well, in his khaki shorts and black tee.

When we came to the end of the vineyard, we crossed a two-lane road lined with more giant oaks. Not far in the distance was the tasting room. The building was quite old and partially covered in ivy. Irregular red bricks formed a picturesque structure with a gallant entry. Beside the huge double doors sat two large copper pots filled with bright yellow flowers.

Parker opened one of the doors and ushered me in. It was cool and dark inside, and it took a moment for our eyes to adjust. We stood there alone in the entryway and looked at one another as if neither of us could believe what was happening. It seemed as surreal as that rainy day in the bar, which had felt like a torn page from a novel, teased by the wind and lost in a puddle.

PARKER

"Come, I'll escort you to a private tasting room." Parker's alluring voice made me realize how much I had missed the sensual tone of it, somewhat hoarse and almost whispered. I would often close my eyes and focus on his genuinely carefree laugh. Miles never laughed and nothing Miles ever did was carefree. Calculated moves were all he knew, in work or play. I thought of this while standing in the entryway with its highly varnished floor that made everything echo, including Parker's voice as he spoke. It gave me chills, as if I'd crossed over into a forbidden world, standing in dark shadows with a man I shouldn't have been craving for a decade. The bright sun was locked out and seemed a lifetime away on the other side of the tasting room doors. An army couldn't knock those solid wooden doors down without a lot of effort.

"Where is this tasting room you're taking me to?" I asked.

"You'll see." Parker guided me along a corridor to the right of the entryway. Voices followed us. They were muddled but cheerful and came from the open and airy room beyond the shadowed entry, where I'd noticed a bar bathed in sunlight beneath a high vaulted ceiling. People had been standing at the bar while someone on the other side of the counter poured wine into stemware lined up in front of them. Miles and I had done a lot of tastings in similar settings when first moving to Napa Valley. We'd never agreed on the wines or come to this particular tasting room.

Parker led me into a room at the end of the corridor. It was flooded with light from a long rectangular window. Bottles of wine were displayed on a small bar in the corner of the room. I wandered over to see the labels more closely. They all looked like miniature paintings of grapes. Each label had gold trim around it. I'd never seen such fine artwork on a label.

Parker slipped behind the bar and set up stemware. "What do you think?" he asked, gesturing to the wall beside us. I glanced up and observed a large oil painting of half-eaten cheeses on a silver tray, surrounded by crusty breads and glasses of sloppily poured wine. It seemed to give the observer permission to live in the moment, to relinquish all forms of protocol and guardedness.

"It's wonderful," I said.

Parker handed me a tasting pour and I tried to look away from his dark, earthy eyes that drew you into their warmth, opposite of Miles, whose icy blue eyes made you shiver. Parker's whole demeanor was like an open book, honest and real. How could this man be so different from my husband, whose hard gazes were unreadable?

"Let's try it," he said, swirling his wine in the large, delicate stemware. Then he sniffed the aroma and held his glass up to the light to study its "legs." The streams fell slowly, and so I knew it was a full-bodied wine.

"Shouldn't we start with the lighter wines?" I asked.

Parker grinned. "I skipped to one of my favorites."

I took a sip while thinking about how inappropriate it was for me to be here. It would have been fine for two old friends to meet and share an afternoon together, but we were hardly friends, having met just once a long time ago. I didn't know how to define what we were, or maybe I didn't want to. "This wine has a spicy nope I especially like," I added.

"I thought you might." Parker seemed pleased with himself that I enjoyed the cabernet he had chosen. He filled my glass, and then his.

"The labels are unique. Who did them?" I inquired.

"An artist friend of mine." He picked up a bottle from the counter and showed it to me, pointing to where it was signed ZA in the lower right-hand corner.

"What does ZA stand for?"

"Zachary Austin."

"He does very nice work." I studied the array of bottles on the bar top again, wondering how my sketches would look as wine labels and envisioning KR for Katya Rose in the lower right-hand corner. Scanning the rest of the room I observed a white leather sofa on the opposite side from the bar. A heavy glass table sat squarely in front of it. The table held a vase of blood-red roses. There was no other furniture and nothing else hung on the walls, yet the room exuded warmth from the dark wood floors and ornately framed window. I walked over and sat on the sofa, sinking into the buttery leather. Parker sat beside me, and our knees gently touched. It should have felt awkward since we were not old friends, or even new ones, but it wasn't awkward at all. It was as if we'd done this every day for the last decade.

"Tell me about your marriage, Parker."

He shrugged. "I've known Julia my whole life. Our families wanted us to marry and so we said why not. Neither of us met anyone else while in college, at least no one we could find again." Parker shot me a meaningful look.

"That doesn't sound very romantic," I commented.

"I guess not. Julia was fun to be with but in the end, we were neither one happy. Our love was too complaisant, and we knew it." Parker took a sip of his wine and added, "We have remained friends."

"How long were you married?"

"Five years. No children. We were careful not to get pregnant. Maybe we knew all along our marriage wouldn't work, that it was more to please our families than ourselves. We've been divorced for two years."

"Now you're free to find true love. Someone you can't live without." I finished my wine and placed the empty glass on the table with the roses.

"Yes, maybe. Let me get you another pour." Parker retrieved the open cabernet from the bar and refilled our glasses. "Funny you should mention true love, Rose. The time you and I spent together felt like the beginning of exactly that, even though it was so brief I often wondered if I'd dreamed it. But then I couldn't find you again and now here you are, married to someone else."

I stared into my wine glass and couldn't look at him. Parker continued as if nothing significant had been said. "It's your turn. Tell me about this lucky man you married. You say that he's an attorney right here in St. Helena?"

I was no more eager to share than Parker had been. "Miles and I met our freshman year of college. We dated on and off while at the university, but I lost track of him when I left because of my father's passing. Then out of the blue he came to my one and only gallery show a couple years later. We were together nonstop after that. Grandma Rose had passed a few weeks before Miles showed up that night at the gallery. She had a friend who was an art dealer and they had conspired to show my work at a very trendy place in Portland. I missed my grandmother terribly. She and I had face-timed nearly every day after my father's death. I had immersed myself in art to cope with grief. My father had meant the world to me. Then Grandma Rose passed too, and it felt like I had no one, until Miles appeared out of nowhere."

"What about your mom?" Parker asked.

I shrugged. "My mother had a low tolerance for all the time I spent drawing. I think she struggled to understand why I loved art so much instead of doing whatever other children did. Our relationship became more distant once I entered high school. I was painting in oils by then and writing poetry. I had become quite withdrawn from the outside world. Other than attending classes I rarely left my attic studio Father had set up for me. It had a dormer window that looked out onto the high desert, which was our front yard. There was endless inspiration out that window. Juniper and Aspen, Douglas Fir and Ponderosa Pine. Mountains framed the distance. Broken Top and Mt. Jefferson, The Three Sisters and Mt. Bachelor.

"You must have loved where you grew up," Parker commented.

"Very much," I agreed.

"Your father was quite thoughtful to nurture your gift for art."

"He loved my paintings," I admitted, "but he especially loved my poetry. He is why I minored in English Literature, although art seems to possess me now, and leaves no time for writing. Once Father passed, I rarely saw my mother. When she died from bronchitis a few years ago I felt especially bad that I hadn't given her grandchildren. Perhaps it would have bridged the gap between us, and she would have forgotten what a disappointment I'd been as a daughter."

"It isn't possible for you to be a disappointment to anyone," Parker commented. "I'm sure your mother loved you very much. Some people are terrible at communicating their feelings."

I hesitated to say anything else. I couldn't bring myself to admit I'd felt the same as he, that our brief time together in college might have been the beginning of true love. If only I hadn't left the next day, as fate would have it. After a long pause I shared how Miles had convinced me to marry him, so we could raise a family, only to end up childless after seven years of trying."

"It could still happen, Rose." He took my hand and squeezed it. "Until then you have your art. Why haven't you had any gallery showings here?"

"I just haven't been motivated to secure a location for my work, and anyway, I've been distracted lately—obsessed really, with sketching on the hill above your vineyard."

"So that's what you were doing when I found you on the hill."

"Yes."

"What other vineyards have you sketched at?"

"Only yours," I confessed. "Of course, I didn't know it was yours. But this is where I first came and then I returned because I felt comfortable here. It's fairly secluded up on the hill by the old oak tree, which has become like a good friend. Sketching is my therapy, you see, and your family's vineyard is where I hold my therapy sessions. The pencils and sketchbooks are my therapist. They speak to me, and I listen." I smiled at him, although I was dead serious.

Parker had a thoughtful look on his face, as if trying to understand. I wondered what expression he would have if I'd told him how connected I felt to this winery, simply because of a fleeting comment he'd made in the pub that day about his family's vineyard in St. Helena.

"Why do you need therapy sessions?" he asked.

I shrugged. "Doesn't everyone need a place of respite to sort out the meaning of life, especially their own?"

"I only wish I'd agreed to come help my brother sooner." Parker grew quiet then as if lost in thought. Perhaps he was questioning what good it would have done to help with the winery before now, because even though he was free, I was not.

"What do you do for a living, besides coddling grapes?" I asked.

"Coddling grapes is what I do to feed my soul, like drawing must feed yours. I guess it is *my* therapy. To make a living, I write articles for corporations."

"Do you enjoy writing articles?" I asked.

"There is usually a lot of research involved, and I enjoy it immensely. Especially because I can do it remotely."

"So, this is what you're doing with a psychology degree?"

"I went back and got a master's in journalism."

"I'd like to earn a master's in art history one day," I confessed. "Then I could teach what I love to study, when my fingers are sore from weeding plants and sketching grapes."

"Weeding plants?"

"I'm a micro farmer. The patch of land behind my grandmother's house is where I grow everything. I sell my crops to the best restaurants in Napa."

"You must grow superb produce if high end restaurants want it."

"I enjoy nurturing plants and watching them grow," I confessed.

"Me too," Parker admitted. "That's why I'm here now, helping with the vineyard."

We studied one another again, me enticed by the calmness of his earthy eyes and he apparently lost in the storminess of mine. I was suddenly uncomfortably warm, no doubt from all the wine I'd just consumed. "I should go," I said, grateful I hadn't leaned forward to kiss him, which had been more than a fleeting thought. I was not the kind of girl to take marriage vows lightly. I'd made a commitment to Miles, and it had been a decision I was prepared to live with. Now, however, my feelings for Parker were confusing everything and turning my orderly world upside-down. I glanced at my watch. "I can't believe how late it is. Where did the day go?" I stood up, and nearly fell back down. I hated being such a lightweight when it came to drinking.

"Let me call a ride for you." Parker stood and gently held my arm to steady me. Waves of regret washed over my body like the sea rushing to the shore.

Something about his kind gesture took me back to Oregon, to the university, to when I was still young and naïve and had fallen so hard for Parker upon first sight. Now all those feelings were rushing back, and I couldn't deny a renewed desire for this man. I hadn't thought about him when fervently pouring myself into art to push away the pain of my father's death, or when Miles appeared at my gallery showing on opening night, rescuing me from long reclusive hours in my studio. It was easy to focus on Miles and his life while he helped me through the pain of Grandma Rose's passing. If only it hadn't led to a marriage that I wasn't fully present to embrace.

How strange that lately my mind had been wandering back down memory lane, back to Parker's arms that night, and now here he was in the flesh. I couldn't, however, share any of this with Parker. We somehow managed not to fall into each other's arms and back onto the sofa, although part of me wished we had. I took one last look at the oil painting, with its message to abandon all rules of convention, before heading down the hallway and into the open tasting room. Parker was right beside me as we stood watching the small crowd that had gathered, typical for this time of day. Laughter and the clinking of glassware bounced off the ceiling, nearly mimicking a church choir in the cathedral-like setting.

Tall, narrow windows overlooked the west side of the vineyard, where the sun was just beginning to set. Something about it was spiritual. I thought of Christ changing water into wine at the wedding. It was a scripture reading I'd heard often as a child. Everything about wine country was a blessing from God. I felt His presence in this tasting room, lofty as any high-ceilinged sanctuary. God seemed to permeate the air here, where grapes were turned into wine.

I felt exposed, knowing where my heart should be as opposed to where it was; caught up in this moment, with a man I didn't wish to say goodbye to. We stood side by side, delaying that goodbye, and observed the happy tasting room scene. Parker had a quiet way of just *being* and *observing*. Miles was never content or quiet. Whenever in my presence he was multitasking while criticizing or lecturing. I rarely listened, so it was hard to be offended. He equally judged and berated the world, which made it easier to not take personally.

I glanced up at Parker, wondering how long we'd been standing there, with the sky turning a rosy pink out the windows, until suddenly I spotted a familiar face in the crowd. It nearly made my blood run cold, seeing him there with a woman. Could it really be Miles and his secretary, or was the wine causing me to hallucinate?

MILES

I blinked to be sure my eyes weren't deceiving me, that I wasn't imagining Miles standing at the bar with his young secretary. Their arms and legs were twisted together like the vines out the window. They kissed in a way that looked comfortable, as if they'd had a lot of practice. I wanted to take a step closer, to be sure I wasn't imagining it, but there really was no doubt. It was Miles. His impeccable Gucci suite was unmistakable.

I ran out the door in somewhat of a daze, after pushing it open with all my strength. I couldn't escape fast enough. It shut quickly behind me, cutting off laughter and clinking of glass. Running through endless rows of grapes to the top of the hill left me breathless. Pink tones in the sky had darkened and fragmented. How was it possible I'd met up with Parker again, after all these years, on the same day my husband appeared to be having an affair? *I won't be home until late, Katya. I have a dinner meeting tonight with a client.* How many times had I heard that? How many times had Miles gone on overnight trips to San Francisco to meet with clients, or wine tasting on Sunday afternoons? Miles and Meghan intertwined at the bar flashed through my mind again, the familiarity between them . . . the crassness of flaunting a kiss in public.

What a fool I'd been.

All this time while laboring over the validity of my relationship with Miles, he'd been busy moving on. He must have decided we couldn't conceive a child, and therefore our marriage was a farce. I sat against the tree and hugged my legs while calculating the last time we'd made love. It was months ago, right before I thought I'd gotten pregnant. Now I knew why making love was usually my idea. I'd been so obsessed with having children, I hadn't noticed. Tears began to flow as if a dam burst inside me. I made mournful sounds that caused the oak tree to tremble, or perhaps I was the one trembling. This is the sorry state Parker found me in when he approached my quivering body, curled into a fetal position beside the tree. Despite everything, I had been faithful to Miles. I thought we shared the hope of a family. How naïve was I?

Parker knelt beside me and ran his fingers through my hair in a comforting way. "Rose, what is it? What happened?"

I didn't respond.

Parker lay next to me in the field of grass beside the tree. I spoke to him then, in a muffled voice. "Miles is in the tasting room."

"Your husband?" Parker sighed. "I take it he was not alone."

I didn't answer.

"Was he the fellow at the end of the bar, medium build, sandy hair?"

"Yes," I squeaked.

"Oh no, Rose, that man has been there many times with the same woman. I'm so sorry."

I sat up in the long grass. "I am such a fool," I said. "Even my husband thinks so."

Parker sat up next to me. "Rose. Never say that. Why would you think such a thing?"

I shrugged. "I don't know. I was a disappointment to my mother and now, clearly, I am a disappointment to my husband as well."

"You could never be a disappointment. I'm sure your mother loved you very much." Parker smiled. "My own mother wished for a little blond angel like you. Instead, she had a dark-haired boy who was always causing trouble."

We both laughed until I remembered Miles and Meghan, and their hungry kiss. Tears spilled down my face, which I angrily wiped away. "Why didn't he just tell me he wanted out of the marriage, that he'd found someone who can have the children we couldn't?"

"I'm sure he still loves you, Katya. I can't imagine any man not being madly in love with you, given the chance. It's hard to say why some men cheat. We are a dishonorable breed in general, thick headed and uncivilized." Parker furrowed his brow.

I reached out and touched his face. "I don't believe there is anything about you uncivilized or dishonorable." Perhaps in protest to my words, Parker reached over and kissed me. I wanted to resist, but my entire body had other ideas about it and at this precise moment, there was no clear reason to uphold honor, so I didn't.

The minute our lips touched sanity eluded us. We gave in to our passion right there beneath the oak tree. Soon the sky was cloaked in darkness and stars rose to shine upon our tangled naked bodies. We lay side-by-side on the soft grass with our discarded clothing strewn about. I would like to say we came to our senses and parted ways, but that was not the case. Every time our passion resurfaced, we clung together more intensely, and so it was we held one another into the wee hours of the morning on the hill above the vineyard.

We gathered our clothing at first light of day and stood together, disheveled and damp. We kissed one last time and then said nothing. Our eyes, however, spoke volumes. They expressed the depth of our feelings. I slipped silently away and down the hill, but not without stopping halfway to glance back up. Parker was merely a shadow against the rising sun. What had I done? There was no time to ponder this, not here, not now.

Maybe never.

THE FALL

All the way home I tried to think of what to say to Miles, but nothing entered my head. My thoughts were completely consumed by the touch and feel of someone *who was not my husband.* Miles was still sleeping when I arrived at Genevieve, so I draped myself across the guest bed and stared at the ceiling. There were many nights when I would fall asleep there while reading, so as not to disturb him with the light. He'd probably arrived late and full of wine, and not checked to see if I was home.

I hadn't thought of anything to say if I'd found him pacing the floor. Surely betrayal was written all over me and therefore no lie could suffice. My flesh still tingled from Parker's touch. My lips still felt his pressed there. Nothing could hide the storm swirling behind my gray eyes. If Miles were to investigate them, it would all be clear; my feelings of disgust for *his* betrayal, my still fresh lust for someone else. I can thank fate that my husband apparently didn't bother to look for me in the guestroom when he arrived home the night before.

Just as I had thought he might, Miles peeked his head in the door the next morning, but I pretended to be asleep. Truthfully, I wouldn't sleep soundly again for a very long time. Miles and I spent the next couple months as if nothing happened. It made me realize how far apart we'd grown. I never returned to the vineyard to sketch again. I couldn't become involved with Parker while still married to Miles. That wouldn't be fair to anyone, least of all to the baby growing inside me. Parker's baby! How ironic that one night above a vineyard would give me the child I had failed to conceive year after empty year of my marriage.

I wanted a quiet divorce. No accusations. No revelations of infidelity. I was waiting for the perfect moment to simply say we had grown apart. I doubted Miles would resist such a proposal. Why would he? With me gone he could have his young naïve secretary with the bobbed off platinum hair and whoever else he was sleeping with, if there was anyone else. On the other hand, Miles was an attorney, and quite a clever one at that. He had always coveted Genevieve and especially the property she sat on. It was prime real estate situated in the heart of downtown Napa. Miles had been asking me to sign a living will ever since we'd married.

I had managed to hold him off all these years, hoping to have children we could leave the house and property to. How could I explain to Miles that I didn't want to leave Genevieve to anyone but my children? My grandmother had often said she wanted her home to stay in the family. She meant me and any offspring I might have, but not Miles, or any other spouse who did not carry our lineage. And there was no other lineage. I was the last of our family.

Asking for a divorce could begin a battle I didn't want. Just the thought of selling Genevieve and the land she sat on so Miles could reap half the profit kept me awake at night. I wasn't sure he had any right to the land and property I had inherited, but there was no telling what loopholes he might come up with. For nights on end, I had nightmares about Miles sailing a big white yacht out of the San Francisco Bay. Meghan's platinum bob would blow gently in the offshore breeze as I watched them sail out of sight. I would be standing alone on the shore, rubbing my swollen belly, knowing my child would never step foot in Genevieve. Grandma Rose would be looking down from heaven with disappointment on her face. It was a look I dreaded more than any other as a child. I loved her so much it always broke my heart to fall short of her expectations, which fortunately, didn't happen often.

And I didn't want it to happen now.

I'd taken a pregnancy test, because unlike my recent false pregnancy, the changes in my body were glaring. Now I wanted my circumstances to change as well. I needed time to find out if I could keep Grandma Rose's home and property, and how to go about getting a divorce. Miles knew every attorney in Napa Valley. I would need to go to San Francisco to see someone he didn't know. Even that would be risky since I had no way of knowing exactly who he had worked with or knew socially. The last thing I needed was for my snooping to get back to him. I wanted to do everything possible toward an amicable divorce, and then have Parker's baby in peace—perhaps even Parker, if dreams really did come true. In the meantime, I couldn't tell either of them about the baby, which would have complicated everything.

I didn't have the courage to approach Parker even if I'd wanted to. How could I explain to him that we were having a baby? How could I tell Parker I was completely in love with him after one isolated afternoon in a college pub followed by wine tasting ten years later? There was, of course, our two random nights of steamy sex, one of which had led to this pregnancy. Nonetheless, it seemed presumptuous of me to think he loved me too.

I decided not to share any of this with Lorelei, not until I could sort out a plan for leaving Miles. Harvest was the busiest time of year for upper end Napa restaurants, which made it easy to skip our Friday nights together on my porch.

We were both overworked with me delivering produce and Lorelei juggling VIP reservations. It was also a time of elaborate parties, which I attended to network with clients. Lorelei and I ended up at some of the same parties but were never alone to discuss anything of consequence. I simply drank a lot of sparkling water with a twist of lime and became a master at hiding all the unrest in my heart, and the baby in my womb.

One especially stressful afternoon I needed to see the infant wear in the high cabinet. I wanted to feel the soft fabric, in hopes that it would untangle the knots in my body. Life was unimaginably tense, wondering when and how to leave Miles. What would I say? Anything but the truth wouldn't matter because the truth would soon be showing. I was only two months pregnant, but no closer to any answers I could live with. I hadn't heard from Parker, not that I expected to. He was the sort of man that would give me space to either fix or dissolve my marriage. Of course, he might have decided our story had come full circle and want to leave well enough alone. In my heart of hearts, I didn't think so. I knew he believed in true love as much as I did and was waiting patiently for me to come back to him.

I envisioned Parker at the winery, perhaps climbing to the top of the hill and standing beside the oak tree where we'd made love, hoping I'd finally appear and throw my arms around him. Instead, here I was, dragging a ladder from Genevieve's cellar and up the back porch steps. I leaned it against the wall and climbed to the top. It took a firm tug to pull open the cupboard door, but then I immediately smiled when seeing the pile of clothes. Something about the sight of them calmed me. I brought a onesie up to my face, lightly touching the softness to my cheek. This time, the baby clothes brought a smile to my face instead of tears.

Soon I could forget about all the nights alone in Genevieve these past couple months, reading books and listening to music while Miles was out gallivanting about. I no longer believed he was working long hours or away on business trips. I knew precisely what he was doing, and probably with whom.

I didn't care.

I buried my face in the onesie and saw flashes of Parker and I lying beneath the oak tree, staring up at endless stars. I felt his hot flesh against mine, as if reliving it. The pastel yellow onesie smelled fresh and new, like hope itself. I heard an infant cry and saw a flash of me and Parker holding our wiggly newborn between us, but then I looked up and spied the doorknob at the back of the cupboard. What could it possibly be there for?

I remembered discovering the doorknob when first placing baby clothes in the cabinet, forlorn that I had not been pregnant. Miles came home just in time to prevent me from opening the secret space. Reaching past the pile of baby clothes I was still a few inches short of that knob. Pulling myself up onto the edge of the shelf allowed my hand to easily reach the knob and I eagerly turned it. Just as I pulled the door open, I heard a loud rushing sound and then suddenly I was motionless in midair, until falling in slow motion. The rushing sound continued to fill my head until I woke up in a grassy field, with a big blue sky towering over me.

RUBY ROSE

Lying in damp, fragrant grass while staring up at an intensely blue sky was mind-boggling. I couldn't recall my name, or where I was, or why I was there. The azure sea of blue overhead held me captive and gave a sense of peacefulness as I lay there. Soon I heard a dog barking, and voices. They were happy voices. I was sure that I heard a child's carefree giggles and a grown man's hearty laugh. A kite soon appeared in my field of vision. It was emerald-green with a purple tail and looked quite bold against the expansive sky. There was a golden retriever chasing it and then out of nowhere two people rushed up and knelt beside me. I studied the uncomfortably close faces while they stared wide eyed at me. Glancing between their worried looks I saw the kite fall drunkenly behind them. The golden retriever barked in protest.

"Rosy, are you okay? Can you move?" I blinked and looked at this man again. It was Parker. I would know that husky voice and those dark eyes anywhere, in any world.

"Daddy, is Mommy okay?"

"I think so, Ruby. At least I pray she is. Rose! Can you move sweetie? Should I call an ambulance?"

"I'm fine," I said, finally. "Where am I?" I added, almost regretfully when peering up at their confused faces. The retriever had wiggled in between them for a closer look. He whined nervously and licked my hand.

"Rose, you're right here in the meadow. Remember? You insisted on painting a mural for people to see from the highway." Parker glanced at the two-lane road across the wide green meadow. I slowly sat up and stared at the barn beside me. It had a slanted tin roof and was painted with a partial scene of junipers. The junipers were a backdrop to horses running in a field speckled with orange jewelweed.

"I painted that?" I asked.

"Mommy, don't you remember? I helped you pick out the paint." Ruby gently touched my face. Her hand was soft and warm. I took a good look at her. I didn't know what my life had been before knowing this redheaded child sitting in a grassy field, nor did I care. I never wanted to leave. Her eyes were the color of emeralds and she had Grandmother Rose's smile.

"I don't remember anything," I confessed.

We all sat in the field with the wind teasing our hair and looked at one another, at a loss for what to say. Ruby hugged the retriever, still whining nervously. "It's okay, Goldie. Mommy will be fine."

"Rosy, think a minute. What's your full name?" Parker asked.

I stared at him while trying to recall. "Katya? I think it's Katya . . . Harrington."

He visibly cringed.

"Who are the Harringtons?" Ruby looked at her father.

"Rosy, you haven't been a Harrington for seven years."

I blinked and was too stunned to ask why not. Parker reached out and ran his hand through my hair, which felt like a familiar gesture. He kissed me gently on the cheek and whispered in my ear, *"Your name is Katya Mancini, but to me, you are Rose . . . my rose."*

"Mommy, who *am I*?" Ruby looked apprehensive and I laughed.

"You, my dear, are something more precious than rubies to match your hair." I reached out and touched her fire-red locks. We all laughed. It relieved a lot of tension, but nonetheless, I had no recollection of those past seven years married to Parker. The memories flooding back ended with falling through Genevieve's cupboard, which sounded absurd even to me in my dazed state. Had I fallen into another realm or a wormhole in time, or was I simply dreaming?

"Let's get you home, Rosy." Parker held a firm grip on my right arm as we crossed the field, while Ruby ran ahead with Goldie. When we reached the house I turned around, hoping the view would trigger something in my consciousness. Staring into the bright sun beyond a sea of grass only made my eyes water. The familiar scents of juniper and pine brought back memories of my childhood. I noticed an aspen grove in the near distance and a barn just beyond it, a larger barn than the one I'd supposedly fallen from. I could hear chickens clucking and a horse whinny.

"Where am I, Parker?" I asked.

"You're home, Rosy, on Desert Sky, our small ranch in Central Oregon."

"Ohhh please remember, Mommy. Please, please!"

I knelt down and kissed her cheek. "I will remember, sweetie. I'm just a little dazed from the bump on my head." It felt familiar to be close to her, as if she were flesh of my flesh, which obviously she was. It seemed too good to be true, like a fairytale. I couldn't help but wonder what the catch was.

"Let's go inside. You can rest while I call Ellis." Parker opened the door and ushered me in. I felt like a child at Disney World, mesmerized and in awe. My head hurt, however, and everything was blurry, so I sat down as directed. Ruby fluffed a pillow behind me on the overstuffed leather chair and ran into the kitchen, shouting she'd fetch a glass of water. Goldie dutifully lay down on the floor beside me.

"Who is Ellis?" I asked.

"Our family physician. He's also a friend," Parker added.

I studied him while standing there on his cell phone. His thick brows were scrunched together and his coarse, dark hair was in utter disarray. He'd never looked more handsome. He was staring at me, perplexed, waiting for the doctor to answer. Parker's eyes reflected a warm place filled with comforting things I couldn't quite remember, and they were also ablaze with urgent concern. It grieved me to know I had caused him such stress.

"Rosy, Ellis says to meet him at his office. Do you feel up to the trip?" He looked at me beseechingly and it occurred to me that I hadn't been listening. I was lost in thought about how surreal this felt, as if I were a silent observer in someone else's life. "Rose? We need to go. Ellis wants to see you."

"Yes. Okay," I whispered, clumsily standing. Parker and Ruby helped me to a Land Rover. Goldie jumped in the back of the vehicle and barked approvingly. I stared out the window at stretches of green pastureland dotted with tall, red barked Ponderosa Pine. Mountains jutted up from the far side of the fields, which were speckled with horses and cattle, alpacas, and llamas. Parker had the windows down on the Land Rover, allowing the scent of pine needles to rush in. I decided I couldn't be dreaming. No one feels the wind in a dream or inhales the scent of pine needles. Besides, I had never felt more awake than at this moment, staring out the window, nearly crying from the beauty of it. Maybe I had died, and this was heaven.

OLIVER

My first thoughts when observing the unconscious woman were not of head trauma. No, she looked more like a sleeping beauty lying there. I detected a faint smile on her face. This was not typical, mind you, for coma patients. Blond hair floated about her face like downy feathers, and her tiny frame showed no signs of stress. It was as if she were more in a dream state than a coma. I checked on her in the intensive care unit frequently, when not attending other emergency room calamities. Taking the night shift for a colleague who didn't feel well had allowed me to be there when the ambulance dropped off our fair maiden. It was fortuitous because she would be my patient anyway, by the next morning. I was the head neurosurgeon on staff.

There was something exhilarating about the unpredictability of working in the ER, aside from the fact I enjoyed helping people in crisis. I'd originally been trained as a trauma physician before realizing my true passion was neurosurgery. This patient was intriguing from the moment she arrived, having appeared to be in a blissful sleep rather than tragically injured. She coincidentally looked alarmingly like the only woman I had ever loved. It was many years before, but I had regretted losing Amelia ever since. If I am being completely honest, having lost her was still painful.

The husband had said Ms. Harrington fell from a ladder in the kitchen of their home. He found her crumpled on the floor when arriving from work. He hadn't gotten home until nearly eight o'clock, which certainly didn't help her condition any, considering she'd fallen hours earlier. I made this assessment during my initial exam. Something about her touched me deeply. Maybe it was the memories of me and Amelia rushing back, all those feelings doctors try to avoid. Emotions can interfere with important decision-making regarding a patient's condition, so I tried desperately to block visions of me and Amelia walking hand in hand, enjoying a bottle of wine in a vineyard on a sunny day, making love all night with the moon streaming through the window.

Instead, I focused on helping Katya Harrington make it through the night with her severe head trauma, and I wondered why no one else seemed to care. Miles Harrington, her husband, had gone home hours ago. Either he hadn't told anyone of her condition, or there was no one to tell. I stared at her slender, chalk-white face and wondered why her husband would not be here. He'd reacted with disbelief when I informed him that his wife lost the first trimester baby she'd been carrying. He'd seemed very agitated about that, claiming the child couldn't possibly be his, due to a childhood illness that left him sterile.

Nonetheless, I tried to make it clear to Mr. Harrington that his wife's blood pressure was unstable, and she might need emergency surgery before the night was over. Her MRI had shown a tear in the Dura mater (outer membrane) surrounding the spinal cord and brain. Leaking spinal fluid was causing intracranial hypotension and was probably causing her coma. Until that tear healed, she would likely not awaken. We could only hope it would begin to mend on its own and surgery would not be required.

I did something I had never done before when my shift was over, I pulled up a chair next to this comatose woman in ICU and simply sat there. I wasn't sure if I was waiting for her to pass into another world or return to this one, but whichever the case, something deep within me couldn't allow her to do either alone. I took her pale hand into mine and found it to be the softest thing I'd ever touched. It was cool and listless. She didn't respond to my grip. Around seven a.m. the next morning I caught sight of a dark shadow at the door. It was her husband, impeccably dressed in an expensive suit. His sandy-colored hair was slicked back, and his average height seemed taller somehow, with the pretentious airs he exuded. Obviously, his visit was not going to be a lengthy one. I tucked Ms. Harrington's hand in the blanket and stood up.

"Still in a coma, I see." Mr. Harrington stood at the foot of the bed and looked sternly at his wife, as if disappointed to find her alive.

"Yes, she made it through the night. I've run a few tests and can tell you her brain activity indicates hope, but her physical condition is quite critical." I reached over to shake his hand. "I'm Dr. Easton. I'm a neurosurgeon and I was working the night shift when your wife arrived."

"You can call me Miles." He shook my hand firmly. "Why would a neurosurgeon work the night shift, and what does any of that mean, regarding Katya's condition?" Miles looked over at me and I noticed his eyes were an icy blue, which gave me an odd chill. Perhaps it was his unemotional demeanor rather than his eyes causing me to shiver.

"It means that her brain waves are quite active. The blood supply must not have been cut off completely in the fall, or the long period of time she spent on the kitchen floor. However, physically, aside from the tear in her membrane and spinal fluid leakage, there is significant swelling in the brain and severe bruising, all of which is causing her blood pressure to be unstable. As for me being a neurosurgeon on a night shift, that's because I was filling in for a sick colleague," I explained.

"When will her condition stabilize?" Miles asked.

"There's no way of knowing. We just have to wait and see and hope for the best."

"I'll be back this evening." He turned to leave and nearly ran into an attractive woman with auburn hair.

"Hello Miles."

"Lorelei."

Like ships passing in the night (or in this case the early morning) Miles was gone as soon as they had acknowledged one another. Lorelei, I assumed, was a close friend. She observed our patient from just inside the door while clinging to a tote bag. It wasn't long until she looked up to contemplate who I might be.

"Hello, I'm Dr. Easton," I said while holding out my hand, which Lorelei shook passively, being somewhat in a daze.

"I'm Lorelei De Luca, Katy's friend. When I called Miles this morning to see why Katy wasn't answering her phone, he informed me she'd fallen off a ladder and was in a coma. Will she wake up soon, doctor?"

"We have no way of knowing for certain, but let's hope so," I answered.

Ms. De Luca nodded slowly. "She's really more like a sister than a friend." She glanced at the tote bag. "I've brought a few of Katy's things."

I didn't comment, since it was clear to both of us Katya only needed prayers for now. I felt much better leaving, knowing Ms. Harrington was with someone who cared about her. Should there be any change in Katya's condition I would be paged, so I went home to sleep. Unfortunately (and uncharacteristically) sleep eluded me. I finally rose from my restless bed and spent several hours reading about comas. I could find nothing to explain such active brain waves, considering the amount of head trauma caused by the fall. It was a rare case indeed.

No patient had ever affected me this much. God knows there was always more to learn in my profession. Nonetheless, there seemed to be an aspect of her situation that went beyond explanation. While a student at UCLA I'd been told some cases defied all logic and wondered if I would ever run across such a case. The only thing I knew for certain is that I'd be haunted by this patient until she either passed or fully recovered. If I had any say in it, she would wake up rather than not, and my plan was to spend the coming days accumulating all the knowledge necessary to make that happen.

After some endless and obsessed reading of medical journals, I finally slept, with an open book on my chest, which slid to the floor at some point mid afternoon and woke me up. I drank half a pot of coffee and resumed my reading about comas, but nothing earth shattering appeared on the pages of my thick medical books to explain Katya Harrington's ill matched symptoms.

By four o'clock I was weeding and watering my garden. I brought in a few fall vegetables—parsnips and kale, which I sautéed and ate with salmon I'd caught and froze on my Alaskan fishing trip the past spring. I was still on the night shift for my ailing colleague and probably wouldn't eat again until the wee hours of the night when I'd most likely forage something from the hospital kitchen. I'd learned how to access it when unattended and found comfort in the solitude there, somewhere after the dinner rush and before the busy morning bustle.

When I returned to the hospital that evening, I peeked into Ms. Harrington's room and saw that her friend Lorelei was there. She wore different clothing than when we'd met that morning and so I knew she hadn't been there all day.

"How is our sleeping beauty doing?" I asked.

"I think that fairytale character had dark hair," she mused.

I shrugged my shoulders. "It fits otherwise though, doesn't it?"

Her expression became quite serious. "Yes, I suppose it does."

"I've checked her chart at the front desk. There is no change in her condition," I shared, while coming in for a closer look at our patient. She could have been frozen in a block of ice, or a glass case, like the woman in the Grimm's book.

"You just missed her husband," Ms. De Luca offered up.

I detected a dislike for him in her tone. "Was he here long?" I asked.

"No." Lorelei looked dismayed. "I don't know what's causing him to be so disinterested in Katy's condition. He seems to be more angry than sad."

She glanced at me, as if perhaps I could solve that puzzle for her. I wanted to tell Lorelei why Miles was annoyed with his wife, but of course, doctor-patient confidentiality prevented me from explaining that she'd suffered a miscarriage in the fall, and the baby wasn't her husband's. "It's not that uncommon for some people, when feeling helpless in a situation, and scared, to project the emotion of anger rather than sadness."

She nodded. "Well, he did mumble on about how he'd told her she'd fall and break her neck the last time Katy was on a ladder in the kitchen." Lorelei sat beside our patient while I checked Katya's pulse and IV.

"I can't imagine why Katy was on a ladder in the kitchen to begin with," Lorelei commented. "I know they have some very high cabinets. Maybe she decided to use them for storage."

"Maybe," I agreed. "Does Ms. Harrington have any family we should call?" I asked.

"No. Her parents have passed, and she has no siblings. I've never heard Katy mention any other family that she's close to." Lorelei paused there and looked at me, really studied my face for the first time. "Why are you still here Dr. Easton? Usually doctors duck in and out of patient rooms in a nanosecond, leaving you to wonder if they were merely an illusion."

I laughed. "It's a slow evening in the ER. They'll page me if I'm needed."

"Do you always work nights?"

"No, but I do enjoy the break in my regular routine. I might ask the same of you, Ms. De Luca. Why are you still here?"

"Please, call me Lorelei."

"All right then, Lorelei. Do you have someone waiting for you at home?"

"Just Leo, my cat. There's nowhere else I'd rather be than here, wringing my hands and praying until my prayers are just one long rant to God, begging him to heal Katy." Her eyes started to water. "When might she wake up?"

I sighed deeply. "We don't know. Her brain waves are quite strong, so if she does wake up, she will probably be fine mentally." I stood over Katya and observed her eyes. It appeared there was movement under those creamy white lids and blond lashes. It startled me, but I didn't let on that I was confused by it. Most coma patients with a traumatic brain injury did not appear to be merely dreaming.

"I must go," I said. "But I'll check back later if I have a chance." I turned to address Lorelei. "The best help you can be to our patient is to get plenty of rest yourself. Then, when you're here, talk to her as if you expect your friend to answer. And maybe read to her. Just hearing your voice could make a difference."

Lorelei nodded slowly, taking in what I said. "I will do anything to help her wake up."

"Good. Then be sure you aren't exhausted or starving yourself from worry. The more cheerful and energized you are, the better the chances of her responding to your voice, and perhaps to your very presence." I took a last look at her. Lorelei was already showing signs of sleep deprivation and I was betting she couldn't remember when she'd eaten last. "It wouldn't be in Ms. Harrington's best interest for you to end up in the hospital yourself."

Lorelei nodded. "Of course. I promise I'll take care of myself, so I can read to Katy enthusiastically every night after work. I will also talk to her, incessantly. I will demand that she wake up because I need her to be okay." Lorelei laughed through her tears. I squeezed her shoulder and smiled. Then I left for the ER, where I planned to read more about comas, between cuts that needed stitching and babies with croup.

DESERT SKY

It felt a bit odd, and yet oddly comfortable, to be seated between Parker and Ruby while waiting for Dr. Ellis Canton. Downtown Sisters had stirred memories in me, not from the past seven years, but from growing up in the area. Quaint shops, cafés, and brew pubs stood along both sides of the two-lane highway that ran through the heart of town. The doctor's office where Ellis worked was one block over. We'd turned down a side street to park. Ruby had grabbed my hand after scrambling out of the backseat to open my door. She and Parker had led me to Dr. Canton's office, while Goldie waited for us in the Land Rover. We hadn't been in the waiting room long when Dr. Canton's nurse took all three of us to an examination room and informed us that the doctor would be there shortly.

"How long have you known Ellis?" I asked, after his secretary left.

"He has a ranch up the road, and we bought a horse from him. Your horse, Rose. That's how we met Ellis. We'd only lived here a short while and he offered to show us all the best trails, so we rode with him a few times and still do on occasion."

I nodded, trying to absorb this knowledge of which I had no recollection. Ellis appeared right then and greeted Ruby first, then Parker. Finally, he looked at me. His smile waned a little and concern flooded his hazel eyes. Ellis was short with thick brown hair neatly combed. He looked quite preppy, especially for the town of Sisters whose inhabitants were mostly ranchers, small business owners, and reclusive writers or artists needing wide open, sparsely populated spaces.

Ellis, I decided, was a very nice man. He poked and prodded me in various places, asked a lot of questions, and pronounced with a stern face that my lost seven years might be temporary. He concluded I had a concussion. He instructed Parker and Ruby to fill in all the blanks as best they could. He said their stories about our shared history these past seven years might trigger something and make it all come rushing back. Ellis was silent for a minute and then added, "I find it peculiar how Katya is only missing the last seven years. Such an odd thing, her amnesia being so concise like that." He folded his arms. "Make sure she rests for a few days and call me if she experiences any nausea or dizziness. No horseback riding or mural painting until she has fully recovered."

We thanked our rancher neighbor and headed back to Desert Sky with nothing more resolved than when we arrived. Before leaving the town of Sisters we stopped for ice cream, and even Goldie had a small vanilla cone. It made us all laugh to watch her eat it in one fell swoop. As we drove down the long driveway to our ranch house, I took note of the half-painted mural on the small red barn where hay was stored. "I should finish it," I said. "The mural."

Parker glanced at me from the driver's seat. "I don't know, Rosy. I don't like the idea of you being on that roof again."

"That's silly, Parker. I need to finish what I started. I'll be much more careful next time I'm up there." I studied the slanted roof as we drove by and questioned whether I was even capable of finishing it. I had no idea about the original concept for the mural, nor did I fully believe my skills were so vast. It was almost as if I was impersonating someone else, that without a vivid imagination I could never fathom how to be this person everyone believed me to be. How could I finish a mural I never sketched a plan for? How could I be a proper mother to Ruby without knowing her likes and dislikes, her daily habits, her fears?

Anxiety began to replace confusion. By the time we'd walked back into our cozy high desert home, I was more concerned with navigating my future than recalling my past. The only thing real to me was my splitting headache. Parker gave me ibuprofen and a glass of water. He took my hand and led me into the master bedroom while insisting I lie down and rest. But I was too fascinated with the lovely room. I watched him fluff massive pillows stuffed into dark green cases with gold edges. They rested on a king-size bed covered with a forest-green comforter sporting an evergreen tree pattern. One could sink into that bed and never rise again. It caused me to wonder how many times we'd made love in this luxurious setting. I couldn't recall any of them, no matter how hard I tried. Only flashes of making love in the vineyard beneath the stars came to mind, which caused me to remember being pregnant with Parker's child. Was Ruby the baby we conceived that night? I glanced at Parker. "When is Ruby's birthday?"

"November eighth. You've already started planning her party, Rose. Ruby wants to bake sugar cookies together, using the leaf cookie cutters you found at Logans Market. She'll be six." Parker tried not to show concern, but I could see the worry in his eyes.

"Hopefully it will all come back to me soon." I smiled briefly to reassure us both, but I hated that the timing didn't work. It was six months off. Ruby should have been born at the end of April, not the beginning of November. Where did those six months go? Were they lost forever? Did they never exist? I decided this must all be a dream and I was simply imagining what life would be like living with Parker and raising our child together. The last thing on my mind before opening the door at the back of the kitchen cupboard was a vision of Parker and me holding our wiggly baby between us. Now here I was, dropped into the perfect life as if I'd willed it to happen.

"Rosy, please lie down."

"This room is lovely," I commented, ignoring his request. Instead, I studied the etchings on the walls of horses and mountains, and high desert flowers. It was all quite intriguing. "Who is the artist?" I asked.

"You are, Rosy." He scrunched his eyebrows together and looked at me with concern. I stared back at him blankly, at a loss for words. To avoid his pained look, I glanced out the high, arched windows flooding us with sunlight. It was a stunning view. The Three Sisters and Mt. Jefferson loomed proudly in the distance, at the far end of a grassy field. A patio filled with empty clay pots could be seen from the double glass doors.

"What grew in the pots? I asked.

"A variety of flowers the deer won't eat, which is something you'd researched quite extensively. The daffodils come up in early spring, and then brilliant orange foxgloves and red poppies. You have a very green thumb." He smiled and my heart soared to see him relax a bit. He'd been so tense ever since I'd awakened in the field, believing myself to be Katya Harrington.

"Please, Rosy, lie down while I make dinner." He gently embraced me, kissing my forehead.

"I will. I promise."

Parker left and I lay on the bed just as I said I would. I stared at the ceiling fan whirling above me and waited for the ibuprofen to ease my pain. I dozed a little and felt much better when I woke up. Instead of looking for Parker I stepped onto the patio off the master suite and admired the snowy peaks in the distance. They were exactly as I remembered them from my childhood. The ranch I'd grown up on wasn't far from here. I felt an urge to revisit it one day, although they say you can never go home again, to look forward, not back.

I decided it must be mid-October considering the angle of the sun and the bright yellow leaves on aspens in the distance. I'd fallen through the cupboard in mid-October, so that made sense, if anything at all made sense, which nothing really did. In fact, I had no idea if I'd fallen through the cupboard or not. I wasn't even sure I was awake. Whatever I looked at was slightly blurry, while sounds echoed slightly. Ellis had told me this was due to the concussion and would clear up. My biggest concern was that when everything cleared up, I would clearly not be here anymore.

Staring into the distance at the majestic peaks, I wondered when the first snow had fallen. I would need to ask Parker later at dinner. Goldie came running up from around the front of the house just then. She barked happily, wagging her tail, and joined me on the patio. I petted her as she lay down beside the rattan chair I'd slouched into. Ruby soon appeared as well and watched us shyly from a distance. I motioned for her to come and hesitantly she made her way over. "Daddy said not to bother you," she confessed.

I smiled at her. "You could never bother me, sweetie. Just having you near brings me more joy than you could ever know."

She grinned widely at that and finally relaxed, plopping into a rattan chair identical to mine. Together we stared at the mountains. I silently prayed this moment would never pass, but then Parker appeared at the doorway, announcing dinner was ready. Ruby and Goldie seemed dismayed to have been found sitting beside me, but Parker merely grinned at them both.

Dinner was slightly awkward. I had to force myself to eat because I wasn't the least bit hungry. I couldn't take my eyes off Parker and Ruby, whom I barely knew but loved more than I'd thought possible. I watched Ruby take tiny bites of her grilled steelhead trout while Parker told us how he'd caught the fish himself on a trip to Coos Bay. He said Ellis had come, and a few others, while Ruby and I spent the weekend baking cookies and watching Disney movies. I told him it was delicious and then he mentioned there was more in the freezer. He also told me the kale for the salad had come from the garden I planted. My eyes wandered to a calendar hung beside a bowl of freshly picked apples. A shiny photo of a pumpkin patch meant I'd guessed the date correctly. It was October.

We all helped clear the table while Goldie stretched out on the cool tile floor and watched. The rest of the evening Ruby and I played records on an old turntable, which I recognized from my childhood. I hadn't forgotten the artists or songs, and the unfamiliar ones I assumed were Parker's. A few of the records were children's collections that Ruby informed me I had bought for her at an old record store in town. But her favorites were my father's that I had inherited along with the turntable. Peter, Paul and Mary, Simon and Garfunkel, Helen Reddy. She especially liked The Beatles. We sang along to some, interspersed with dancing and laughing, while Parker sat in the over-stuffed leather chair and tried to read a book. He spent more time watching us and grinning broadly than he did reading.

I couldn't interpret the look on his face. I didn't really *know* Parker, only that I felt so completely drawn to him from the first time we met. We'd spent a total of two days together and two nights, ten years apart. I recalled how compelled I was to be intimate with him in college, even though I'm a shy and reclusive person and had never slept with anyone but Miles. The night in the vineyard was just as impulsive. And then I thought of Ruby again and how I'd gotten pregnant under the stars. Surely Ruby was the child we conceived in the vineyard and if not, then perhaps she was no more real than any of this. Perhaps I made her up, and if so, I did a very good job.

LORELEI

"Dr. Easton, this is my secretary, Meghan." There was no warmth in the introduction. Miles looked more annoyed than pleased to see me. Meghan smiled and I nodded in return. Judging by the flirtatious way she looked at Miles, I guessed their relationship to be more than professional.

"It's past visiting hours," I said, while viewing Katya's chart.

"I know." Miles nodded. "We were just leaving."

They nearly flew out the door, as if quite uncomfortable in my presence. I wondered what kind of husband would screw around with his secretary and then bring her to see his wife, who was in a coma.

Miles and Meghan had been standing at the foot of the bed and looked up sharply when I'd entered the room. I doubt they expected to see me so late in the evening, but I was on the night shift, filling in for someone again. I stood beside Katya and studied her facial features, which told me so much more than her underlying condition. It was intriguing the way her lips turned up slightly, and her eyelids gently fluttered. She appeared to be asleep, and there was no indication she desired to be awake. I shook my head. I wouldn't want to be awake either if I was a woman so unfortunate as to be married to Miles Harrington.

None of the latest tests I'd run had given me any conclusive knowledge about her current condition. Fortunately, she had stopped leaking spinal fluid, which meant the tear in her dura mater was healing. Swelling in the brain was subsiding. She'd suffered quite a severe concussion. It would take time for her bruised and battered brain to recover. There was no way of knowing how complete that recovery would be.

Before leaving my night shift early the next morning I stopped by Katya's room again and found Lorelei there. I didn't say anything but the look on my face must have indicated my surprise.

"I thought I'd talk to her before work." Lorelei looked at me with pleading in those big blue eyes, knowing it was nowhere near visiting hours.

I smiled. "Let's get you a special pass to come whenever you want. Your visitations are instrumental to Katya's recovery."

"I'd appreciate that."

I studied Lorelei's lovely face for a minute and decided something was off. She looked tense, maybe just concerned for her friend, but I felt it was more than that. "Are you okay?" I asked.

She shrugged. "I stopped by late last night to see Katy, just like I always do." Lorelei glanced at me sheepishly. "But I didn't enter the room because I heard Miles's voice, so I waited outside the door for a minute. I don't know why I did that, but then I heard a woman speaking. She asked Miles how long it would be before Katya died. He told her he didn't know but that when she did, he'd inherit the house on First Street, which Katya's grandmother willed to her. Miles said the property alone was worth a fortune."

Lorelei walked over to the window and peered out. "It really shook me. I knew Miles was a bit strange. He's never been an especially warm and friendly person, but I had no idea he was cheating on Katy and calculating how to get her Napa real estate."

"What makes you think he's cheating?" I asked.

"I ducked around the corner in the hall just as they were leaving. The woman was laughing about something before they even reached the elevator, and then they kissed right when it opened. The hall was deserted except for me spying on them, but I'm not sure they would have cared if anyone had seen them."

I sighed deeply. "I ran into Miles last night, too. He had a woman with him and said she was his secretary. Why do you think Katya's husband is strange?" I asked.

Lorelei shrugged. "When I look into his icy blue eyes, they're cold as steel, and he never cracks a smile. He always seems to be slightly angry, either upset with Katya or life in general."

"She looks like an angel lying there," I confessed. "It's hard to believe anyone could ever be upset with her."

"Miles was never a happy person," Lorelei offered up. "I didn't see a lot of him, but when he was around, he seemed to always be full of nervous energy. He thought Katya was too distracted by her art and her micro farming and for that matter, he had strong opinions about everything. Katy tuned him out most of the time. Somehow, she appeased his intensity and lived in harmony with him, although her feelings seemed to fall short of love. Honestly, I don't think he ever loved her, either."

"That would be hard, living in a loveless marriage. Katya, by the way, is improving," I offered up, to change the subject. "Barring any complications, I don't anticipate her dying."

Lorelei nodded and looked relieved. "I need to get to work." She grabbed her purse from the chair. "I'll be back later."

It occurred to me how this vivacious woman didn't seem to have a life outside of work. How many women like Lorelei had I run into lately? Women that lived and breathed their vocation, with no tolerance for dead-end dates and online matchmaking? But then here I was, in the same position. The only damsel in distress I felt inclined to save was this fair maiden in the bed beside me. I only hoped she would wake up and end her dysfunctional marriage.

After checking over my garden and eating breakfast I went to bed. It wasn't long after I'd fallen asleep that I had a strange dream. It was about Katya. She stood in the middle of a vineyard with a breeze teasing the clouds of gold that hugged her face. She seemed to be looking for someone, or something, but then her image changed into that of Amelia, my love that got away. The clouds of gold turned into long silky strands and suddenly all trace of Katya was gone. It was only Amelia who stood looking out over the valley of grapes. We had done a lot of wine tasting back when our relationship was new. Maybe this was just a memory of her that I'd forgotten. We did love to walk along the vineyards and admire the fruit before harvest. I couldn't remember specifically why we'd broken up. Something to do with my career taking too much of me and not leaving enough for her.

I'd never dreamed about a patient before, or Amelia. It was disturbing how much Katya was affecting me. Here she was, someone I'd never met, and nonetheless I couldn't get her off my mind. After taking a few sleeping pills I slept soundly, but my brain was in a fog when I awoke, so I decided to take a walk in the brisk fall air. I was surprised to find Lorelei watering plants on a front porch just a couple streets over. She saw me as well, so I paused beside the historical home. The house had fresh white paint and lovely intricate trim. "Is this where you live," I asked?

"No. Katy lives here." She put down her watering can and leaned on the railing. "Why are you walking down First Street like a tourist?" she asked, and then she laughed. I almost didn't recognize her in such a cheerful state.

"I live here, just a few streets over," I answered. "I didn't realize our patient lived in Old Town Napa. Why doesn't Miles water the plants?"

"He left for the weekend. No doubt headed to San Francisco with his secretary, who is with him all the time now." Lorelei rolled her eyes. "He asked if I would care for things while he was gone. I've been harvesting her produce and feeding the cat, so he thought I might not mind watering the plants."

"I see. Katya is lucky to have such a faithful friend," I said, knowing I should move on. I'd already been too invasive regarding Katya's personal life, but my feet were hesitant to leave. Something about Katya Harrington and her life intrigued me.

"Why don't you come sit for a minute and I'll get us a glass of wine?" Lorelei asked, obviously aware of my desire to linger. "It's four o'clock afterall. Almost Happy Hour." She smiled down at me from the porch.

"I'd like that," I answered, while ascending the half flight of steps. Lorelei went inside to pour the wine and I observed Oxbow Public Market across the street. I could smell fresh baked pizza dough from the bistro two doors down. This home and its location were worth a small fortune, just as Miles had said. I left the railing and sat on a rattan loveseat surrounded by palms in large blue pots. A colorful throw rug adorned the porch, and the sweet scent of plumeria flowers filled the air from various shaped pots, which Lorelei had been watering. Being mid-October I knew the flowers would soon be spent, even in ever-sunny Napa. It made me appreciate them more. Soon she returned with a tray that held a bottle of cabernet and an assortment of cheeses. Freshly washed grapes glistened in a white bowl beside a crusty baguette.

"What a lovely feast," I commented.

"I bought it all at the Oxbow earlier. I'm happy to share it with you, Dr. Easton. Consider it a small token of my gratitude for your care of my Katy."

We looked each other in the eye, and hers were moist.

"Please, call me Oliver."

Lorelei nodded and handed me a glass of wine. She looked different in her torn jeans and white t-shirt, much more approachable and carefree. "If you don't mind my asking, why hasn't a worthy man snatched you up by now?"

"I don't see a ring on your finger, either." Lorelei looked at me accusingly and took a sip of wine.

"I seem to be married to my work," I admitted.

"As am I," Lorelei confessed.

"How did our Katya end up with a fiend like Miles?" I inquired.

Lorelei shrugged. "I'm guessing they were just ready to settle down and have children, although Miles never seemed like the type of person who would want kids, but then my time with him has been fairly limited."

"What do you know about her, Lorelei? She is the most mysterious patient I've ever had: no family, no friends except for you, and then there is a husband who seems to care less about her and more about her property."

Lorelei pulled off a piece of the baguette and sliced a hunk of cheese. She laid them on a small plate with a clump of grapes and handed it to me. "Katy is a gifted artist."

"So, she paints?"

"No. Our Katy does intricate etchings and lovely translucent silk screens, that is, when she's not sitting in a vineyard filling leather journals with pencil sketches."

I felt a shiver at how close to my dream this sounded, picturing Katya in a vineyard. "As I might have expected, she is quite the creative recluse," I commented.

"Yes." Lorelei nibbled on a purple grape while observing First Street. "I miss her terribly. Katy has wonderful insight into almost everything. She's very nurturing and kind, you know."

I nodded, but honestly, I didn't know. The woman I knew was still as a church mouse. Only her eyes fluttered, as if she were dancing somewhere behind them.

"Will my Katy wake up and be who she had been before the tragic fall?"

"I can't answer that," I said. "I hope so. We don't have any reason to believe she won't, but then, I ask myself every day, what is keeping her unconscious? The swelling in her brain has gone down and the bruising is subsiding. The tear in her membrane is healing nicely. I don't believe any of these issues are severe enough to keep her asleep at this point, but then, comas can be quite mysterious." I had finished the scrumptious bounty I'd been served and swallowed the last of my wine, which was quite good. I lifted the bottle and studied the label. "Have you been to this winery?"

"It's where Katy went almost every day to sketch. I'd never known her to enter the tasting room there, but she always bought their wines at the market, right there at Oxbow." Lorelei tilted her head toward the large brick building across the street, with patrons sitting under umbrellas out front.

"I should go," I said, and stood up.

"I'll see you around, doc."

"Please, call me Oliver."

"Oliver, then." She smiled, which lit up her whole face.

On my walk home I thought about the many times Katya and Lorelei had spent on that colorful front porch. It caused me to see Ms. Harrington in a new light; buying cheese and wine at the Oxbow Public Market, along with local produce and fresh bread from other vendors housed in the brick building. I envisioned her choosing meats from the butcher on the corner, and pastries from the renowned Model Bakery, which sat next to the butcher shop. Katya was a person to me now, one who sketched in a vineyard and labored over detailed etchings, an ancient art form to be sure, and one that had only recently been revived. Katya Harrington had width and breadth, and incredible dimension, just as I had imagined she might. She didn't deserve to lose her baby or be in a coma or have a husband that didn't care. It caused me to loathe Miles Harrington. *Keep dancing*, I thought to myself. B*eneath those fluttering ivory eyelids, keep dancing until I can figure out how to free you from your deep sleep.*

In the meantime, I would keep a close eye on her husband, whom I didn't trust.

LABELS

It was nearly the end of my first week with Parker and Ruby at the ranch. My headaches were not as severe, and I was sleeping less. I took those as good signs. Parker and I sat on the front porch swing after dinner, sipping a glorious wine I assumed was from his family's vineyard. The swing gently rocked us, each lost in our own thoughts. It was a comfortable silence, intimate and familiar, just as one might expect after seven years of marriage regardless that I had no recollection of it.

Living with Parker and Ruby this past week had been surreal. It was as if my fantasies had come to life but were so fragile they might vanish like a mirage. At night I would listen to Parker's steady breathing and feel at peace with a world that had somehow unaligned itself. Was it temporary? Would it fall back into place and reset my reality? The thought of returning to Napa made me shudder.

Parker and I hadn't made love since my fall, but the memories of our lovemaking in the vineyard were always on my mind. I wanted to reach for him in the night so we could undress each other, just like we had done beside the oak tree. I longed to kiss and caress him, feel his response to my touch, and mine to his. Instead, I cuddled against his chest each night in the king-size bed beside the mountain view and only dreamt of lovemaking. Confused and somewhat dazed both mentally and physically, it was all I could muster.

While sitting with Parker on the swing I shared how Ruby diligently guided me all day through the house and property. She told me everything she could think of about our life at Desert Sky. Parker had spent most of the day in his den writing articles, but he joined us periodically to see how we were doing. I wondered if he saw me the same as he did before the fall, because I had no recollection of that person or what she had been doing for the last seven years.

Parker slipped off the swing and said he would return with more wine. He kissed me on the cheek before leaving. While he was away a slight breeze picked up and blew in fragrances of juniper and sagebrush. One of the horses in the field beside the porch whinnied contentedly. The other two nibbled on thick grass. Ruby had said the sleek black gelding belonged to Parker, and the dapple-gray was hers. She'd also informed me that the spirited chestnut mare was mine. A shiver had exploded up my spine at the thought of riding her.

My last memories of riding a horse were as a child, growing up on my father's ranch. I didn't believe anything could compare to wine country for width and breadth of all God's finest artwork, until being among evergreens and snow-covered peaks again. I'd taken all of this for granted while growing up, but now I saw it fully for the majestic place that it was.

"Here you go, my Rose." Parker had come back and refilled my glass. Something about the label caught my attention and I asked to see the bottle. He filled his glass and handed it to me. I couldn't believe what I saw. It was one of my vineyard sketches. I stared at him in disbelief. "You used one of my sketches for this label?"

"We've used a lot of them. Your artwork is now on all our labels. People line up to buy the new releases. We can't decide what our patrons are more excited about, the new wines or the new labels sporting your sketches." Parker laughed and it was a delightful sound, one I had heard in my head many times since meeting him on that fateful college day.

"Do you remember when you took me to your private tasting room, a whole decade after our chance meeting in college on that rainy day?" I asked.

"Of course I remember." Parker squeezed my hand.

"I couldn't stop staring at the labels by your artist friend, Zachary?"

"Zachary Austin. Do you remember everything about that day?"

I looked up at him and smiled. "And that night."

"Rosy, do you remember why I didn't see you again for all those months?"

"No. Do you know why?" I asked.

Parker shook his head. "You've never been willing to talk about it. All you have told me is that Miles divorced you, and how you were fine with that because you never loved him to begin with."

"Tell me about when we met again, many months later," I asked, eager to know.

"I never stopped thinking about you the whole time we were separated." Parker got a faraway look in his eye, which reflected how this whole dream world felt to me. "Every day, every night," he continued. "But it wasn't my place to interfere in your life. You knew how to find me, just one town over in St. Helena." Parker ran a hand through his disheveled hair. "It was agonizing, not searching for you, not seeking you out to see how you were." He moved closer and put his arm around me, as if afraid I might disappear and never be seen again, or maybe it was more my fear than his.

"Rosy, you just showed up one day. I was pouring wine for a tasting when you stepped inside the entryway. It was a slow afternoon and the couple I poured for had been our only patrons. I stared at you, standing there in a rose-colored sundress with those blond curls hovering about your head. You looked like an angel straight from heaven, especially with the sun streaming in the window and lighting your hair on fire. I was speechless, as if watching a visitation from beyond this world." Parker shook his head. "I will never forget how pale your skin was, as if you were a ghost, or had just seen one."

Parker kissed my forehead. "I would have thought you a figment of my imagination, except the couple I'd been pouring for were equally captivated by your presence. When I finally came to my senses, I hurried to greet you."

"What happened then?" I asked, frustrated at not remembering this pivotal moment.

"I took your hand and led you out the back door, into the vineyard, slowly, because you almost seemed to be in a trance. It was as if you didn't know why you were there. We sat on a bench, and I asked if you'd been ill because you didn't look well. I remember how your gray eyes were dark, filled with thunderstorms of uncertainty."

"What did I say?" I asked.

"You caught me up on your life and we made plans to come here. After that we kissed, carefully at first, but then hard and long. We felt our need in that kiss. A need for each other, a need to never be parted again, a need to blend all that we were and had been into one inseparable future. And well, the kiss turned into lovemaking, in my bedroom above the tasting room."

"You slept above the tasting room?"

"It's a small apartment, which is where I stayed when helping run the vineyard."

"Where did you live when not helping run the vineyard?" I asked, frustrated by how little I knew about him.

"Writing articles remotely allowed me to travel. That's what I did after Julia and I divorced, I traveled. I'd spend a few weeks here and a few weeks there, across Europe, South America, Asia."

"So, there was nowhere to call home?"

"Just the vineyard. Our parents' house was down the road from it, but after college I only stayed in the apartment above the tasting room. Mom and Dad are gone now, so it's just my brother and I running the winery. He has a wife and kids. They live in St. Helena."

"And what do they think of us, moving to Oregon and having Ruby so soon after?"

"They adore you, and Ruby. They spend Christmas and Fourth of July with us every year."

"I see." It was a dismissive response because I didn't see at all. How could I have spent all those holidays with his brother's family and not know what a single one of them looked like? Trying to contain my confusion was difficult, but I saw no need to share the agony I felt.

"Do we have other bottles with my sketches on them?" I asked.

"Yes, in the wine cellar. Do you want to see them?"

"Yes."

"Let's wait until tomorrow, Rosy. You need to get some rest."

"It's only nine o'clock," I protested.

"Rose, you're just now feeling better since sustaining that concussion, and I know you'll want to linger over those labels in the wine cellar."

I agreed to wait. Ruby had been whisked away after dinner and when I asked Parker about it, he said our nearest neighbors took Ruby for a few days, so I'd have time to rest and recover. He assured me they were lovely people and adored our daughter, who revelled in their undivided attention. I decided exploring the wine cellar would be a nice diversion, something to keep me from missing Ruby. While preparing for bed I wondered if I would recognize the rest of my sketches on the wine labels. Any piece of my past that might be familiar was an exciting thought. I lay awake all night, confused about the timing of my pregnancy. Ruby should have been born right when Parker and I reunited, but she wasn't born for six more months. This new life I had mysteriously found myself in would have been perfect, except for the timing of Ruby's birth.

ALICE'S ADVENTURES

"May I join you, Dr. Easton?"

I looked up to see Lorelei beside me with a tray in her hands.

"Of course," I said, while standing to greet her. "And it's Oliver."

"Yes, I know." Lorelei placed her tray on the table and pulled up a chair. "I feel uncomfortable calling you Oliver." She smiled, which brightened the dull room.

"Why?" I asked.

"I don't know. Maybe because Katy's life is in your hands, which makes you an extraordinary person. Calling you Oliver seems too ordinary." Lorelei lit up the cafeteria again with her infectious smile.

I shook my head and chuckled at her humor. "Extraordinary is one thing I've never been called before. Let's wait and see if I can pull her out of this coma before labeling me anything other than an ordinary, frustrated doctor."

Lorelei studied me for a minute. "Why have you taken such a special interest in my Katy?" I didn't answer right away, and I could clearly see Lorelei's face turn red, as if embarrassed by the question. "I just mean, it seems like you're interested in Katy as much as her condition."

"You're right," I admitted, reluctantly. "Katya reminds me of my first love, who slipped out of my fingers when we were both attending UCLA. She went on to be a botanist which is what I thought I wanted to be, but then I became fascinated with medical botany, and that led to medicine in general. Somehow, I ended up a neurosurgeon. Plants are now my hobby. I get a lot of joy from growing organic herbs and vegetables to share with colleagues and neighbors. Something about working with seeds and soil is very calming. It grounds me, if you will forgive the pun. Gardening is a great stress reliever."

"I can only imagine how stressful it is to be a physician. Especially one that works a night shift now and then. Is that why you're here so late?"

"Yes," I admitted. "I've always been a night owl. It suits me. Caring for people in an emergency is very fulfilling, but also nerve-racking. I often work in my garden for an hour before going to bed, when coming off an all-nighter. I sleep better after gardening. It clears the weeds from my head, which is another terrible pun. I apologize."

We both laughed.

"No wonder you've taken such an interest in Katy. You have the same passion for growing things, not to mention Katy reminding you of a love that got away."

"I am more impressed with your Katy every day. Her produce rivals mine, and mind you, I take great pride in having a garden few gardeners can equal. I have immense respect for her focus and skills."

"You're just the man I need." Lorelei put her water glass down.

"I am?"

"Yes. I've been weeding and watering Katy's small specialty crops, but they're starting to look like orphans without her obsessive care and nurturing."

"Would you like me to take a look at them?"

"That would be wonderful."

"I'll stop by tomorrow afternoon."

"You know, you're not distant and unapproachable like so many in your field. I find it hard to believe no one has found a way to snatch you up, despite your busy schedule." Lorelei had finished her pie and was looking at me curiously.

"I have been in a few relationships, but my job does get in the way," I confessed.

"I could say the same," Lorelei admitted.

We both rose and left the cafeteria together. As it turned out I was headed to Katya's room and so Lorelei tagged along, since she was there to visit her best friend. We entered hoping to find her awake, but instead she was lying as still as the first day she'd entered this room. I checked her vitals while Lorelei brushed a few wisps of hair from our patient's face. Then she kissed Katya softly on the check and spoke to her in a cheery voice, as if Katya could hear every word. Perhaps she could. I honestly had no way of knowing. There weren't any significant changes in her vital signs, and when I returned later Lorelei had gone home. It was a quiet night in the ER and so I decided to stay for a while.

There was a book beside Katya's bed. It was *Alice's Adventures in Wonderland*, by Lewis Carroll. This, I decided, must be what Lorelei was reading out loud to our patient. Maybe Katya was dreaming about adventures of her own. I only hoped she hadn't fallen down a rabbit hole from which she might never return.

GENEVIEVE

Lorelei was there to greet me when I arrived at Katya's house on First Street the next afternoon. She led me through the house to the backyard and I couldn't help but think about how much the home reflected this patient I barely knew, yet somehow did know, by the friend who adored her and the husband who didn't. I also knew her by the way she managed to isolate herself in a small, close-knit town. How else could she have no other visitors?

The front room was streaming with light from long, narrow windows. Sunbeams danced on a plush green sofa and Oriental rug covering most of a dark, wooden floor. A few end tables housed colorful lamps and potted plants that looked well cared for. A floor to ceiling bookshelf neatly displayed rows and rows of well-worn bindings on everything from the classics to a few newly released Pulitzer winners. I tried not to linger too long reading titles, since I was basically a trespasser.

The front room was open to the formal dining area, which housed a heavy wooden table for six, eight if you raised the side leaves. Scented candles were tucked here and there and had obviously been burnt often. It was a home I could sit down in, grab a book to read, and never leave. Everything was neat and organized, yet comfortably worn and inviting. Pictures of what must have been her parents and grandparents were proudly displayed behind the glass doors of a china cabinet. They were tucked beside antique crystal and dishware with a purple grape pattern.

"It was her grandmother's," Lorelei informed me. "Katy's made very little changes to Genevieve, just a few personal touches; the books and candles. I think the floor rug is new and a couple lamps. Basically, she's added some interesting colors and scents, and a lot of literature. Believe it or not, Katy's read every book you see on these shelves."

I nodded appreciatively. "Genevieve?" I asked.

"That's' what Katy calls the house, or rather the spirit within it."

"I see." But I didn't really see at all. It was just one more dimension to this fascinating patient of mine. We didn't enter the other rooms, two of which had doors right off the front room. I couldn't help but glance in through the open doorways, however. The room in front was made up for guests, with an enticing four-poster bed and matching desk by the window. It had lots of light, overstuffed pillows, and a reading lamp on a bedside stand. The second room was filled with art and art supplies. There were different sized silk screens leaning against the wall. A solid, rough-hewn table filled the middle of the room and had various metal etching plates scattered across it. Paints and chemicals for etching had been neatly stored in large tubs, which sat on a shelf below the table.

"That's Katy's studio," Lorelei informed me.

"She does beautiful work," I commented. I couldn't help but stare at the artwork against the wall.

"Yes, she does. I've been after her to approach one of the galleries in town, but she's been distracted by other things lately."

I didn't ask what those distractions were, but I did wonder if perhaps a bad marriage and a pregnancy had anything to do with it. We entered the large kitchen and I stared up at the white highly-polished cabinets, from which Katya had fallen onto a white marble floor. I shook my head, wondering how the fall hadn't killed her. Other than the chill of near death in the air, this room felt strangely inviting, with baskets of fruits and vegetables on the shiny black counter. There was an antique breakfast table with a vase of fresh sunflowers placed in the middle of it. Lorelei must have put them there since Katya had fallen over a week ago now.

"I've been bringing in the produce not perfect enough to give her clients. That's what Katy always did. And I've been picking the apples and pears that grow on the trees at the far side of the lot. We made applesauce and canned pears together every year about this time." Lorelei stared out the window at the fruit trees in the distance.

There were two rooms off the kitchen. One appeared to be the only bathroom. It was typical of older homes to have one large bathroom off the kitchen. The other door led to the master bedroom. Lorelei pointed out how it had been added later along with the laundry room, which led to the back door. There was a small back porch with a half flight of stairs that led to the yard. The porch was perfect for standing on to admire Katya's plant beds. She also had a good number of large pots filled with an array of herbs and microgreens. Some held heirloom tomatoes heavy on the vine. I marveled at the various colors and shapes of the tomatoes. It made my mouth water just looking at them. Lorelei showed me where the gardening tools were in the shed, which sat in the back corner of the lot beside the driveway. A large black cat had jumped up on the wooden fence, startling me.

"That's Crow." Lorelei laughed.

"Katya's cat?"

"Yes. He was born in the cellar, with no trace of a mama or siblings."

I smiled at Crow, while he stared at me with huge yellow eyes. "Do we need to feed him?"

"I feed him once a day, same as Katy did. He hunts for his other meals."

I didn't ask why Miles wasn't caring for Crow. "Will he let you pet him?"

"No. He's quite wild, and Katy hasn't tried to tame him, other than capturing Crow long enough to be neutered and vaccinated."

"He is a handsome boy," I observed. "I hope Katya will be home soon," I said to Crow. "I'm sure you must miss her."

Lorelei kept me company while I fertilized and watered the crops. Then she saw me off with a basket of slightly imperfect fruits and vegetables. On the walk home I couldn't help but think about the baby Katya lost. What a wonderful mother she would have made; patient and nurturing by the looks of her plants, and there was how she looked after Crow, not to mention how much Lorelei loved Katya. I could only wonder how this gifted and nurturing woman ended up with a heartless man like Miles. I made a mental note to ask Lorelei more about their relationship next time I saw her.

ZACHARY

The first day Ruby was at our neighbor's house I took a long walk with Goldie across the field and into the Pine Grove, which was part of our Desert Sky ranch. Ruby and I had taken this walk a few times together. I missed her skipping beside me and chattering on about how she hoped we'd see a rabbit or a squirrel, which inevitably we would. Then we'd see the small creature run lickety-split with Goldie barking her head off. Afterward I sat on the porch swing reading a book until Parker finished an article he was working on and joined me. It was late afternoon by then.

"Are you ready to see your labels?" he asked.

I smiled in response.

Parker held my hand as we crossed the steep concrete steps to the wine cellar. It was perceptively cooler in the windowless room. Endless rows of wine racks lined the walls and gave the dimly lit space an ancient look. Parker pulled bottles from various racks and set them on a rough-hewn table, while one by one I picked them up, studied the label and then set them back down again. It gave me chills to see my sketches on every label. Some had clusters of grapes, or a solitary cluster in shades of green or purple. Others had lush vines. One label had a receding row of vines, another had an old oak on top of a hill. There were as many variations as types of wine and views from the vineyard. The initials KR (for Katya Rose) were on every label, in the right lower corner.

"Whatever happened to Zachary Austin?" I asked, remembering his initials on the bottle we drank that day in the tasting room.

"He lives down the road from us."

I looked up from the wine bottle in my hands and studied Parker's face. How long has he lived down the road? "Are we friends?" I asked.

Parker smiled. "Yes, we are. Zachary and I grew up on the same street in St. Helena. He bought a small ranch just south of here because he fell in love with Sisters when visiting us for our wedding. He raises alpacas."

"Really. How odd that I don't remember," I quipped, wanting to open bottle after bottle and drink them down to forget what I couldn't remember. Parker came closer and gently took the Cabernet from my hands. He set it down beside the others and hugged me tightly to his chest.

"It will all come back to you, Rosy. I know it will." He kissed the top of my head. "There's something I should tell you," he added.

I mumbled *what* into his shirt.

"It's about your best friend, Lorelei."

Just the mention of Lorelei's name caused me to tear myself loose from our embrace. I looked up at Parker. "What about her?"

"She's married to Zachary."

"You're kidding?" I scoffed, staring at him in disbelief.

"I couldn't be more serious. They have a girl named Kooper and a boy named Ryker. They're a couple years younger than Ruby. They're fraternal twins," Parker added, and then he grinned widely.

"Where is Lorelei? Why haven't I seen her since my fall from the roof?"

"She's in San Francisco visiting family. Lorelei grew up there, you know."

I nodded. "Yes, I know. I seem to know everything prior to the last seven years. How did they meet?"

"Zachary and Lorelei came to visit our first summer here. They stood up for us when we said our vows, in the field by the house. Lorelei fell in love with the area, just like Zach, so she moved to Sisters and opened a café. Honestly, I think they fell for each other as much as they did the area."

"I'm happy for her," I said, while trying to digest all this information. "And that's always been her dream, you know, to open a café," I added, feeling more frustrated than ever at not remembering any of this.

"It's also an art gallery," Parker added. "The gallery idea was Zach's doing. Lorelei embraced the idea because she could finally get your work out there for the world to appreciate."

"My work is in their gallery?"

"Yes, and Zachary's of course, and a few other local artists." Parker paused there. "Rosy, we thought it best not to mention your fall to her. Lorelei's mother is quite ill, which is why she went to visit, and well, we didn't want her worrying about you, too."

"Of course," I agreed. "I'm glad you didn't say anything." I shook my head. "I can't believe they fell in love and live nearby." I was sure the look on my face revealed my disbelief because Parker laughed out loud while gazing into my eyes. Our hands were on each other's shoulders, as if we couldn't bear to let go of one another.

"We have them over quite a bit, Rosy. And we go to their place too."

I obviously didn't remember any of our interactions with them. I didn't even remember us saying our vows. The only thing I knew for sure was that if I were going to create a dream world, this would be it, including the part where my best friend lives down the road on a ranch with alpacas. I traced the shape of Parker's face. He felt real. I ran my hand through his dark disheveled hair, which also felt real. I pulled him to me and kissed him. Everything within me stirred.

Parker picked me up in his arms and set me down on a red couch in the corner of the cellar. It was surrounded by other furniture stored there, along with a half dozen boxes. We made love for the first time since my fall. It was slow and exploratory as we savored one another, like a vintage wine set aside for a worthy occasion. I wanted the dream to stand still, and my reality, whatever it was, to not return. I wanted to open every bottle on the rough-hewn table beneath the dim lights and drink them, slowly, on the worn red couch while naked in Parker's arms.

As it was, we only drank one bottle, after rummaging through the boxes scattered around us. Fortuitously, we'd found a wine opener and several oversized crystal goblets in one of the boxes. "These were my grandmother's things," Parker shared. "I packed them myself. It's all from her house on Oak Street in St. Helena. It's everything that reminded me of her the most."

"That's sweet, Parker." I slipped into his flannel shirt and left it unbuttoned. He pulled his jeans back on but left them unsnapped. We got cozy on the faded red couch and I held the goblets while Parker poured the wine. It was cool at first but then warm on my throat. It had a spicy afternote. I savored it, along with the heavy crystal that had been his grandmother's. How I wished I could have known her. Halfway through the bottle we were swapping childhood memories and giggling like children. "I hope your grandmother doesn't mind us sitting half naked on her couch, drinking wine from her crystal," I said, while running my hand down Parker's chest and into his open jeans.

"I'm sure she is smiling at us from heaven." Parker reached out and gently took the goblet from my hand. He slid his hands inside the flannel shirt, and we made love again. By the time we'd snatched our clothing from the floor, it was damp and wrinkled. After placing the remaining bottles back on the rack, we ran up the stairs and flung open the door to embrace the sun sinking fast into the western sky. A breeze blew through the grass in the field where I'd said vows I didn't remember.

Parker took my hand and walked me to the middle of the field. "Right here, Rosy. Right here is where we said *I do*."

I nodded, with tears in my eyes. I felt robbed, not recalling this memory no matter how hard I tried.

"You wore a white summer gown that blew slightly in a breeze just like this one. It fell off your shoulders and had lacy sleeves. You were such a vision. I thought I was dreaming. I wanted to reach out and touch your feathery blond waves shining in the noonday sun. I wanted you all to myself in that field. I felt inexplicable joy when Zachary handed me the ring to put on your finger."

"What did you wear?" I asked.

"Exactly what you chose for me."

We both laughed, and lay down in the field, watching the sun slip lower over the mountains while the sky lit up on fire in vivid oranges and lucid reds.

"I wore a white button-down shirt, open at the neck, with khaki slacks. Everything was casual and loose fitting, and perfect," Parker told me.

"Who married us?" I asked.

"My brother came from Napa with his wife and kids. He married us."

"Your brother's a preacher?" I turned to look at Parker, lying there half hidden in the grass, his face glowing from the sky all ablaze.

"No. He got everything he needed off the Internet."

"Who else was there?"

Parker looked over at me. "Not many people besides my brother and his wife, and their two kids. Just a few ranchers from down the road, along with their families, and of course Lorelei and Zachary. Lorelei had prepared us a feast and wine flowed all night from the cellar. We paid a local rock band to set up and play at the reception, so we could dance under the stars with our new neighbors."

"It sounds perfect," I said, watching the colors in the sky fade.

"It was perfect." Parker rolled over on his side and brushed hair off my face. Then he kissed me. He tasted like the wine we'd been drinking. I recalled our lovemaking earlier, and our night in the vineyard so long ago. Was this real or was it just a fantasy? The only thing I really knew is that I loved Parker and I never wanted to lose him again, having already lost and found him twice. But it wasn't my choice to stay or leave. Fate seemed to have the upper hand and I couldn't see the cards, let alone choose how to play them.

A Lewis Carroll quote came rushing back to me. I had loved the book as a child but had no idea why it popped into my head. *Imagination is the only weapon in the war against reality.* In truth, reality was my only weapon in the war against imagination, but reality was illusive of late.

DELIVERY

Well into the second week of Ms. Harrington's coma I became slightly obsessed with her micro farm. Katya's condition was a wait-and-see situation that I found to be agonizing. Doctors want to heal their patients and feel quite helpless when they have no choice but to monitor a dire situation. It didn't help that Katya looked so much like Amelia lying there, which pained me beyond words. It had been a different kind of loss, a breakup I never realized would affect me as much as it did. Their features were so comparable it nearly shocked me sometimes when looking at Katya. Perhaps part of me didn't want to fail this patient because I had failed to appreciate, and therefore lost, the love of my life.

I had access to the micro farm because Lorelei and I had become friends. We were bonded by our commitment to this comatose woman, whom I had never met but felt as if I knew. Her presence was everywhere in the home she called Genevieve, and in the meticulously groomed produce growing behind it, currently harboring the last of her fall crops. I had come early this morning to hand pick her vegetables for the season and deliver them to Angele. It was something I offered to do because the purple cauliflower and baby kale couldn't wait another day. Lorelei had no time to do it, but I did. It was my day off. I would make my delivery around noon, and so we'd planned to have lunch together. I had a lot of questions for her regarding Katya. Perhaps they would help me understand our patient better, which might in turn help me know how best to communicate with Katya when she awakened. That is, if she did awaken.

I hadn't gotten very far with placing purple heads of cauliflower in a produce box when Miles appeared at the back railing. He made his way down the half flight of stairs, as impeccably dressed as always, and approached me looking somewhat perplexed. "May I ask why are you here, doctor, tending to my wife's garden? Does this have something to do with Lorelei and her meddling?"

"Good morning, Miles," I said cheerfully. "Lorelei kindly let me help with these crops because I shared with her how much I love gardening. It's what I do when I'm not doctoring." I laughed, hoping to put the man at ease.

"I don't know why Lorelei is trying to keep these gardens going. I have no intention of running a micro farm, and I doubt Katya will be back to do it."

"I wouldn't give up hope so easily, Miles. Katya's swelling in her brain has subsided significantly. She could wake up any day now."

"The longer a coma lasts, the less likely it is the patient will recover. That's what I read recently," Miles informed me.

"It's only been two weeks. Patients have awakened up to four weeks and even beyond that time with no long-term effect," I assured him.

"If her swelling has gone down, why isn't she awake?"

"It's more complicated than that," I answered. Truthfully, I had no idea why Katya wasn't awake, because by my calculations, she should be.

"I won't allow her to be in a coma for a prolonged period of time," Miles scolded. "I'll fight to keep that from happening," he added. Miles headed toward the garage, which sat beside the shed Katya kept her gardening tools stored in. He cursed under his breath and changed direction, toward the gate at the end of the driveway. It was closed, and he would have to open it. Crow sat atop the gate and meowed loudly at him. Miles skidded back, out of the cat's reach.

I chuckled quietly to myself and went to help. "Good morning, Crow," I said, while opening the gate.

"I don't know why Katya feeds that cat." Miles shook his head. "It's a wild animal. It wouldn't be hanging around if she didn't feed it, and now I think Lorelei is giving it food just like Katya did."

"Oh, I don't know, Miles. I think Crow hangs out here because he was born in the cellar. It's home to him, and as for Katya, there's still every chance she'll completely recover," I stubbornly insisted, refusing to believe the dreary end Miles feared was possible.

Miles didn't answer me. He got into his vehicle and left. I closed the gate and finished harvesting Katya's crops, which I placed in the back of my dark gray Rubicon—dark like my troubled mood, and gray like Katya's waning hope for recovery. I delivered the produce to Angele around lunchtime, just as I had said I would. Lorelei was quite pleased with the vegetables and after examining them, ushered me onto the patio where she insisted on buying my lunch.

While waiting for her to join me I sipped on an earthy merlot and amused myself watching kayakers in the Napa River float downstream with the tide. They eventually rounded the oxbow, toward Katya's Genevieve in Old Town. I couldn't help but wonder if Katya had sat here and admired this same view. Trees shimmered in their fall colors while the Napa sun lazily warmed everything it touched and nothing it didn't. A new chill was in the air early mornings and late evenings as the days shortened. On this third week of October pumpkins were sprouting up on multiple doorsteps, and while scanning Angele's dessert menu, I noted a pumpkin cheesecake offering.

"I hope you don't mind but I ordered for us." Lorelei sat across from me and breathlessly added, "We have a special today that I think you will like."

"I have no doubt," I answered, closing my menu. "I was looking to see if there were any changes since I was here last."

"And when was that?" Lorelei asked.

"Oh my, probably August. I come here whenever I can't live another day without Angele's Ratatouille."

"I can't believe we've never run into each other." Lorelei shook her head in disbelief.

"The hours I keep are quite odd," I said. "I've often been here when Angele is shutting down at night, which is probably one of the few times you *aren't* here."

"That's true," she admitted.

"I ran into Miles at Katya's house," I blurted out.

"That must have been unpleasant." Lorelei took a sip of her ice water sporting a generous lemon slice.

"Yes, it was. He doesn't believe Katya will ever recover."

"He *hopes* she will never recover."

"Explain to me why they're still married," I asked, obviously annoyed.

Lorelei shrugged. "Why does anyone stay in a bad marriage? Sometimes people don't want to admit failure. I know Katya wanted children more than anything. It made her believe things that weren't true."

"Like what?"

"Like thinking Miles would become this loving, doting husband if she got pregnant. She hoped he'd be so excited about parenthood he would no longer be distant and critical."

I nodded slowly, letting that sink in while the waiter served our main course. "This smells wonderful. What is it?"

"Beef stew. It's divine with Katya's fall vegetables."

I grew silent after complimenting Lorelei's choice for lunch. She had no idea Miles couldn't have children, or that Katya was pregnant when she fell. "You once mentioned how Katya was distracted lately from her art. What was the distraction if you don't mind my asking?"

Lorelei tucked a lock of hair behind her ear. "Ever since I've known her, Katya has spent afternoons sketching in a vineyard out in St. Helena. At least, whatever afternoons she had free. Her micro farming keeps her pretty busy."

"Which vineyard?"

"It's owned by the Mancini's. Three Gates Winery."

"Why that vineyard?"

"Katya had a brief encounter with some guy at her college, and she thought that was his family's vineyard. They never exchanged last names, so she doesn't know for sure."

"Is he there?"

"Parker? No. At least, I don't think so. I think she was only going back at this point because it was a great location for her, with easy access to a hill that looked out over endless vines. Any artist's dream, if obsessed with drawing grapes." Lorelei smiled. "Katya rarely does anything without purpose. It must have felt right, for whatever reason. She's an artist. What else can I say? Artists are intuitive. It's partly why I love her."

I had devoured the excellent beef stew and was savoring another glass of merlot while digesting this new information. Maybe Parker had shown up after all and gotten Katya pregnant. But then why hadn't she told her best friend? I studied Lorelei as she watched flecks of sun sparkle on the water. Angele's river view was the best on the Boardwalk. The French bistro had been a boathouse back in the day. There was something magical about the rough-hewn walls, nautical décor, and white tablecloths in the small dining room. It made for great ambiance, especially at night when candles placed at each table were lit up.

Lorelei turned her attention to me, with sadness swimming in her blue eyes. "Oliver, I feel terrible about Katy's fall. I believe there was something on her mind, but we were both so busy." She stared into space, as if recalling a bad memory. "The restaurant is always packed with tourists during harvest, and there are so many late-night parties. It's essential networking for both our businesses. Katy was working long hours to get her crops delivered for the harvest crowds, and I've been here until late each evening." Lorelei paused there and swiped at a tear. "We never had a single late night on her porch this month sharing our deepest secrets, and I think that's exactly what she needed from me. I failed her."

"We all feel helpless when something bad happens to someone we care about. That can often lead to misplaced guilt," I said in earnest.

"There's more, Oliver." Lorelei sighed. "Katy had thought she was pregnant right before harvest time, but then it turned out to be a false alarm. It really got her down, thinking she would finally have a baby, only to learn otherwise. I'm so upset with myself for not being more supportive."

"The important thing is that you're here for her now." I squeezed Lorelei's hand from across the table and peered into her eyes without really seeing them.

All I could think of was this new information. "Katya thought she and Miles were having a baby?"

"Yes."

"Did Miles know about this?"

"No. She didn't want to tell him until she was certain."

"So, she hadn't taken a pregnancy test or seen a doctor?"

"No."

"I see." Part of me couldn't help but wonder how different things might have been if Katya had shared with Miles about possibly being pregnant. Miles would probably have revealed his sterility and perhaps Katya would have left him. "Grieving the loss of a baby, whether real or imagined, can be psychologically traumatizing," I added, and then I stood to leave. "You certainly don't need to spoil me like this, Lorelei. I'm happy to help in any way I can with Katya's micro farm. But thank you for the wonderful lunch anyway."

"It's I that should thank you, Oliver. I can't tell you how much better I feel knowing Katy is in your hands, and you've been so supportive through all of this."

I told Lorelei it was my pleasure, and it truly was. Something about helping Lorelei and working the micro farm kept me from feeling helpless regarding Katya's condition. In the back of my mind, I continually heard Miles's skepticism about his wife recovering, and I couldn't let go of the possibility that she indeed might not recover. Even more disturbing was discovering that someone Katya loved had no idea regarding her condition. I was torn about finding that person, knowing it could make all the difference in her recovery, yet also knowing I'd be meddling in the life of a patient.

FANTASY

Parker and I had gone to bed as usual at eleven o'clock, but I tossed and turned until falling asleep. Sometime before dawn I was plagued by a reoccurring dream in which I'd be falling through the back of a cupboard. I always woke up from the dream before landing. Then I'd remind myself it wasn't a cupboard I'd fallen from; it was a barn roof. The dream began with me tugging on a shiny brass doorknob inside a dark cabinet. I'd tug on the knob until it opened, tumbling me out into a blue sky. Strong winds would suck me into a vacuum, and for a few seconds, I would be suspended in midair. But then I always began to fall, slowly, as if I were weightless.

This time, however, I heard a baby cry as I neared the ground. It was a newborn cry, angry and loud, which suddenly awakened me. I bolted upright in the bed and stared into the darkness. I could feel Parker beside me. I could see the curtain move at the open window, and I could still hear a baby cry. It was such a distinctive sound, the first cry of a new life. The more I listened, however, the more I realized it sounded more like an animal, a cat to be exact. I slipped from the bed and peered out the sliding glass door. Looking down I couldn't believe what I saw, which nearly caused me to shout out loud.

It was Crow!

I opened the door just enough for him to saunter in, as if having been out for an evening stroll. I stood there unable to move as he gingerly headed for the hallway. By then I'd found my feet beneath me and followed him. Crow strutted into Parker's den and hopped onto the leather couch. Standing in the doorway I stared at him through the first light of day. Was this all a dream? The fuzzy thoughts, the frequent blurry vision, the headaches and exhaustion, the occasional dizziness.

Maybe they were symptoms of a head injury, or maybe I had fallen into an alternate reality. If not a dreamworld, then was this the life I might have lived? Was I merely putty in the hands of fate and never in charge of my own destiny? I sat at the other end of the couch and covered myself with the afghan neatly folded there. Watching Crow wash his face caused me to burst into racking sobs. I tried to smother them with a throw pillow by smashing my face into it, so as not to wake Parker or Ruby. But then, at some point, I began to laugh hysterically because I didn't honestly know if Parker and Ruby existed, in this house, on this high desert ranch. Perhaps they were just figments of my imagination, like Crow.

"Rosy, why are you up so early?"

I nearly jumped out of my skin at the sound of Parker's voice. Turning toward the door I saw him standing there and I knew that if this was a dream, I'd done a first-rate job of making it up. I couldn't, however, answer him. I was too emotionally distraught to speak. Instead, I buried my head in the pillow again. Parker sat down beside me. "Oh Rosy. I'm so sorry. I should have mentioned that we brought Crow with us from California, but he's been gallivanting about for nearly two weeks now. I was afraid if he never came back, it would only make you sad to know he had been here until you fell from the barn."

I raised my face from the pillow and stared at Parker. He looked much older in the gray light of dawn. I couldn't imagine how ancient *I* must have looked. I felt weary from all the little pieces of my life floating about, with no hope of ever connecting them into one coherent picture. Parker reached out and touched my puffy cloud of hair as if it were a sacred work of art. Only in my imagination could I cause a man to love me like this.

"Why is Crow on your couch?" I asked in a small, lost voice.

Parker glanced at the enormous black cat, looking quite handsome in these early hours rather than spent like Parker and myself.

"He's been partially an indoor cat for quite a while, Rose. The winters here are severe compared to Napa Valley." Parker laughed. "Crow was more than happy to accept a warm, dry rug in front of the fireplace. He's always been drawn to Ruby and was quite protective whenever we had our baby girl outside. I think it was Ruby that coaxed him in one winter during a snowstorm." Parker looked at me. "You'd be amazed, Rosy, at how Crow will cuddle up right beside Ruby, as if they've been best friends their whole lives."

I studied the fine lines around Parker's eyes and could feel a slight smile on my face, but I was still unable to speak. All I could think about was this fantasy I'd so carefully created, if not an alternate reality some amazing god had placed me in, probably by mistake. Or maybe that's what heaven is, everything you have dared to wish for.

"Say something, Rosy. Do you need a pain pill?"

"No, Parker. I'm just so confused. I think I might have lost any grip I ever had on reality. Maybe what I really need is a shrink."

"Rose, don't talk like that." He set the afghan aside and pulled me to him. I buried my head in his chest and suddenly all thoughts of Crow vanished. The silkiness of Parker's pajama shirt against his hard chest muscles aroused me. I kissed him between two middle buttons, which easily spilled open, as if preferring to be undone. Parker pulled my face up to his and kissed me tenderly, but soon our soft, sweet kiss turned into a hard passionate need. In one continuous motion Parker lifted my nightie over my head and dropped it to the floor. Crow jumped from the couch just as we sprawled out across the afghan and made love.

I took a long, hot shower afterward. Standing beneath the soothing stream of water I wondered about the fall I'd taken. I remembered being pulled through a vacuum and then freezing in midair before free-falling through a dazzling blue sky. I miraculously landed in a plush green field, complete with the family and home I'd always wanted. There wasn't any way this could all be real. No matter how hard I wanted to believe this was truly my life, there simply was no denying the baby Parker and I conceived would have been born at the end of April, not in November. There was no logic to it. This is how I knew I would wake up any minute, and it would all be over.

VINES

After lunch with Lorelei at Angele I drove to Three Gates Winery in St. Helena. I needed to know who fathered the baby Katya lost. It disturbed me that I'd taken such an interest in this patient, but I couldn't help myself. I'd called a few friends from medical school to consult about her condition but nothing they shared had helped. Katya's tear in her Dura mater had mended, her swelling had gone down, and her bruising was healed. Everything was functioning properly, and still she slept. Obviously, her brain was injured in a way that didn't show on any of the tests we ran. Maybe that damage would heal itself, and maybe it wouldn't.

Lorelei had not grown weary of reading the Lewis Carroll book to Katya every day before and after work. It seemed appropriate for her to be reading a book in which nothing appeared to be as it was. Lorelei didn't know Miles couldn't have children, or that Katya had lost someone else's baby. Parker Mancini had no idea his one true love wasn't staying away to save her marriage, but instead had fallen and lost his baby, which he knew nothing about. None of us knew what was happening behind Katya's fluttering eyes and slight smile, or why her coma was so unlike most, in that she appeared to be only sleeping, as if an actual sleeping beauty.

How does someone as interesting as Katya Harrington end up with no family, a husband like Miles, and only one faithful friend? Artists are known for being reclusive, and Katya certainly fit that mold. Then again, how could she possibly have time to make friends between coddling a yard full of delicate plants and creating some of the most intriguing artwork I had ever seen? I was in awe of her intricate etchings and fluid silk screens, the striking yet unpretentious details and warmth of her home, the luscious and vibrant produce she grew. All evidence of her made me want to know the woman. I could only hope one day I would.

The drive through wine country was stunning. Grapevines lined the road on both sides as far as the eye could see, and then disappeared into infinity. I passed one winery after another, while gentle hills rose and fell along the way. Massive oaks would occasionally jut up in little groves. I'd never seen a bigger, bluer sky with nary a cloud in sight. When turning into Three Gates Winery I stopped the car for a minute to admire the picturesque private drive. Just as the sign indicated, there were three gates from the road to the tasting room. They were all wide open as I passed them one by one, winding around gentle curves in the road. I wondered if the knoll above the tasting room was where Katya sketched. It had a sprawling oak tree at the very top, and a sweeping view in every direction. I could picture her there.

The parking lot was almost empty, probably because harvest was nearly complete and major tourism was winding down. I decided to walk up the hill to the majestic oak before entering the tasting room. It was easy to cross the nearly deserted country road and hike upward, straight between two long rows of grapevines. The leaves on the vines were speckled with tinges of brown, and a certain slant to the sun gave away the changing season. I wondered if Katya had sketched the barren vines and shriveling leaves as enthusiastically as she had other seasons in the vineyard.

When I reached the tree, I stared straight up through its twisted branches and saw patches of blue sky where leaves had grown less dense. I sat against its broad trunk and looked out across a sea of green, dotted here and there with a cluster of willow trees, or maple, or oak like the one I was leaning against. They were all tinged with a hint of autumn. Blackbirds cawed at me while ants threatened to crawl on my shoes. If only I had a leather-bound book and variety of pencils like I'd seen in Katya's studio. I would have penned the inspiring scene, just as she had done.

I don't know how long I lingered there, but I can tell you there is nothing more frightening sometimes than being alone with your own thoughts. Mine were disturbing because they forced me to see how my life was as barren as these stripped and dying vines. Where was my harvest? I had no wife or children, just a few relatives back where I had grown up. My friends were but a few, which I blamed on my intense work schedule. Perhaps one reason I'd been so easily drawn into Katya's world is because it aligned with mine. She was obviously a workaholic, and so was I, yet I bet she never thought of herself as such, just as I'd never considered myself reclusive. Who would read me books if I were in a coma? Surely not all the patients I'd healed, or the colleagues who had admired my work. Surely no one, honestly, no one at all.

At least Katya had Lorelei. And now she had me. I would continue to do whatever I could to heal her, not just because that was my calling in general, but because I couldn't bear the thought of her never recovering. In the deepest darkest corners of my mind, God help me, I was falling in love with this woman I'd never met. Part of me thought I was losing my mind. Doctors are known for walking a fine line between sainthood and insanity. God knows . . . I'm no saint, but insane . . . maybe?

Who would prefer middle of the night ambulances full of accident victims instead of everyday illnesses? Who would weed a garden while watching the sun come up instead of going straight to bed after a harrowing night shift? Only a disturbed doctor obsessed with the personal life of their coma patient.

On that lovely note I walked back down the hill through the rows of grapevines, crossed the deserted country road, and entered the tasting room. I hoped to meet the man who had impregnated my patient, with whom I was obsessed.

A young woman with a ponytail lined stemware up along the counter for me. She poured each of my tastings, after educating me on the grape it was produced from, and which notes I could expect to find in that wine. By the time I'd worked my way through whites and into reds, more patrons had entered the bar area. My ponytailed server became busy with new customers, allowing me time to observe my surroundings. The facility was architecturally impressive. Heavy entryway doors opened onto a low-ceilinged alcove. Beyond the alcove was a large open-beamed room surrounded by massive windows. From those expansive windows one could peer out at grapevines gently rolling down one slope and up another, until disappearing into the distance.

A hallway veered off the alcove and led to what I presumed to be private tasting areas. There were probably living quarters above that part of the winery judging by the outside of the large stone building. I wondered if Katya's old college friend resided in the upstairs living quarters. My thoughts were soon interrupted by someone entering the tasting room, flooding the shadowed entry with sunlight for an instant until the heavy doors thudded shut. A tall, well-built man stood there, glancing over the bar area. His eyes conveyed familiarity with the environment.

Even from a distance I could tell he was brooding about something, ruminating over things unseen and unfelt by the rest of us sharing his space. Then to my surprise he walked my way, slipping behind the bar as if he'd done it a million times. "May I offer you a glass of your favorite tasting?" he asked. "It's on the house, since your server has become quite overwhelmed with customers and left you dry. An empty glass is forbidden here," he added, with a warm smile.

"That's very generous of you," I said. "I especially like the 2018 cab."

"I'm not surprised. In my opinion it's our best wine. My name is Parker, by the way." He poured me a glass of the robust cab and continued to smile, but a sadness prevailed in his eyes. This man, without a doubt, was the boy from

Katya's college days. I envisioned them together, she small and fair, he tall and olive toned. What a lovely couple they'd have been, had fate not intervened.

"I'm Oliver," I responded, reaching out to shake his hand. I felt my own smile to be stiff. How could it not be? Standing before me was a rival, regardless that he didn't know it. "Are you the proprietor?" I asked.

"The winery has been in my family for a long time. My brother runs it. I just help out when I'm in town." Parker studied me while I looked into his eyes, which were as deep and brown as a newly dug grave. I wanted to feel sorry for the man, but I couldn't. If he'd only reached out to Katya in the last few weeks, he'd know her current condition.

"And where is home when not here, at the winery?" I inquired.

Parker shrugged. "Anywhere I choose really. I write articles for corporations, to either promote their businesses or inform their clientele. It's all done remotely, which allows me to travel."

"Interesting. May I ask if it's a lucrative profession?"

"One can become quite successful at it if diligent and motivated. I think I've encountered some luck along the way as well, regarding the inroads I've stumbled upon. At any rate, it's the one area of my life where I've excelled beyond my expectations."

"Are you married?" I asked, already knowing he probably wasn't.

"No. The only woman for me has slipped through my fingers, twice." Parker stared at the endless rows of vines out the window behind me. I could see his eyes rest on the hill with the old sprawling oak tree.

"I'm a doctor," I admitted, "but the one thing I cannot heal is a broken heart. Only time can do that."

Parker shook his head. "I seem to be as inept at love as I am adept at writing for corporations. Facts are easy. Logic is foundational. But love, well that's complicated."

"I wish you the best of luck with figuring it out," I said, while hoping his best luck would be with someone other than Katya.

"What about you?" he asked. "Are you married?"

"No. My profession leaves no time for relationships," I confessed. "I did love someone once, a long time ago. I honestly haven't been willing to put myself out there again."

"I don't blame you," Parker said.

I stood to leave, and we said our goodbyes. I barely saw the road while winding back through the twists and turns between each gate. I felt guilty, despite knowing it wasn't my place to tell Parker where Katya was, or why, just like I couldn't tell Lorelei about Katya losing a baby, one that was not her husband's, who couldn't have children even if he'd wanted to.

It took the entire trip home to reassure myself I was doing the right thing by not interfering in Katya's personal life. Curiosity had led me to the winery, not a desire to interfere in her (or Parker's) decisions. I convinced myself these inexplicable feelings for Katya could only be helpful toward her recovery. I was staying within the boundaries of professionalism. My friendship with Lorelei was acceptable, given that we lived in a small town and were practically neighbors.

Then it occurred to me I didn't know where Lorelei lived. I'd been so focused on Katya that I hadn't thought to ask. Maybe my judgment shouldn't be trusted. Maybe I needed to turn Katya over to another doctor, someone fresh and new, who might be able to wake her up.

By the time I pulled into my driveway I concluded there was no disentangling myself from Katya's case. God help me, I couldn't walk away. I didn't have Parker's ability to stand on the sidelines and hope everything would work out as it should. No, for better or for worse, I would fight for Katya to the end, whatever that end might be.

LAKE BILLY CHINOOK

It had been two weeks since my apparent fall from a barn roof, which supposedly caused the concussion attributed to my memory loss. My best calculation, at this point, was that I didn't fall from a barn roof at all. I fell through a cupboard door in Genevieve, exactly like my recurring dream in this dreamworld. Perhaps this was death, a place you fall into out of nowhere, but is so appealing you don't care. Some might call it heaven. It was a flawed theory, I decided, because *I did care.* Not knowing if this was reality or not, or whether I would wake up or not, was slowly eating away at me.

Ellis had just pronounced me well, mainly because it had been two weeks and concussions were thought to be healed by then, but he had no explanation for the ongoing memory loss. I could tell from how carefully he'd worded his appraisal of my condition that he didn't hold out much hope for it ever coming back, since it hadn't already. "Now what?" I asked Parker, while staring at him from the passenger seat of the car. I had no doubt my gray eyes were stormier than ever, since my inner turmoil was about to overtake me. He returned my stare with those dark brown eyes that radiated warmth, like a freshly hoed plot of earth ready for seed.

"Rosy, don't give up hope. Ellis said your memory might still return."

"He didn't say it convincingly," I retorted. I quit staring at Parker and looked out the window.

"He's never had a patient with amnesia. I think he just feels unqualified to give an opinion."

"I guess so," I agreed. "I can't wait to pick up Ruby and go home."

"Zach called and said the twins want Ruby to stay longer. He suggested we go to the lake. It's such an unusually warm day for October." Parker reached over and took my hand into his, but I kept looking out the window, trying to hold back my tears of frustration.

"Rosy, we can have a picnic and go for a boat ride. I think it would be good for you. Zach said Ruby and the twins are excited about the idea."

"Fine," I agreed. "I'll pretend I remember Zachary and the twins until one day this genuinely feels like my life." I glanced at Parker. "You know, like the velveteen rabbit. Everything will suddenly *be real.*"

Parker kissed my cheek. "Sometimes you're so funny, Rose. Let's run by the house and get our swimming suits. It's going to be in the mid-seventies. That never happens this time of year. And you love Lake Billy Chinook. You always have. It will cheer you up."

"Maybe it will," I quietly answered, but my insides were screaming and having a meltdown. I was mourning the loss of all those memories from the past seven years. I'd have given anything to remember the look on Parker's face when we stood in the meadow and said I do, or when we had our first dance as a married couple. I absolutely hated not remembering my belly swollen with Ruby or holding her in my arms for the first time. I felt robbed of these events.

We drove in silence for a while, both of us lost in our own thoughts. Mine kept circling back to the fall. Did I really tumble out the back of a cupboard? It didn't feel any more real to me than falling from a barn roof, which I didn't recall in the slightest. Why did I recall every painful minute of my seven years married to Miles, but not one day of the past seven years married to Parker? I shivered at the thought of possibly returning to Napa and to Miles, to the mess everything had become with his cheating, and then my cheating. Ruby had to be the child Parker and I conceived that night in the vineyard, regardless that the timing of her birthday was off. It was so hard to convince myself of this, however, because it was the same month here as it had been in Napa before the fall.

After our mostly quiet ride home we put on our swimsuits and grabbed towels, stuffing them into an oversized beach bag. Parker packed a cooler with drinks and snacks while I rooted through Ruby's drawers for her swimsuit. I found a whole pile of them, one more adorable than the next, which reminded me of the onesies I never got to see her wear. I concluded we spent a fair amount of time at Lake Billy Chinook in the summer, but then I remembered there was a hot tub on the master suite patio. That might be another reason for so many swimsuits. I also packed a heavy sweatshirt for my sweet girl, because it wouldn't stay warm for very long this time of year.

We met Zachary at the lake with all three kids in tow. He helped us unpack the car and together we headed toward his private dock where the boat was moored. "I hear you got a clean bill of health from Ellis. That's great news." Zach looked at me as if I were an old friend, while I tried not to stare at him as if he were a stranger.

"Yes. No memories returning yet though," I added, while observing Zach to be quite muscular with eyes as blue as Lorelei's. "When is my best friend coming home?" I asked.

"I'm not sure. Her mother may be passing soon. I know she won't come back until then."

"I'm really sorry, Zach. This all must be so hard on you and the twins." I glanced at Kooper and Ryker, each holding one of Ruby's hands as they walked out in front of us. From the back it was clear that Kooper had gotten Lorelei's thick auburn hair and Ryker was blond like his dad.

"We're fine." Zach laughed. "Maybe not as organized as usual but hanging in there. I'm sorry about your memory, Katya. I haven't mentioned your concussion to Lorelei. She has so much on her plate right now, with her mom, and trying to manage the Studio Café remotely. I thought it would be best to hold off on telling her about your concussion."

"I completely understand. I think you made the right decision."

Soon we arrived at the dock where I watched Ruby, Kooper, and Ryker scamper onto the boat over the open bow. Parker and Zachary climbed in next, shoving coolers and beach bags into out-of-the-way places before securing life jackets on Ruby and the twins. The sun glistened on the water like lit up fairy dust.

Maybe I didn't remember Zach or his boat, but I'd been coming to this lake my whole life. It was full of memories. My mother never came. She didn't like water, but my father and I would tootle around in a fishing boat most Saturdays in good weather. We'd motor up the arm of a river when tired of fishing. We had three choices, since three rivers flowed into the dammed-up canyon: the Metolius, Crooked River, and Deschutes. Zach owned a lot on the Metolius, which was where he had his private dock. It was a huge lake, surrounded by rock walls jutting up into the sky. As a child I would see mountain goats perched on the cliffs, and wild horses grazing at the top of the ridge. I wondered if they were still there.

"Rosy? Are you coming?"

I scrambled over the bow and sat beside Ruby while Zach steered us out to open water. We anchored in a cove to eat our picnic lunch after the short boat ride. Zach had brought sandwiches and it wasn't long until all three children had peanut butter smeared across their cheeks. When cleaning up their faces I looked into Kooper's and Ryker's eyes, and I saw my Lorelei there. Looking into Ruby's eyes I saw Grandma Rose. Goosebumps broke out on my skin. I smoothed them away while hoping to never wake up, if this was a dream.

Perhaps I was healed from my head injury, but nonetheless fractured light and wavy lines blurred my vision now and then. I had lapses in coherence, merely seconds where only a void existed, and then all the sights and sounds of life would rush back in. Voices often echoed in my head. It was happening now as I wiped peanut butter off Kooper's cheeks, but I didn't mention it to anyone, for fear that acknowledgement would awaken me.

After lunch Zach and Parker put on short wetsuits and took turns wake surfing while the children and I watched, cheering them on. Hardly any boats were on the lake. It felt as if we had the entire dammed up canyon all to ourselves, which made it feel even more magical. A bald eagle swooped down right in front of us at one point, snatching a fish from an osprey and flying away flapping its long white wings as if nothing at all had happened. I marveled at the barren beauty of the rough-hewn cliffs, and the starkness of the bold canyon walls. Nature's creatures had so expertly adapted to the wild, unforgiving terrain.

"Rosy, you should wake surf." Parker looked at me encouragingly. "Ellis said you can return to all your regular activities."

"I wake surf?" I asked.

"Yes, Rose. You're a master at it. Zach and I are both jealous of how easy you make it look."

"I've never been athletic," I protested.

"Surfing the wake is more about balance, and in your case, elegance and grace."

Zach agreed.

I stared at them for a minute, trying to recall ever having wake surfed.

"Please Mommy!" Ruby clapped her hands in anticipation. She crawled into my lap and hugged me tightly.

"All right then, let's give it a try." I kissed Ruby on the forehead and sat her down beside Kooper and Ryker in the bow. Parker handed me a short wetsuit and life vest, which Zach said were Lorelei's. I smiled at her good taste and suddenly missed her more than I could ever have imagined. After jumping in the water and getting over the initial shock of how cold it was, I felt strangely comfortable with the entire situation. Zach pulled me up easily on the first try. I threw the rope onboard almost at once and surfed as if competing for a championship title. The only disconcerting thing about the exhilarating run was wondering if this was simply a beautiful dream. If so, then at the precise moment I woke up, my worst nightmare would begin.

OYSTERS

I had a strong desire for Hog Island oysters and so I stopped off at Oxbow Public Market Place on my way back from Three Gates Winery. It would be the perfect ending to a lovely afternoon. Sitting at the counter facing First Street made me think about Katya and Genevieve. I couldn't see the house from where I was. It was out the front door and on the other side of the building, nonetheless I could feel Genevieve's presence. No matter how everything turned out, I was certain the home would always haunt me. Maybe because it felt so mysterious and alive whenever I was there, even if only in the gardens working with the plants. Katya's presence in the home itself seemed to blend with the remnants of her grandmother's spirit. Perhaps I was a bit daft, but I truly believed there was a *feeling* in the house that resonated with both women, neither of whom I had met.

"Well hello stranger. Didn't I just see you at lunch?" Lorelei had slid onto a stool beside me.

I quit staring across the huge, high ceilinged Market Place, filled with patrons buying dinner at various food venders. "And so, I guess we meet again, only over oysters this time," I exclaimed, and then I laughed.

"It would appear so," Lorelei agreed. "I generally have oysters here once a week. I'm heading across the street to Katya's afterwards to water the plants."

"May I tag along?" I asked.

"Certainly. Miles is in San Francisco for a few days, again." Lorelei rolled her eyes. "Sunsets are gorgeous from Katya's front porch. We could watch it with a bottle of wine."

"That sounds lovely. It seems I'm always meeting you at Katya's. Where do *you* live, Lorelei, if you don't mind my asking?"

"Of course not. I have a little house that butts up against a winery on the other side of town. Why do you ask?"

"Oh, no reason. It just occurred to me I had no idea where you called home." Was I still paranoid about all things Katya? Undoubtedly, but at least I now knew where Lorelei lived.

"Home for me was originally in the Bay Area," Lorelei added. "I was raised there, but ever since getting my MBA I've lived here." Someone behind the counter brought her a glass of wine and our oysters appeared soon after. By the time we'd finished our feast, guilt had set in.

"I just came from Three Gates Winery," I confessed.

"Really? So, after our lunch you took a drive out there?"

"I did."

"Are the vines shriveled yet?"

"Not shriveled at all but the leaves are starting to turn, like the trees. Have you been to Three Gates?" I asked. A handful of young employees were shucking oysters behind the counter. Lorelei and I both watched this painstaking task unfold as she answered.

"Yes. Quite lovely. Did you have a specific reason for going there?" she asked.

"Curiosity, mainly. I know I'm getting too involved in Katya's life. I'm not sure why. Her situation is as fascinating as she is, maybe that's why," I confessed.

"So, what did you think?" Lorelei asked. "Did you see any potential knights in shining armor to awaken our sleeping beauty?"

"No," I said. I could never tell Lorelei about having met Parker in the tasting room. It didn't appear that she had any inkling about Katya having met up with Parker at some point, or that Katya had been pregnant with his baby. Our patient had managed to weave herself a very tangled web before that fateful fall. I only hoped she would have an opportunity to untangle it at some point. "I did see what a perfect area it is for sketching," I shared. "There are endless views from the hill across the street."

"I know." Lorelei finished her wine. "I never climbed the hill to see the view, not until after Katy's fall."

"Why did you climb it then?" I asked.

"I just wanted to feel close to her."

"Did you?"

"Yes. Her presence is so strong there I wasn't sure if it gave me peace of mind or added to my frustration."

"Frustration about feeling helpless, regarding her condition?"

"Yes."

"I know exactly how you feel," I said, while paying the bill. I insisted on buying Lorelei's dinner, especially since she was going to let me rummage through Katya's art. We meandered through the market and stopped at a few vendors on our way out. Lorelei bought wine and cheese. I bought nuts and chocolates. It would be fun to relax on Katya's porch and watch the sun set, but more importantly I would have a chance to study Katya's etchings and silk screens. I'd merely glanced at her art when first seeing it. Now that I'd been to the vineyard where the sketches for her printmaking had originated, I couldn't wait to re-examine her work.

Once at the house we put our purchases on the counter. Together we sat on the floor of Katya's studio to sort through her art stacked against the wall. One piece was more thought provoking than the next. The silk screens were layers of transparent color in either warm or cool tones. The layers gave the art great dimension. She perfectly captured spring in the vineyard with soft greens and delicate yellows. Mid-summer vines were bolder, darker green, with intense lighting. Harvest was glorious, with shades of purple mixed into the greens and yellows.

The etchings couldn't have been more different. The gently flowing translucent layers found in her silk screens were all sharp lines and hard edges in the etchings. Vivid details overshadowed the lush colors. One might get lost in a Katya etching, tracing each line with your mind. I found them stimulating, perplexing, whereas the silk screens gave me a sense of calm. The art of dreamers.

Clearly, two very different women lived within her.

"What do you think?" Lorelei glanced at me, but I couldn't tear my gaze from the art.

"Her work is so contrasting. If she were to make a silk screen of oysters, I have no doubt I'd want to devour them. Katya would make a plate of oysters appear sensual and succulent, like a perfect juicy feast. You would probably swear you could smell them and even taste their sweet nectar. Quite the contrary, if she did an etching of those same oysters, I'm sure I'd want to hold them in my hands and feel their rough, sharp edges and their smooth, round shells. I'd wonder why I'd never noticed their exact shape and texture before, each one different from the next."

Lorelei laughed. "You do love oysters, don't you? But alas, Katya seems to be obsessed only with her vineyard. Don't you find that odd?"

"Not really. Her subject matter within the confines of the vineyard is so diverse I honestly don't think I could ever get bored with her work."

"I agree." Lorelei began straightening the art, placing every piece where it had been. "What I love about her art is how I can literally feel every season. She somehow puts me there. And her interpretation of the various views at her beloved winery makes me wonder if I've been looking at the same landscape."

"True," I agreed. "But I must say I find it intriguing to see it all through her eyes, which is almost other-worldly."

"Other-worldly?" Lorelei smiled.

"You know, as if she's viewing it in a different reality."

"I think we call that abstract art."

"I suppose it's all a matter of interpretation," I admitted. "Her silk screens are somewhat abstract, but her etchings are very exact. It's her etchings, that stark portrayal of reality that makes me feel as if her universe is altered from mine."

"What do you mean?" Lorelei glanced at me curiously.

"I mean she sees details in a way I never have, and I'm a doctor. I admire how exacting she is. It's something we have in common."

"Aside from gardening?" I could have sworn there was a twinkle in Lorelei's eye when she said this. Was she making fun of me, and my obsession with Katya?

"And reading," I added, refusing to acknowledge her mocking tone.

We ate chocolate and drank wine as the sun went down, each in our own space on the generous porch. Lorelei and I were quite comfortable with one another by this point. Conversation didn't need to happen. Our own thoughts were enough to fill our heads for quite a while. Neither of us seemed to relish leaving, so we delved into the nuts and cheese, and opened another bottle of wine. Why not? It was a lovely October evening. The lights on First Street made the late evening crowd quite visible to us as they mosied into wine bars or restaurants. Lively music began to play a half a block away where a new brewpub had recently opened.

When I finally went home it was on foot. I'd left my car in the parking lot next to Oxbow Public Market, because I was slightly drunk, and grateful I could sleep it off before needing to see patients by mid-morning the next day. I tried not to think about how I could change outcomes of Kaya's life. I could tell Parker how she fell off a ladder and not only ended up in a coma, but also lost *his* baby. When we'd discovered blood seeping from between her legs, I'd had tissue examined. I don't know what caused me to do this, but if I hadn't, no one might ever have known she'd been pregnant. I wouldn't have told Miles about the baby, if I hadn't known about it, who in turn might not be so angry with Katya now.

It made me realize how instrumental we are in the lives that touch ours. We have opportunities to be discreet, or to not use discretion at all when dealing with what could be life-changing knowledge for someone. The fate of others sits in our hands more often than we'd like to admit. Our conscience is our guide. For whatever reason, Katya chose not to tell Parker or Miles about the baby she was carrying.

I couldn't think of a worse nightmare than waking up from a coma and finding out your best kept secrets had fallen into the wrong hands. I could only hope I'd be there when Katya awoke, and Miles would not.

BEARINGS

It had been over two weeks since my fall from the barn roof, or through the cupboard door, whichever way I chose to recall it. Now it was mid-October. The mountains outside my bedroom window hinted of the season. Mt. Jefferson and The Three Sisters had a light dusting of snow, but otherwise it had been an unusually warm autumn. Parker had vanished into his den quite early to finish an article. I was lingering over the coffee and toast he'd brought me on a breakfast tray. The toast was smothered in blackberry jam, which Parker said I made myself last summer. He told me there were lots of thick, thorny blackberry bushes growing along the property fence. No doubt Ruby was eating cereal in the kitchen while Goldie lay at her feet. It all seemed so normal, so status quo. It was a morning most would take for granted, but not me. Nothing about my life seemed normal. It felt more like someone had dropped me into a movie set and I still needed to get my bearings.

Eventually I crawled out of bed, despite a temptation to stay there all day staring at the mountains outside the window. I slid open my closet door and ran my hand across the neatly arranged clothing. Shirts and sweaters were hung from cool to warm tones. It looked like something I would do, arrange my clothes in such a manner, but I had no recollection of doing it. Every morning for the past two weeks I had stared at one piece of clothing or another, trying to recall having bought it or worn it. But I couldn't recall a thing regarding *anything*, not for the last seven years.

For whatever reason, I decided to look at the far end of the closet today. There were skirts and dresses there, once again arranged by color. I scanned the items and then froze when seeing a rose-colored dress. I touched the fabric and it slid off into my arms. The sundress was sleeveless and fitted. It hung just below the knees when I held it against my body. The material was a soft, dusty pink and the design simple, yet elegant. It had to be the dress Parker said I wore when entering the tasting room, on that day when we were finally reunited after our night in the vineyard.

I closed my eyes while holding the dress against my chest, and tried to envision that day, in this dress, seeing Parker again. Nothing came to mind. My head was empty, void of any thoughts whatsoever. I carefully hung the dress back up and then something on the shelf above it caught my eye. It was a white photo album. I pulled it down and looked at the cover. It said "Our Wedding" in gold print. Sitting on the bedroom floor I lingered over each page. Everything Parker said about that day came to life in the pictures. And then it occurred to me I hadn't seen any wedding photos displayed around the house. Ruby appeared in the doorway and my attention was immediately drawn to her. "Good morning, my little angel." She was a vision in her pink nightie with thick red locks cascading everywhere. Goldie stood beside her, tail wagging. "Come and look at wedding pictures." I didn't have to ask twice. Ruby scampered over and joined me on the floor. Goldie sat beside us. "Have you seen this album?" I inquired, while running a hand through her messy curls.

Ruby nodded her head. "Yes, Mommy. You love looking at this book." I stared into her emerald eyes, at a loss for what to say.

"You love the ones in Daddy's den, too."

"In Daddy's den?"

She nodded her bedhead again and I was sure I'd never seen anything more precious than this child I had no memory of. "Let's look when your daddy takes a break from his work," I suggested.

Ruby's face lit up and she clapped her hands. "Okay, Mommy!"

"Now let's get you dressed." I stood up and set the album on the bed, not willing to stash it away on the closet shelf where it had been. Goldie led the way down the hall and into Ruby's room with its Disney Princess theme. The cheery colors everywhere made me feel as if wrapped in a rainbow. Together we chose something for her to wear and then I left, with instructions to brush her teeth and make her bed after getting dressed.

It wasn't long until Ruby ran back into the master suite with Goldie at her heels. I had dressed and made the bed. She crawled up on it and I brushed her hair. It was becoming a routine, a welcome one, something familiar I could look forward to. Sometimes I would French braid her silky red locks the way Grandma Rose used to braid my wispy fluffs of blond. Other times I simply pulled it off her face with barrettes. She never flinched or fidgeted, as if this had been our ritual prior to my head injury, although I had no recollection of it.

The order of each new day was becoming familiar to me. Mornings were quiet and unhurried, with Parker working in his den. By noon he would resurface and together we'd fix lunch. The autumn days were still warm enough to eat on the patio. Today Ruby had wolfed down her PB&J so she could run back off the patio and play again. She had a bottle of bubbles, which the wind blew from the wand while she ran as fast as she could. Goldie nipped at the floating balls of soap, barking nonstop. Occasionally she jumped up and broke one with her nose, causing Ruby to laugh uncontrollably. After a while they lay down in the grass, looking quite winded. Parker and I observed all this as if it were the best show in town. I reached for his hand under the table. "Our life feels like a dream," I confessed.

Parker laughed his deep hearty laugh. "It *is* a dream, Rosy, and I hope we never wake up."

"Me either," I said, realizing he had no idea how desperately I meant that. "Why isn't Ruby in school?" I asked, wondering why it hadn't occurred to me until this very moment to inquire. "Shouldn't she be in kindergarten?"

"Her teacher and I decided you need this time to get reacquainted with your daughter, since you have no memory of her. There's also the possibility that having her here will trigger your memory to return. Ruby is bright, Rose. She excels at school, and with a November birthday she's one of the oldest in her class. Her teacher has shared that it's hard to keep her challenged. Missing a few weeks won't hurt her academically."

"Selfishly, I'm glad she's here for a while," I commented, smiling, but deep inside I was dismayed once again that her birthday didn't align with the one night we'd made love before my fall from the cupboard.

Parker kissed me on the cheek. "I knew you would be happy to have her here."

"Ruby will be six soon. Why doesn't she have a sibling by now?" I asked, knowing I had wanted more than one child. I honestly didn't know what Parker's thoughts were on the subject. I didn't know his thoughts on most subjects, which was disconcerting to say the least.

"Rubes was a difficult birth for you, Rosy. You're so tiny. Thank God Ruby was also tiny at only five pounds, but the doctors didn't think you should have any more children, and so I have refused to try. It isn't worth the risk, despite your arguments otherwise. We've discussed adopting but haven't really done anything about it. Ruby seems to fill our lives up just fine."

I couldn't disagree with that because I didn't feel a bit deprived by only having Ruby. Whatever this was, dream or not, it couldn't have felt more perfect than just the way it was.

After lunch I slipped into Parker's den while he cleaned up the kitchen from lunch. I told him I wanted to see our wedding pictures, asking why they were all in his den. He shrugged and told me it had been my idea to keep them there. It did sound like a decision I would make, displaying our special event in shrine-like fashion somewhere I could have a sweeping view of every major moment. I discovered the framed photos on a shelf at the far corner of the room. I hadn't noticed them when brooding over Crow's mystical visit in the middle of the night.

Parker soon appeared and I reluctantly ushered myself out. It was time to explore my studio, which I had been avoiding. Ruby had resurfaced from the yard for a glass of water and while she drank it, I asked if she wanted to accompany me to the studio. Her response was an eager *yes*. We exited the house together and climbed a stairway above the garage, which led to what could have been a small apartment. A counter with a sink and microwave sat in one corner of the large airy room, full of light from several generous windows. A table for two had been placed below one of them, looking out onto the meadow behind the house. The rest of the space might have held furniture, but instead it was full of art supplies and equipment. There was also a bathroom, with a door that opened onto a cozy bedroom.

I couldn't have designed a more perfect studio, which eerily, I somehow believed was exactly what I'd done. I stared at my sketchbooks and pencils scattered across an art table in the middle of the room. My thoughts were so heavy I felt glued to the floor, unable to move. Why was all of this so foreign to me, and yet so familiar?

"Mommy, are you okay?"

I glanced at Ruby and saw the worried look in her eye. "Yes, sweetie. Just taking it all in." Slowly I ran my hand across the worktable that had shelves below it, filled with everything one might need to do silk screens or etchings. And then I realized it was *my* table. These were *my* supplies, exactly as they had been in the Napa house, in *Genevieve*. But how could that be?

Ruby ran to a child-size easel beside the table for two. "This is where I paint, Mommy!" she announced.

I barely had time to respond when someone behind us said "Hello, stranger" in a low smoky voice. I knew immediately it was Lorelei, which meant her mother must have passed recently. We collided into a tight hug as if two magnets drawn together by a powerful source.

"Parker told me you were up here," Lorelei said in a muffled voice, with her head in my clouds of hair.

"I'm so sorry about your mom passing," I whispered.

"Me too," she answered, with an audible crack in her voice.

Lorelei slowly let go of me and took a good look at Ruby. "Ryker and Kooper are in the yard if you want to see them." Ruby grinned and ran out the door. It was only then I noticed a tote bag on Lorelei's arm. "I come bearing food and drink." She smiled, at last, although her eyes had a weary look. Lorelei proceeded to grab a plate from the cupboard above the microwave and put fresh baked lemon scones on it, fresh from the Sisters's bakery. Then she pulled two large chai teas from the bag and sat down at the table below the window. I joined her, nearly pinching myself to see if this moment could truly be happening. My best friend didn't look any different. It was as if she hadn't aged at all in the past seven years. Perhaps there were a few more lines around her eyes but losing a mother could do that to you.

"Will the twins be okay in the yard?" I asked.

"Ruby is wonderful with them, but then you know that." Lorelei looked at me strangely. "I was annoyed with Zach for not telling me about your concussion until I arrived home this morning."

I shrugged. "My head injury is supposedly healed."

"He said you still can't remember the last few years."

"Last seven years, to be exact." I took a drink of the tea, which I hadn't realized I liked. It was delicious.

"That's so odd, Katy."

"I know."

We both took a scone from the plate and marveled at how wonderful and lemony it tasted. I felt more like myself than I had since the fall. I had a lot more history with Lorelei than I did with anyone else in this alternate world.

"I'm so sorry I wasn't here for you." Lorelei studied me with her weary eyes.

"Don't be silly. You needed to be with your mom. Did you have some quality time at the end, and did she pass peacefully?" I asked.

"Yes, to both." Lorelei began to tear up and I reached across the table to touch her arm. "Let's change the subject before I break down and bawl again. I need to be strong for Ryker and Kooper." Lorelei smiled through her tears.

"Of course. But if you ever need a cry fest, I'm your girl. We can take a hike in the woods and have a meltdown in front of small creatures who will never tell."

Lorelei laughed. "It sounds like you're mourning your memories as much as I'm mourning my mom."

"Life has been a little frustrating, to say the least," I admitted.

"What's the last thing you remember?"

"Falling through a door."

"A door?"

"There was a door in the back of a cupboard, in Genevieve."

"Katy, you fell off a ladder in Genevieve, and that was a long time ago."

"Seven years ago?"

Lorelei thought for a moment. "Yes, I guess it was about seven years ago. You don't remember anything since then?"

"No."

"How strange."

"Very."

"Parker told Zachary you fell off the barn roof a couple weeks ago."

"Lorelei, I only remember falling through a door in the back of a cupboard, but I do remember waking up in a field, staring at a barn roof."

My best friend studied me for a few seconds, while popping the last bite of lemon scone in her mouth. She raised a perfectly arched brow and something about her demeanor made me recall the Mad Hatter from *Alice's Adventures in Wonderland*. Perhaps it was a rabbit hole in time I'd fallen through. Why had Lewis Carroll's book come to mind? It had been at least twenty years since I'd read it.

BITTEN

Katya was beginning her third week in a coma. Overall, her appearance reminded me of a porcelain doll, pale and gaunt, with perfectly chiseled features that never moved but were nonetheless captivating. There was a faint rosy color to her lips. That might have been Lorelei's doing. She put lip-gloss on Katya every day and rubbed lotion into her hands and feet while singing in a hushed tone. Her voice was enchanting. I found myself checking on Katya at the same time each morning so I could listen. Not one golden hair on Katya's head had been altered. It was as if the seven dwarfs placed her in an invisible dome for safekeeping. If she was fated to be this way until her prince showed up, then I should have alerted Parker Mancini of her condition.

"I've never seen a more groomed patient," I commented.

Lorelei placed the *Alice's Adventures in Wonderland* book on the nightstand. Then she positioned Katya's hands and smoothed the blanket they rested on.

"I see you're still reading to our patient," I added.

"I love this woman like a sister. She would do the same for me."

"Do you have a sister?" I asked.

"No. I am an only child, just like Katy. It's one of many things we have in common. What about you, Oliver? Do you have any siblings?"

"I have a sister on the East Coast. We haven't seen each other in years. Our aunt and uncle raised Emma and me after our parents died in a plane crash. We were eight and ten."

"That must have been hard." Lorelei looked me in the eye, which she seldom did. I doubt she realized just how focused she always was on our patient.

"It was a long time ago. It is odd, however, that neither of us married or had children, at least not yet. I wouldn't want to delve into the psychology of that."

"Were your aunt and uncle good to you?"

"Yes. It was our mother's older sister and her husband. They were intelligent and kind, but it isn't the same you know. They'd never had children and were quite busy with their careers. Aunt Ginni was a historian. She worked at the Autry Museum of the American West. I can tell you anything you want to know about Annie Oakley."

"I'd love to hear about her." Lorelei laughed. It was nice to see her eyes light up and sparkle, since I mostly saw a furrowed brow and sad look on her face. "What did your uncle do?" she asked.

"He was a botanist. Maybe that's why I wanted to be one, until discovering my love of medicine."

"I think I understand now why you're such a great gardener. Speaking of which, will I see you at Katya's later?"

"Yes, I'll be there. She has golden beets and purple carrots ready to harvest."

Lorelei said goodbye and disappeared into the hallway. I wasn't far behind, eager to finish rounds with my patients and get on with my day, so I could leave early and harvest Katya's vegetables.

I arrived at Genevieve around four o'clock and found Lorelei by the back gate talking to Crow. It was a typical October day hovering around seventy degrees, although by this time the sun had lowered in the sky.

Together we harvested the baby root vegetables, hurrying to finish before dusk. Crow watched from the fence while we worked. Miles pulled up just as we placed the last box of golden beets in the back of Lorelei's SUV. It was a silver Lexus, which fit her personality, elegant and eye-catching. Miles stepped from his BMW to open the gate and shot an unwelcome glance our way. Meghan was in the passenger seat, looking uncomfortable. It was an awkward moment to say the least.

After parking the car and closing the gate they walked past us while staring straight ahead and entered the backdoor. Meghan finally glanced our way when climbing the half flight of stairs. I'm sure our curious looks unnerved her. Why would she believe it okay to be in Katya's home, with Katya's husband, while Katya lay fighting for her life in a coma? Of all the odd behaviors I had seen in my profession this seemed the least sensitive, but then I'd never taken such a personal interest in a patient.

"They're actually grocery shopping together and playing house," Lorelei mumbled.

"I hadn't noticed the groceries," I admitted. "I couldn't get past the idea that Miles brought her here," I added, while we stared at the closed door. It had been a troubled marriage and Katya herself had not been faithful, but there was something inhumane about ignoring her condition altogether. Lorelei and I continued staring at the back door, as if we couldn't comprehend their brazen behavior, until suddenly we heard a loud scream from somewhere inside the home. After a quick glance at one another we ran to the porch and up the stairs. I knocked loudly before we barged into the laundry room. From there we had a clear view of the kitchen. Lorelei and I stopped dead in our tracks while Miles and Meghan glanced our way from the kitchen sink. "Is everything all right?" I asked.

"A black widow just bit Meghan," Miles exclaimed.

I stepped through the laundry room door and over to the sink where the spider was hovering near the closed drain.

"I didn't kill it," Miles said. "I thought we should be sure it's a black widow, which means she'll need some medical treatment, right?"

"It *is* a black widow, but she'll be fine," I assured him. I asked Lorelei to fill a plastic bag with ice while I coaxed the spider into a jar Miles had found under the sink. After instructing Meghan to wash the bite thoroughly with soap and water I took a quick walk outside, through the back gate and across the alleyway. I bent down and let the spider crawl from the jar. I doubted it would return to Genevieve.

"Why not just kill it?" Miles asked when I reentered the house. He appeared to be more irritated at me than sympathetic toward Meghan's injury.

"Black widows are not normally aggressive. Meghan must have startled it."

Meghan stared at Miles through glassy eyes. "I don't want to be here another minute." She grabbed her purse with the uninjured hand and headed for the door.

"Do you have some antiseptic cream and a clean bandage you can put on that bite?" I asked.

Meghan looked at Miles, who went to retrieve both.

"You'll want to take some Tylenol. Your hand is going to hurt a lot and you might get achy all over. I'd take it easy for a day or so," I suggested.

After Miles returned, Meghan set the purse down and rubbed cream into her palm. "I want to go home, Miles. Now!"

"There won't be any spiders next time you come," he assured her. "I'll have the house fumigated."

Lorelei stared at Miles as if he were suggesting murder. "I don't think you should fumigate unless there's a nest of them somewhere. Katy wouldn't want that."

"Well, she isn't here, is she? And might never be again." Miles returned Lorelei's stare.

"Why don't we stick around and look for any indication of more black widows?" I suggested. "Lorelei is right. There's no need to fumigate if this was a fluke thing."

"Fine." Miles guided Meghan out the door and asked us to lock up when done spider hunting. Once they'd gone Lorelei looked at me with dread. "Katy will be so upset if Miles has this house fumigated. She's never killed a spider, or any insect for that matter. She cups them in her hands and puts the tiny creatures out in the garden."

"That's impressive," I said, while chuckling. "Let's start looking for friends of the intruder." We began busily searching the entire home, looking in every nook and cranny that might appeal to a spider. I used the ladder Katya had fallen from to look in the attic. When I replaced it in the cellar, I thoroughly investigated that area, too, and then the crawl space. Nothing appeared anywhere except a few small, harmless house spiders.

We sat at the kitchen table when finished searching. Lorelei looked puzzled. "I have no idea where that black widow came from."

"Maybe Genevieve doesn't like Meghan and conspired with a black widow to run her off," I suggested. We both laughed and it cut through the tension still lingering in the house from all the earlier drama.

"I halfway believe it," Lorelei confessed. "Doors in this house only stick for Miles, you know."

"Seriously?" I shot her an incredulous look.

"I'm not kidding. Doors stick, books fall off shelves and hit his toes. Once he nearly caught on fire from lighting a candle."

"You honestly think there's a spirit in this home who has it out for Miles?"

Lorelei shrugged. "I think it's possible."

I wanted to disagree based on conventional logic, but nothing about Katya or her situation was either logical or conventional. One thing I could presume, however, is that Katya's grandmother would not approve of Miles for her granddaughter. If you looked at it from that perspective, then it did indeed make sense that Miles (and now his secretary) were targets for mean-spirited mischief, orchestrated by none other than Grandma Rose herself.

SNOW

"Mommy, let's build a snowman!"

Ruby stared out the window with her nose against the glass and I smiled at her enthusiasm. "It's just starting to fall, Ruby. There isn't enough snow on the ground to build a snowman." I ran my fingers through her silky red hair while she stared up at me. "Maybe in a couple hours," I added.

"Can I go watch it snow with Goldie?"

"Yes." I barely answered before she bolted out the door. I had no doubt she was on a mission to see if Parker would let her bundle up and chase snowflakes with Goldie. I knew he'd say no. How did I know that? How did I know Parker and Ruby so well without really knowing them at all? When I played music for the first time in my studio, how did I know it would be piano music? In Napa I only played cello and string music, piping it through the whole house. There were so many things I didn't know about this new home and my new family, but more and more there were a lot of things *I did know*. I just didn't know why I knew them. It was mind boggling.

I sighed and poured more wine into the crystal stemware I'd found in one of the studio cabinets. It reminded me of Grandma Rose's antique crystal back in Genevieve, but this was not her stemware. I needed to ask Parker about Genevieve. It hadn't occurred to me yet to inquire. Maybe I didn't want to know for fear the knowledge would somehow thrust me back there, with Miles. I watched large puffy snowflakes saunter to the ground as if in slow motion while another Lewis Carroll quote came to mind. *I wonder if the snow loves the trees and fields, that it kisses them so gently? And then it covers them up snug, you know, with a white quilt; and perhaps it says, 'Go to sleep darlings, till the summer comes again.'*

Why these quotes kept creeping into my head, I had no idea. I must say the snowflakes were mesmerizing as they swirled about and danced in the breeze. They seemed to be falling in perfect harmony with the music streaming through my studio. I always played melancholy tunes, soul searching, sometimes heart wrenching. I wondered why this type of music was my preference when creating etchings or silk screens. Would people feel melancholy and search their souls when they observed my art?

It had been three weeks since supposedly falling off that barn roof. I'd spent a lot of time lately pondering the unfinished mural, thinking about the master plan for its creation. So much had happened in the past three weeks. I'd gone from being nearly helpless and quite clingy to brooding for hours in my studio, alone. Ruby would dash in and out from time to time, maybe paint at her easel or devour cookies and milk at the table by the window. I kept all her favorite snacks tucked away in the mini kitchen. I didn't know why I knew what she liked and disliked.

Occasionally Parker would text me to meet him in the hot tub, or on the front porch swing. He never asked me when I planned to resurface. Instead, he created rendezvouses, or tempted me with something wonderful he'd made in the kitchen. *Are you coming down for pulled pork tacos? Otherwise, we'll let Goldie have yours. She's eyeing them up and licking her lips.* This was the text I had just received. I didn't know how long I'd been staring out the window trying to make sense of this new life, not to mention creating a plan for finishing the mural.

By the time Parker sent the text I'd had an idea for completing the barn roof. Just knowing I had a plan cheered me up immensely. I nearly ran down the studio steps and into the house, which smelled like roasted bell peppers and green chiles. I took in the whole lovely scene with a smile. Parker was busy at the counter stuffing shredded pork into a tortilla he had warmed in a skillet. Ruby was dropping a piece of pork for Goldie, who promptly licked it up. She had taco sauce smeared on her face and instantly looked guilty about sharing her lunch with Goldie. I pretended I hadn't seen a thing. I was getting good at pretending about everything from knowing people I should know, to knowing my exact role in this family, when in fact it was something I grappled with hour by hour.

By the time we cleaned up the kitchen lots of snow had accumulated. It was time to wreak havoc on the lawn making snow people and snow angels, so we bundled up while Goldie barked and wagged her tail. She was impatient for us to secure hats, scarves, and gloves. I had no sooner helped Ruby with her mittens than she was out the door with her faithful companion. They ran around in the field, just past the landscaped yard, while Parker and I rolled balls of snow into a family of three. After a while Ruby quit running in circles and stared at our snow people.

"Oh, it's a family like ours!" Ruby shouted. "Can I help?"

"We thought you'd never ask." Parker looked at her and grinned.

All three of us scoured the yard for useful items to complete our snow family. Ruby found black rocks at the edge of the road for their eyes and mouths. For their noses I pulled out carrots left in the garden, just inside the fence we'd built to keep deer and other foragers away. Parker snapped off pine boughs for arms and I went inside for spare hats and scarves. Ruby made snow angels while I was gone.

"Look Mommy!" she shouted when I returned with the scarves and hats. Goldie barked and pranced around the snow angels, and then suddenly all the laughing and shouting and Goldie's barking sounded far away. It became nothing more than faint echoes, overshadowed by a loud buzzing in my ears. I watched Rubes and Goldie fade in and out. Soon I was squinting to see them at all. I panicked thinking they would disappear for good. I wanted to believe it was the sun shining on the snow that blinded me, but it was more than that. It was as if they weren't quite there, or maybe I wasn't. Obviously, these episodes of blurry vision and fading sound were getting worse instead of better. The buzzing in my ears was growing louder with each new episode.

For some strange reason whenever my reality started to fragment like this, Parker would remain solid and clear. He never faded in and out like everything else and his voice never diminished or echoed. He was my anchor to this illusive world and so I looked for him over by the snow people in the meadow, at the edge of the lawn. The minute he came into view my anxiety subsided. I stared at him, at the clear unwavering vision of him, with beads of sweat on my forehead despite the frosty air.

"Rosy! Bring me the hats and scarves and then we'll take some pictures," Parker shouted, while waving to me. I quickly made my way over to him and didn't mention what had just happened. While arranging hats and scarves on the snow mommy I studied the blanketed white field glistening in the bright sun. Standing at the edge of the meadow felt peaceful and serene. It was as if God had lovingly covered the dead, lifeless field with his snowy gift to protect the dormant plants awaiting spring. It calmed me somehow, made me believe I was in control of my own destiny, and that this was all quite real, not a dream.

Parker had placed a thick woolen scarf on the daddy snowperson. It was forest green and went well with the black cowboy hat I'd chosen to go with it. I'd wrapped a rose-colored scarf around the snow mommy. It was long and flowy and had a rose-colored beanie hat to match. Ruby had trudged over in her snow boots and wanted to adorn the snow child. We watched as she wound the pink scarf around its neck and carefully placed the matching beanie hat (sporting a big fluffy pink pom) on the snow child's head.

We stood back and admired our work before Parker took a barrage of photos. First Ruby and Goldie posed beside the snow family and then we used the timer on the camera to take a few family shots. I thought about all the photo albums I'd browsed through in the den. There were pictures of Ruby and Goldie beside a snowman every year since she was about two. No matter how hard I studied the pictures hoping something would trigger my memory, nothing did.

After traipsing inside and peeling off our layers, I made a pot of mac & cheese using Grandma Rose's recipe. It was the one recipe I knew by heart, because she would make it for me whenever I visited her. Ruby set the table while Parker grated the cheese. "I love Mommy's mac and cheese!" Ruby exclaimed, while carefully folding paper napkins.

"I've made this here before?" I asked.

Parker and Ruby looked at one another and grinned.

"Many times," Parker assured me.

"I wish I could remember." I looked at them and rolled my eyes.

"But you remembered the recipe," Parker pointed out. "Maybe that's the first step to regaining your memory.

"Maybe," I agreed, but in my heart I knew better. The things I recalled had more to do with rote memory than events; Ruby's favorite snacks, what drawers their clothes went into, recipes, etc. These things I somehow knew, but that was it. I couldn't recall Ruby's face as a baby, or lovemaking here with Parker. Lost to me was horseback riding among the fall colors or planting my garden in the spring. It was maddening to say the least.

After dinner we drank hot cocoa in front of the fire Parker had built. Ruby soon fell asleep on the sofa with a chocolate mustache. I draped a blanket over her. Goldie was already napping on the floor nearby. I sat back down beside Parker, who whispered in my ear *let's sneak away to the hot tub*. I enthusiastically agreed. After tiptoeing out of the room we dashed down the hall to put our suits on.

It felt good to soak in the warm bubbly water, letting the jets massage our weary muscles. Running around for a couple hours in the fresh snow had been more tiring than we'd realized. We both watched as the sun lowered in the sky. Where had the day gone? Aside from my unfortunate episode of fading images and sounds, it had been the most remarkable day so far since my concussion. Our family had felt more real than ever before. I convinced myself the episode of fading images and sounds was nothing more than a few lingering symptoms from the concussion. I put the whole incident out of my mind. What I couldn't stop thinking about, however, was Genevieve. Despite not wanting to talk about my past with Miles, my curiosity was growing about what happened to Grandma Rose's house in Napa.

"Parker, who lives in Genevieve now?"

"She is still yours, of course. We stay there a couple weeks every spring for the Bottle Rock Festival, and a couple weeks during harvest."

"I've never been to the Bottle Rock Festival. Miles never wanted to go. He didn't like rock bands, street food, or crowds. Some of the area's best chefs have booths there, but not even that could sway him." I regretted saying this the minute it spilled out. Parker looked a little hurt.

"That's really interesting, Rosy, especially since you've never shared anything at all with me about your marriage to Miles."

I wanted to dive beneath the hot tub. "I'm sorry, Parker. That was a thoughtless thing for me to say."

"Don't be sorry. Maybe it's taken a bump on the head to finally talk about your marriage to Miles."

I studied Parker, trying to determine if he truly wanted to hear about my marriage to Miles. It was intriguing to me how I'd had some clarity of thought about that while living at Desert Sky. Nothing about my life here was clear, yet the life I left behind was becoming clearer to me than while living it. "What is it you want to know?"

"Why did you say *I do*, Rosy? What did you see in Miles, in a future together, that appealed to you?"

I shrugged. "It was more about how he adamantly pursued me all through college and then reappeared one night at my gallery showing. I've already told you that."

"You married a man simply because he pursued you?"

"Maybe I thought it was our fate to be together."

"Your *fate*?" Parker looked genuinely confused.

"Okay, the truth is I never loved him, and I feel terrible for having cheated someone out of love. I broke up with him several times in college, but he kept coming back like a bad penny. By the time he came to my gallery showing I had a very tainted view of true love."

"And why was that?"

I didn't answer.

"Rosy?"

"Okay, Parker. Once upon a time I thought I might have found true love, but then it slipped away. After a while I gave up on the whole concept and decided it must be a myth."

"You decided true love was a myth, so you settled for Miles?"

"Yes."

"Was I that true love you thought you'd found?"

"Yes."

"I'm sorry, Rose. I was a fool not to track you down. I've always regretted it."

I shrugged. "It isn't as if I made more of an effort myself. My father had just died. He was everything to me. I was emotionally distraught about his passing and there was no room in my heart for anyone else."

"Until Miles reappeared," Parker pointed out.

"Yes. He was witty and clever and can be quite charming when focused on a conquest," I admitted. "I wanted children and a family of my own. For whatever reason, Miles seemed to be my only option. Other men never seriously pursued me. They'd dance cautiously, as if around a flame, and then dash away."

Parker smiled. "I can understand that. You're quite complicated, you know."

"I am?"

"It took a determined lawyer to court you, Rose. I'm sure most men saw you as an unconquerable quest, reclusive and completely focused on your art. You quietly flutter from one art project to the next. This is who you are. Delicate, reclusive, yet bold and determined. Like a butterfly."

"Is that how you see me, Parker?" I grinned and splashed water on him.

"The only difference between me and every other guy is how I couldn't possibly live without you, so instead I hold you fluttering near my fingertips. Sometimes I worry that I've bent your wings, or you might suffocate, but I can't quit trying to make you happy. *I* can't be happy unless *you're* happy."

"Am I really that difficult?"

"It isn't like you try to be. It's just that you're often withdrawn and distant. You do most of your communicating through those stormy eyes. No one knows where they stand with you, except a handful of people you've let into your inner world."

"Somewhere along the way Miles tired of my fluttering about 'in a bold, determined way,' as you put it, so he found solace in his secretary. End of story."

"I think it is you that tired of him. The woman I met in the vineyard long ago was searching for something beyond the dead-end road looming before her."

"I didn't think of my marriage as a complete disaster until the day I saw Miles with someone else. At that same moment I realized true love *did* exist, and it wasn't foolish of me to think our chance meeting in college was fate. We were meant to be. The timing just wasn't right, but now we have fulfilled our destiny."

"I couldn't agree more." Parker swooped me up into his arms and kissed me as if it was our first and we had been waiting far too long. When we came up for air, I suggested we check on Ruby. Parker threw a towel around his waist and slipped through the master bedroom door. While he was gone, I wondered if this really was our destiny or just a fluke moment in time that would soon disappear.

Parker returned to say that Ruby was fast asleep, and Goldie was curled up by her feet. He laid his towel beside the hot tub while I watched. My stormy eyes must have communicated how I felt about his well-toned body, because Parker slipped his suit off and effortlessly stepped back into the spa. He then carefully peeled off mine. We became tangled together like that day in the vineyard beneath the stars. Afterward we shared a steamy shower, bundled up in terry cloth robes, and put our sleeping princess to bed.

I smoothed red wisps of hair off Ruby's face and kissed her softly on the cheek. Parker took my hand and together we shuffled out the door in our spa slippers. Then we read for a while in our enormous king-size bed, until Parker turned the light off.

If only I could have turned my mind off.

What I didn't share with Parker in the spa was how humiliating my marriage to Miles had turned out to be. It was only recently that I realized Miles hadn't loved me any more than I loved him. All this time I'd thought he loved me enough for both of us but instead, he had ulterior motives for the marriage. Thinking back now made it all clear. Miles knew my father had died before attending my gallery showing. He'd told me at the gallery how sorry he was. Miles also knew my Grandma Rose had recently passed and I'd inherited her house in Napa. We'd barely reestablished our relationship and he was already applying to a law firm in St. Helena, where a colleague had just made partner. We hadn't been married long when Miles suggested we use my inheritance to pay off his college loans. I happily complied. At the time it eased my guilt for not loving him.

And then there was Grandma Rose's house, sitting on a piece of real estate in the heart of Napa worth a small fortune. Gaining possession of the house, of course, had never come together for Miles. I couldn't agree to a living will in which he would inherit Genevieve, should anything happen to me. I never had the heart to tell Miles Grandma Rose wanted the home to stay in the family, and technically, he wasn't family. I was going to leave the house to our children. But then we never had any. And according to Parker the house is still mine.

What I couldn't figure out while lying there staring at the ceiling in the dark, was why didn't I have to sell the house and land, and pay Miles half when we divorced? He had a reputation for being a shrewd attorney. There were those who thought his shrewdness was a clever gift, while others saw it as underhanded. I tried to give Miles the benefit of the doubt, but the longer we were married the harder it was to respect how he manipulated the law. In his case, it would be in his own best interests.

That's what had worried me the most after discovering I was pregnant with Parker's baby. Once I started to show, Miles would divorce me and figure out a legal way to make me pay half of what Genevieve was worth, not to mention the land she sat on. I had no means to do that. I'd have to sell. It's why I didn't demand a divorce on the spot, even knowing Miles had cheated. It's why I didn't go running back into Parker's arms, which was where I wanted to be.

It was eye opening to realize Miles had never been in love with me either. Quite the contrary, I was his ticket to California and a way to pay off his law school debt. It was a difficult reckoning, both embarrassing and maddening. I couldn't share with Parker what I now knew to be the truth about my sham of a marriage.

I justified this complete ignorance about Miles, and his true motivations for marrying me, because of my withdrawal from life in general at that time. I was blinded by grief for Grandma Rose and my father. They were my rock whenever the sands of life would shift beneath my feet. The art in that gallery showing had been an outpouring of love for my dad. I painted all my favorite memories of him—camping beside the Metolius, fishing at Lake Billy Chinook, picnicking at the base of the mountains. There were a couple pieces I had done as a tribute to Grandma Rose, who was so looking forward to the showing, but passed a few weeks prior. Every piece sold for a price I could never have imagined asking. That was when I realized I had become an accomplished artist and it was time to fulfill my only other dream, which was to have a family.

I had thought Miles wanted that too. I had thought a lot of things that were simply not true, things that were less real than this fantasy world, which had brought these truths to light. Maybe that's why I was here. They say the truth will set you free, and I had never felt freer than at this moment when I could finally let go of my guilt for marrying a man I did not love. I had finally decided his intentions were more devious and misleading than mine.

Thank goodness we were divorced, but why didn't I have to sell the Napa house and property, and pay Miles half its worth?

TREASURE

Lorelei and I sat in Katya's kitchen while I tried to process how her home might have a spirit living in it. Apparently, it was a ghost that not only looked out for Katya but also took every opportunity to derail Miles. I didn't believe in ghosts or spirits, but I wanted to. It gave me comfort to think someone (or something) was looking out for Katya. God knows her husband wasn't. "Lorelei," I said finally, "why don't we look up in that cabinet while we're here? For all we know, there could be a nest of spiders there. At the very least we can see what Katya stored up so high."

"I've been wondering what's up there." Lorelei shook her head. "I don't know why I haven't already looked."

"I'll get the ladder," I suggested.

"Let me help." Lorelei followed me to the cellar and together we brought the ladder upstairs to the kitchen, leaning it against the wall beside the cabinets.

"I'll climb up," I said. "The last thing we need is for you to be sharing a bed next to Katya."

"Not funny." Lorelei gave me an exasperated look.

"Want to make any guesses about what's in there?" I asked.

"I have no idea what goes on in that head of hers. Katy has always been a bit mysterious." Lorelei stared up at the cabinets, as if they could solve the mystery of Katya.

I shimmied up the ladder and paused briefly before opening the cupboard door. Looking down it was clear to me how she'd hit her head on the edge of the counter. I'd examined the marble carefully my first time in Genevieve and observed lingering blood stains. The fact that she survived such a nasty fall was almost a miracle. I'd never believed in mystical powers or guardian angels any more than I believed in spirits or ghosts, but there was no logical explanation for Katya's surviving the fall. There was even less of a logical reason for why she was still asleep, having healed from her wounds. Maybe it was time for me to believe in something other than science.

"Stop looking down and open the door." Lorelei was steadying the ladder while scolding me. I pulled on the doorknob, which opened with a faint squeak. What I saw caused me to take pause. It was a pastel rainbow of hopes and dreams, in the form of infant wear.

"Oliver, what did you find?"

"Baby clothes."

Lorelei didn't respond and so I looked at her from atop the ladder.

"I should have known." She sighed. "The baby clothes must have been too painful to look at once Katy realized she wasn't pregnant."

"I'm just beginning to understand how badly she wanted kids," I confessed. I couldn't share with Lorelei how tragic it was that Katya's sterile cheating husband had been giving her false hope about conceiving a child for their entire marriage.

It was just as tragic that she had lost Parker's baby. I wasn't looking forward to telling her this when she awoke. I only hoped I would be the bearer of that bad news rather than Miles. My blood nearly curdled at the thought of how nasty he would be regarding the whole situation of her infidelity, and how he knew she'd cheated because he was not able to have children. My heart ached for our sleeping beauty and just how harsh her realities would be when awakening.

Lorelei and I put the ladder away without saying a word, feeling Katya's disappointment in not bearing children with silent solidarity. After locking up we delivered the vegetables, most of which went to Angele. We stayed for a drink since it was our last stop, and both ordered bourbon on the rocks. It had been a sobering afternoon looking for black widows and then finding Katya's stash of baby clothes. In unison we downed our first drink and ordered another.

Just as I began to relax, Miles strolled in. I don't know why I turned and looked at the entrance, but there he was. Maybe I was developing a sixth sense. I honestly hoped the man wouldn't spot us at the bar, but how could he not? The lavish mahogany bar was part of the cozy dining room filled with tables illuminated in flickering candlelight. He marched straight over to us and sat on the barstool beside Lorelei.

"I thought I might find you here." Miles waved down the bartender. "I'll have whatever they're drinking," he said, while rooting through his pockets.

"Did you lose something?" I asked.

"I was hoping to find you here so I could give you a copy of Katya's advanced directive not to resuscitate in case she quits breathing."

"That's something you need to share with the hospital administration, not me." I felt a rush of adrenaline at the very thought of Miles taking Katya's fate into his own hands. Thankfully Lorelei sat on the barstool between us, or I might have decked him. Katya's situation had me tied up in knots emotionally and it made no sense whatsoever. I was tempted to get psychiatric help with sorting out these feelings for a patient I hadn't technically met.

"Damn." Miles quit rummaging through his pockets. "I must have left it on the table by the door." He took a swig of his drink, which the bartender had quietly set in front of him. "Did you find any black widows?" he asked.

"No," Lorelei confirmed.

"And we searched quite thoroughly," I added. "How is Meghan doing?"

"Meghan is miserable. Her hand is quite swollen and her whole body aches. Damn spider." Miles finished his drink in one angry gulp and ordered another. "If I could catch that feral cat, I'd drown it in a bucket of water."

"You mean Crow?" Lorelei studied Miles as if he were a serial killer, and a smug one at that, still in his Gucci suit this late at night. He'd obviously had a harrowing evening trying to appease Meghan and her spider bite, which I couldn't help but find amusing.

"I guess that's its name," Miles said. "Stupid to name a cat after a bird. Katya was always illogical. I've never understood her."

"How could Crow possibly be a bother to you?" Lorelei asked.

"He hisses and growls at me every time I go to lock or unlock the gate. I'm afraid one of these days he's going to scratch the hell out of me."

"Miles, the cat never gets close enough to anyone to do them harm. His biggest goal in life is avoiding people, especially you." Lorelei rolled her strikingly blue eyes.

"I don't know about that. Why does he wait every morning and night on the fence to harass me?"

"Maybe he suspects you've done something with Katy," Lorelei quipped. I had never heard sarcasm from her before. It took me by surprise. I had to stifle a laugh, especially since Miles was clearly annoyed.

"Look," Miles began, "I know you two think Katya is going to wake up one day but you're both crazy. Even if she does, she'll never be the person she was, and I don't think she'll want to live without quality of life."

"There is every chance Katya will completely recover, Miles." I said emphatically.

"I don't believe you. Everything I've read suggests she could be very damaged *if and when* she wakes up."

"Well then you're reading the wrong articles," Lorelei interjected. "Research successful coma recoveries. The odds are pretty good for waking up and being just fine after rehab." Lorelei finished her second drink in one gulp.

I smiled. This woman was a rock. She not only managed Angele but found time to dote on Katya and her plants. She could also sing quite nicely and hold her liquor well. If I didn't have a psychotic crush on her best friend, I would be tempted to date Lorelei. "I have surgery in the morning, so I need to get home," I said, rather cheerlessly.

"I'm delivering Katya's will to the hospital tomorrow," Miles informed me.

I nodded and held my tongue, instead of questioning Miles about why he had suddenly come up with an advanced directive for Katya. The hospital should have had that information when he checked her in.

"I need to call it a night, too." Lorelei stood up to leave and I stood with her. I put a wad of cash on the counter, but Lorelei stuffed it back into my pocket. She told me the drinks were on the house. We walked out together, without saying goodnight to Miles.

The next morning when I arrived to check on Katya, Miles was waiting for me. He jumped up from the chair beside the bed and handed me a copy of what I assumed was Katya's advanced directive. "I thought you should have a copy, too," he barked.

"Tell me something, Miles. Why would Katya have an advanced directive? Most people our age aren't worried about premature death."

Miles shrugged. "I'm an attorney, so of course I would be on top of such a necessity." Before I could respond he left, without so much as a glance in Katya's direction. I wondered if ice water ran through his veins instead of blood. Leaning over Katya's bed I put my face close to hers. I needed to feel her faint breath while looking for any signs at all that he might have caused her harm. It was so quiet in her room you could hear the hum of her IV drip. Somewhere in my head Lorelei's lovely voice was singing one of her songs for Katya.

TRIUMPH

Our snow had melted and once again the sun shone high in the sky. It had been a sign that the real winter was coming right behind this teaser. Soon the pumpkins on the porch would rot and the dead leaves would blow away in a classic Central Oregon windstorm. This would be my last chance to complete the mural on the barn roof unless I wanted to wait until spring. I didn't know if I'd be here in the spring. I didn't know if I'd be here tomorrow. It didn't feel as if I was completely here right now.

The incomplete mural was as much a mystery as my own life, with one foot in this new world and one in the world I'd left behind. All my memories were prior to my life with Parker, but everything I had always wanted was in this world of missing pieces. Instead of agonizing over a mystery I couldn't solve, I focused on a master plan for completing the scene on the barn roof. It was such a picturesque barn, small and red, with white trim. The roof itself was black metal. The barn mostly housed saddles and other paraphernalia for the horses. I must have thought it would be fun to paint a black metal roof facing the road, although I could never be sure what my motives were, since I couldn't remember.

Parker had taken Ruby and would be gone all day helping Zachary winterize his boat out at Lake Billy Chinook. I was grateful for some time alone and that Parker had such a good friend in Zach. I still couldn't wrap my head around the idea of Lorelei being married to Zachery. Even more mind boggling were their twins. The Lorelei I knew in Napa had not expressed much interest in settling down or having children.

Parker would not approve of my climbing back up on the barn roof. I needed to have the mural done by the time he returned. I honestly had no idea if that was possible. I'd found a pair of running shoes with excellent tread and laced them tightly before entering the barn where the ladder was stored. I placed it against the roof and then carried out the cardboard box of quart-sized paint cans and brushes. I'd found them in a corner of the barn and concluded they'd been used for the first half of the mural. Why else would a box of colorful paints be in the barn? It was heavy and awkward, and I fretted about whether I had stuffed enough rags into it.

I carried my supplies up the ladder and set them on the sloping roof before scrambling onto it myself. I had been eager to see the mural up close, but instead of being drawn to it immediately, my eyes canvassed the incredible view. The endless sky was a show-stopping blue. The mountains were snow-capped from our recent storm. The aspen grove was at its peak of amber perfection. The leaves shimmered in the slight breeze like gold dust in a shallow brook. I stared at the panoramic view for several minutes, and it felt like something bigger than me was pulling the strings of this new and elusive world I'd been dropped into.

Maybe I had traveled in time when falling through Genevieve's cupboard. If so, my biggest fear would be returning against my will. I hadn't chosen to travel here in the first place, so why would I have control of my exit? Maybe this was a vision of what might have been, if only I hadn't run off after that night with Parker long ago, and then again in the vineyard. Maybe this would have been our life if I'd contacted him when discovering I was pregnant. All the *what-ifs* kept swirling around in my head, along with guilt, because I was responsible for the what-ifs never happening. Regardless of why I was here, how I got here, or for how long, I was determined to finish the mural. I had managed to brush the last stroke of paint when Parker drove up the driveway. He had barely stopped the SUV when jumping out and running over. Ruby and Goldie were still in the vehicle, their noses against the windows.

"Rosy, what are you doing? You shouldn't be on that roof!"

"It's fine, Parker. I'm finished."

"Then let's get you down from there."

I let him help me with the box of paints, and then he insisted on accompanying me off the roof and down the ladder. "I'm not an invalid," I protested.

"Maybe not, but your track record for falling off the barn roof is terrible."

"I've only fallen once."

"You've only been up there twice. That's half the time."

As soon as we were on solid ground, Parker pulled me to him in a tight hug. "Promise me you'll stay off the roof," he whispered into my hair.

"I won't need to climb on the roof again, Parker." I looked at him and smiled. "Unless I did a terrible job and need to adjust something."

We strained our necks to see the finished mural, but we were too close to it. Parker took my hand and together we walked back to the SUV. From there we could clearly see my finished work of art. While we stared up at the mural, Ruby tumbled out the door of the Land Rover. Goldie was right behind her.

"It's so pretty, Mommy!"

"Your mural is beautiful, Rosy," Parker agreed.

Even I was amazed at what a good job I'd done. It made me think of authors I'd read about, who said their books sometimes wrote themselves. Their hands only tapped the keys while the story unfolded, and they were often as surprised as the readers by the outcome. Without a doubt, *this* outcome surprised me. You couldn't tell where the juniper trees had been interrupted midstream in their creation, or where the orange jewelweed started and stopped between pre- and post-fall from the roof. The wild horses running across the field were perfectly formed with mouths half open and tales flying in the wind. My favorite part of the mural was the aspen grove I added. Maybe that was because I created it from beginning to end, with a clear memory of the entire process. It felt like progress, like a puzzle piece I was in complete control of connecting to the whole picture.

"I don't think there is anything you could do to make it better. Rosy. It's amazing."

"Thank you," I said, grinning ear to ear.

We held each other for a long, precious moment. Parker smelled like aftershave and juniper berries, which had fallen into his hair while on the barn roof helping me down. They fell from the trees like crazy this time of year. Rubes and Goldie had run down the long driveway to the house, which reminded me of my plans with Lorelei. "What are you and Ruby doing while I'm at Lorelei's café?"

"We're eating pizza and having a Disney movie marathon." We both laughed. Then Parker helped me put the ladder and paints back in the barn. We drove the SUV up to the house and I got ready for my dinner with Lorelei. It felt odd to be leaving Desert Sky by myself. I hadn't driven anywhere alone since my fall. It was silly, but I felt as if in a foreign country despite having grown up in the area. I had turned inward even more than usual these past few weeks. I'm not sure I would have left my studio at all if Parker hadn't enticed me. Ruby spent a lot of time there with me and I cherished the bubble we'd created. She would paint the most delightful pictures in bold colors. Sometimes we'd sit at the table together and mold clay, setting our creations on the windowsill in the sun to dry.

Oddly, Parker never came to my studio. I thought about that as I drove down the long driveway. Maybe he didn't want to interrupt my creative energy. Truth be told, except for the mural I hadn't felt inspired to do anything but brood and sulk. I nearly swerved off the gravel road while staring at the barn roof. I could never look at the mural without remembering that day I woke up in the meadow, with Parker and Ruby staring down at me. At least now it was finished.

When I arrived at my best friend's restaurant, I had to laugh out loud. Her special touches were obvious, even from the outside of her establishment. The décor fit perfectly with the town of Sisters. Lorelei's remodel of the building was rustic and quaint, with an unobtrusive sign that read, "Studio Café." I parked right in front and spent a few minutes admiring her storefront. Once I entered it was exciting to see so much art hung on every wall. Tables adorned with white linen and lit candles were scattered throughout the floor area. The combination was stunning. A pianist was playing something light and whimsical.

"You're right on time."

I turned to see Lorelei standing in the doorway to the bar area. "This is quite impressive! I love all your special touches," I added.

"I'm so glad you approve. That means a lot to me." Lorelei's blue eyes lit up. "Did you notice your work on the walls?"

I hadn't. I'd only taken in the whole captivating concept. Once I focused on the details it was obvious a lot of this art was mine. I didn't remember creating it, but the style was very familiar. "This is so touching, Lorelei, that you would feature my art like this."

"Nonsense. Your work is divine and you're a renowned local artist. I sell a lot of your pieces, which is profitable for both of us. No sentiment involved, my friend. You are so gifted. It frustrates me how much you question that."

I didn't have a response. Lorelei was truly a blessing to me. Having her believe in my art was probably the main reason I hadn't given up on becoming an accomplished artist. Miles had never appreciated my right-brained thinking or my obsession with art. He saw my creative gifts as more of a nuisance if not an outright inconvenience. My mother had felt the same way. Miles and my mother both saw imagination and creativity as something that derailed you from practicality and survival in the real world. Perhaps they were right. It was never an easy path. Life can be a cruel beast when you choose to take the road less traveled, becoming engrossed with intangible things that can drive you crazy. Anyone in the arts can attest to that.

"I hope you're hungry." Lorelei took my arm into hers and led me to the table reserved for us. Piano music from the bar area floated through the room as she poured the wine. It was a Beatles song that brought back memories from the day I'd skipped class and met Parker. The song teased me, like a gentle breeze, while flashes of rainwater running down the street gutter flashed through my head. Lorelei made a toast to friendship while my mind replayed Parker opening the pub door. The tune played eerily on.

I didn't hear anything Lorelei said after that. I just watched her lovely face fade in and out, along with her voice, and the piano music.

LIVING WILL

Watching the Napa River ebb and flow with the evening tide gave me pause to reflect upon my patients, and especially Katya Harrington. My table this evening at Angele had a perfect view of people walking by in the chilly autumn air. At some point in the last three weeks this French bistro had become my favorite place to frequent for dinner. Knowing I might get a chance to chat with Lorelei was a bonus. If she was too busy to sit for a minute, the view out the window could sustain anyone for quite a while. Aside from people bustling down the boardwalk, I had a perfect view of sea birds swooping in for a tasty fish beneath the meandering river. There was also the Napa sky, which lit up most evenings at sunset in fiery reds or smoldering oranges.

"Hello, Oliver."

I turned to see Miles standing beside me. He hadn't been to the hospital in nearly a week. "Hello Miles. Have you found any more black widows?"

"No."

Miles stood beside me until I asked if he'd like to sit for a minute, which he readily did.

"When do we quit kidding ourselves about Katya waking up?" Miles maintained an icy stare while waiting for my reply.

"Coma patients have been known to wake up after four weeks and completely recover." I tried my hardest to say this with confidence, but my resolve was waning. Katya had entered her fourth week with no change at all in her condition. "Miles, why did you marry Katya? Pardon me if I am incorrect here, but it doesn't seem as if you love your wife. You never visit her, and you seem hell bent on ending her life."

A waitress stopped by our table and Miles ordered a glass of wine. He waited for her to leave before answering. "It's Katya who never loved me. She just wanted to have kids."

"Why would you marry her knowing full well you couldn't give her the family she wanted?"

"I thought she'd give up on the idea, but she never did."

"You could have used donor sperm or adopted, had you been honest with her," I pointed out.

Miles shrugged. "I never wanted kids."

I didn't know how to respond to that, especially knowing there was nothing I'd rather do than raise a family with someone like Katya, if not Katya herself. The moment I thought this I tried to put it out of my mind, considering how inappropriate it was for me to feel this way. "Look, Miles, I realize how hurtful it must be that your wife was unfaithful, but from what I have observed, she isn't the only one who sought solace in another."

"If you mean Meghan, the truth is she fell for me head over heels, which is something Katya never did."

"It doesn't appear that you loved Katya any more than she loved you," I said rather dryly.

Miles sipped his wine and didn't look the least bit insulted. He stared out the window and returned to his original subject. "I don't want to be burdened with a wife living for years in a coma or waking up permanently damaged. I need to move on."

"Katya deserves a chance to recover."

"If at some point my wife needs a ventilator, you have a copy of her advanced directive which allows me to prevent that. Thank god I'm executor of her estate. It can get messy when someone passes without legally indicating what should be done with their assets." Miles said this with conviction, but his eyes indicated he was hiding something, like the truth. His fidgeting and obvious discomfort while sitting across from me was very different behavior for him. What happened to the *cool as a cucumber* assertive Miles I'd known until now? His weird behavior was confirming my belief that he'd recently faked estate planning and a living will with an advanced directive for Katya.

"Let's hope it doesn't come to that." I stood to leave, since I had already paid for the meal. "Good evening, Miles."

I didn't wait for a response, but I did see him nod stiffly as I walked away. He was such an incorrigible human being. I couldn't be in his presence another minute. It was late and I would normally have headed home but something caused me to return to the hospital. I entered Katya's room and stood just inside the door, more like a silent observer than her doctor. Why did this woman and her life shake me to my very core?

I slowly inched closer and sat in the chair I had so often found Lorelei perched in, reading from the Lewis Carroll book. Hesitantly I reached out to hold her hand, still as ice and not much warmer to the touch. I had never been a religious man, but I asked God to heal her, because I couldn't.

There was something so tragic about Katya's loveless marriage to a man who never understood or appreciated her. Katya's very name meant pure. It suited her.

Despite her frustration at not having a happy marriage or a house full of children, she managed to make stunning art through precise detail on metal plates, or on her stretched silks that bled emotion. She grew the most well-nurtured and luscious plants I'd ever seen. I couldn't let her die, or worse, waste away. She had too much to live for. I wanted her to wake up and leave Miles. I wanted her to find true love and bear children. I wanted her to continue making exquisite art. I wanted so much for her that it hurt.

I felt so helpless standing there watching her eyes flutter under the dim light. I could only hope she was dreaming the sweetest dreams imaginable. I hoped they were so intense and filled with light and love, that if she never came back to us, it would be by choice. Ever so gently I touched Katya's smooth, delicate cheek and grieved over the stillness of it, the coolness of near death. Then I rose to leave, crestfallen and nearly drained of hope for this miracle of her awakening that had so far eluded us.

I drove home disheartened and feeling sorry for myself, that I might never meet Katya, at least not in this world. I despised myself for not being able to find the key to her recovery. I opened a bottle of wine and drank it slowly on the front porch while staring at the stars in the heavens. They winked at me as if hiding celestial secrets. What defines mortality? Had Katya already left us in every way that mattered? Had she moved on to something better? Would we ever have the answers we all seek? It was with these disturbing thoughts that I fell into bed for a restless sleep. When I reached Katya's room the next morning on my rounds, Lorelei was singing to her as usual. She stopped the minute I walked into the room. "Oliver, Katya is starting her fourth week in a coma."

"I know."

Lorelei's eyes were full of questions she dared not ask.

"Don't give up hope," I said. "Katya still might surprise us all and wake up as if nothing ever happened."

"Do you honestly believe that?"

I shrugged. "Anything is possible as long as her vital signs and brain activity remain strong," I said unconvincingly. "Did Katya ever mention having a living will to you, with Miles as the beneficiary?"

Lorelei studied me for a minute as if the answer was written on my forehead. "Katy did mention wanting Genevieve to stay in her family, and that she should probably have a will drawn up. She wanted to be sure her children inherited the home." Lorelei sighed. "Katy never gave up hope that she'd have kids one day."

I had no immediate response for Lorelei. I didn't believe Katya had gotten around to having that will drawn up, regardless that her husband was an attorney. If she had, Lorelei would know. Katya would have shared that with her best friend. "I have a hunch Miles has drawn up a fake will for Katya," I said, rather angrily.

"Do you really think so? It does sound like Miles. I don't know the man that well, but he's always struck me as a bit shady."

"Yes, I think he might try to kill her by throwing legal papers at us, to stop caring for her basic needs. It would be hard for him to justify. I certainly wouldn't allow it, and he'd have to go through me to make it happen." Walking down the hallway to my office I tried my best to believe what I had just told Lorelei, but in all honesty, I wasn't sure I could prevent Miles from ending Katya's life. He would have the law on his side, and I would have no way to prove it was a forged will.

STUDIO CAFÉ

I stood in Parker's den and studied the etching on his wall. I had created the artwork, but I didn't recall doing it. This is how I felt about all the art in the house, and in Lorelei's Studio Café. It was strange to recognize my style and my signature but not remember the act of creation. Parker walked up behind me and wrapped his arms about my waist. "It's one of your best pieces, or at least it's one of my favorites," he commented.

"Did I sketch this at the coast?"

"Yes."

"Do we go often?"

"We generally go three or four time a year."

"I love the ocean."

Parker laughed. "I know. That's precisely why we go three or four times a year."

"Where is this house?"

Parker studied the house beside the beach in the etching and I was jealous of his memories, of whatever he was lost in thought about. "It's in Newport. We always rent the same beach house."

"I see." My heart suddenly felt heavy with inexplicable sadness at not knowing this. "Can we go next weekend?" I asked.

"If it's available. I'll call and see." Parker kissed the back of my neck. "We'll make new memories Rose. Maybe some old memories will return while we're there."

"Maybe," I halfway mumbled.

Parker returned shortly and said he'd booked the beach house. We'd leave early Friday and return Monday morning. Ruby was ecstatic when we told her. She pulled out her pink duffle bag from the front closet and filled it with sand toys.

"Where will your clothes go?" I asked, trying not to laugh.

Ruby shrugged. "In the bucket!" she declared, pulling a big plastic pail from the duffel bag for me to see.

"Maybe we could put the sand toys in a beach bag, along with some balls and a frisbee for Goldie. What do you think?" I asked.

She nodded her red head in approval.

I spent the next day, before our much-anticipated trip to the ocean, mulling over my time with Lorelei at the Studio Café. Our first course had been steamer clams with Italian sausage. I could still smell the savory sausage and taste the sweet clams. We dipped warm French bread in the lemony broth and Lorelei told me all about falling in love with Zach.

"You kept throwing us together," she professed. "Pizza Fridays and Sunday barbeques at Desert Sky. Saturday night brew pub hopping in Bend. Our only choice was to become a couple, so that hanging out with you and Parker all the time would be less awkward."

"Are you serious?" I'd asked. Then we both laughed. It felt good to laugh with Lorelei again. All those Friday nights on Genevieve's porch had flashed through my mind, all those bottles of wine we drank while inhaling fresh baked bread slathered with creamy brie. "I miss the tasty treasures you brought from Angele after work on Friday night," I'd said.

Lorelei had looked sad when I said this, as if her mind couldn't go there. She changed the subject by saying I had just disappeared one day and then showed up in Oregon, with Parker. No one had any idea where I'd gone, or why. I'd asked her if Miles looked for me, but she seemed to be at a loss for words. "Don't you remember anything about what happened?" she'd asked.

This had taken me aback, even now as I ruminated over her words. "No," I'd replied. The conversation was still so clear to me, so chilling.

"I don't think we should discuss it right now," she'd insisted.

"Why not?" I'd asked.

"It would be better to give yourself more time."

"More time for what?"

"To remember."

"Lorelei," I'd said emphatically, "if I haven't remembered by now, I doubt I ever will."

She'd reached across the table and put her hand on top of mine. "Let's just enjoy our dinner," she'd said. Then Lorelei smiled her famous smile that could light up a room. "I'll fill you in on everything if your memories don't come back soon," she'd promised.

While dragging our suitcases out of the closet I thought about the Oregon pinot Lorelei served with the clams. It was divine. Oregon pinots rivaled Napa's cabernets. The seasonal beet and goat cheese salad had been delicious. When I asked how she found such an incredible chef she told me about meeting Hilary shortly before running off to live in Oregon. She'd convinced her to come and be a partner in the Studio Café.

"Parker never mentioned a third partner," I'd commented.

Lorelei had shrugged. "I don't think he wants to overload you with details."

I thought about that the whole time I was packing Ruby's suitcase, and then my own. What else was Parker streamlining for me? And Lorelei? What didn't they want me to know? I was suddenly feeling paranoid. I sat on the bed and stared out the window. The mountains in the distance began to fade in and out. Was it my imagination, or was the room beginning to darken? In my head the dinner with Lorelei kept unfolding. "What about Ruby?" I'd asked, right after the waiter refreshed our wine glasses.

Lorelei had raised an eyebrow. "What about her?"

"She should have been born at the end of April according to my calculations, but her birthday is in November," I said, nearly tearing up. It was my biggest frustration, not understanding this mystery surrounding Ruby's birthday.

"That's silly," Lorelei had scolded. "Why would her birthday be in April?"

Our main course had arrived and so I didn't press the matter. It was Pasta Bolognese. Lorelei knew it was my favorite Italian dish. My mouth watered recalling the rich, meaty sauce. She had wisely paired it with a Napa cab. I clearly remembered sight and sound fading in and out, just like now, while sitting on the bed in the master suite. Blurry, muted colors filled the room and the view beyond the window. Was I running out of time or running away from the truth, and what was the truth? Was my memory blocked by a head injury or some other trauma I simply did not wish to recall?

NEWPORT

The drive to the coast on Friday was festive. We listened to an oldies station on the radio that played songs from my record collection at Desert Sky. We couldn't dance in the car and fall down laughing the way we had at home, so we sang along instead. When we tired of singing, I pulled snacks from the lunch cooler. It was a three-hour drive to Newport from Sisters, which is a very long time for a five-year-old. Ruby fell asleep during the last leg of the trip, with her head tilted to one side in the booster seat.

"Parker, when were we in Napa last?" I asked, after turning around to cover our sweet princess with her favorite well-worn blanket.

"That would have been Stephanie's wedding."

"Stephanie?"

Parker glanced at me. "She was one of your produce clients."

I recalled that Steph was an independent vendor for The Culinary Institute at Copia, in downtown Napa. Copia was the name of the Institute's public campus offering culinary classes and housing a restaurant. Students, however, lived at the campus in St. Helena, where their credited classes were held. Steph sold note-worthy sandwiches and salads from what used to be the ticket booth, when Copia was privately owned by Robert Mondavi. They'd had a lot of movies and concerts there back in the day. Mondavi was friends with Julia Child, who used to whip up French cuisine in one of Copia's state-of-the-art kitchens. I'd learned all this from the museum upstairs. The CIA at Copia wasn't far from Genevieve in downtown Napa. "What time of year was the wedding?" I asked.

"Last harvest season, at a quaint winery called Calistoga Ranch."

I remembered visiting Calistoga Ranch for a wine tasting with Miles, but I had no memory of attending a wedding there with Parker. Steph didn't have a significant other seven years ago, which is where my memory stopped. "Tell me about the wedding, Parker."

"What I remember most is how alluring you looked in your blue dress. It was soft and flowy and short."

"What about the bride, silly, and who was the groom?"

"I don't recall his name, but Stephanie's dress was quite elegant. Perfect for that setting."

"In the vineyard?"

"Yes. It was a gorgeous evening. The grapes were fat and juicy and ready to be plucked from the vines. The sun was a perfect backdrop for their small intimate wedding. It melted slowly into the horizon and made the sky seem as if on fire with brilliant shades of red and orange all mixed together."

"Why were we invited if it was a small, intimate affair?"

Parker shrugged. "Everyone loves you, Rose. You try to hide from the world, but the people you can't avoid become fans."

"I'm just glad *you're* my fan." I leaned over and kissed him on the cheek. "Tell me more."

"When we arrived, there were servers walking about with silver trays offering everyone a glass of champagne or a tasty delicacy. A string quartet was set up among the vines and they played romantic tunes."

"It sounds exquisite." I sighed, wishing I could remember.

"It was a wonderful time, Rosy. After the short ceremony in the vineyard, we were offered more champagne off silver trays. The string quartet played more tunes and it all could have ended there, but it was just getting started. We made our way to another part of the vineyard where one long table was set. Four amazing courses were served, all with different wine pairings. It was dark before we finished. The last course was served beneath a starlit night."

"How could I forget something so amazing as that?"

"Maybe you'll remember one day."

"Did we dance?"

"Oh yes. They transported us to a cozy wine cave after dinner. It was ancient I think, but they'd filled it with soft lights and plushy chairs. The main room of the cave held the band and dance floor. There was a smaller room with fruit and nuts and cheeses for snacking. I don't think anyone was hungry though after such a lovely meal in the vineyard. We danced until midnight while the servers with silver trays offered us tiny pastries and other sweet bites, in lieu of a cake, and of course there was an open bar."

I was silent the rest of the way to Newport, wondering about the many other things from my past seven years that were a blank slate now. Did Parker and I ever fight, and what did we fight about? All couples have disagreements, but we hadn't had any since my fall. More and more all of this seemed to be too good to be true. Looking out the window was evidence I might be right because the scenery was suddenly blurry.

We arrived by lunchtime and stopped at Mo's Chowder House. I didn't recall having been to Mo's with Parker and Ruby, but I did remember visiting the well-known restaurant a couple times a year growing up. My mother loved the ocean. It might have been the only thing we had in common. Fresh crab off the docks made her face light up like Christmas morning. She'd gather treasures along the shoreline and then sit in a lawn chair staring at the waves for hours. I'd play in the surf up to my knees, but any further would get me scolded. Neither of my parents were the adventurous type. For such strong independent people, I thought them unusually fearful of the physical world.

My father didn't like water. Any kind of water. He did brave Lake Billy Chinook in a fishing boat, but that was as far as his courage went when it came to tackling the natural world around him. He lived in his books and his music when not stressing over business ledgers. I could still hear him reciting poetry to me. I could still see his face take on a tranquil pose when listening to his favorite music, which ranged from Johann Bach to Willie Nelson. He was a huge Elvis fan. *This is Elvis, King of Rock and Roll* he would tell me, when playing his 33 RPM vinyl records louder than my mother preferred.

"We're here," Parker announced. Ruby wiggled out of her booster seat and jumped from the Land Rover with Goldie at her heels. I sat and studied the beach house from the vehicle. It was a good likeness to my etching hanging in Parker's den. The artwork couldn't quite capture how quaint the setting was, with the sun shining brightly on it. The house was the same color as driftwood, with white trim around the windows. A couple seagulls were perched on the roof, as if to greet us. Their gray feathers and white bellies blended right in with the house. I exited the car and cupped my hands over my eyes to look for Ruby, who was already running down the beach. At least she was a safe distance from the tideline. Goldie was prancing about right beside her. Parker had unlocked the door and was watching me from the generous front porch. He had a suitcase in each hand. "Are you coming, Rosy?"

"What about Ruby? I don't think we should leave her alone on the beach."

"I'll watch her." Parker set the suitcases just inside the door. "Go inside and see if any of it looks familiar." Without another word he took off down the beach in the direction Rubes had gone with Goldie.

The house was set back far enough to be safe from high tides during coastal storms. I looked skyward as if expecting one any minute. There were a few dark clouds in the distance. Maybe they'd continue to hover out at sea or maybe they'd work their way here. It was impossible to tell, but storms were not uncommon this time of year. I was guessing we might get at least a shower. After entering the front room, I stood still for a moment, admiring the light, airy feel of the house.

Sand-colored throw rugs were scattered across the dark wood floor. Curtains the color of the Pacific blew gently at the open windows. Vanilla scented candles had been placed here and there with seashells scattered about their base. A well-used stone fireplace filled one corner of the living room, with a wraparound leather couch the color of wet sand. There was a shiny black vase on the mantle. It reminded me of the large lava rocks just offshore. The vase held dried coastal flowers in every color of the rainbow. Whoever furnished the home didn't want you to feel separated from the beach outside the door.

I put the suitcases in our master bedroom, which was small but cozy. There was a plush teal green comforter on the king-size bed and a generous window with an ocean view. I peeked into Ruby's room. It was cheerful and bright with blue and yellow seahorses on the curtains and bedspread. Before heading out to the beach I unloaded everything from our cooler into the fridge. I nearly got lost in the expansive view of the dunes from the kitchen window. A light oak table with six chairs filled the nook area. Someone had set a glass vase filled with wild daisies in the middle of it. How could I not remember such a perfect beach house?

On my way out the door I hesitated at the bookcase beside it. Staring right at me was a copy of Lewis Carroll's *Alice's Adventures in Wonderland*. The book had been on my mind a lot lately and I was tempted to page through it, but decided I'd wait until after dinner.

Dark clouds were moving closer, but the beach was calling to me like an old friend. I didn't have to walk far to find Parker and Rubes playing fetch with Goldie. They must have grabbed the frisbee from the car while I was in the house. I joined them for a while. We ran after the frisbee and laughed when falling in the sand. Soon Parker and I were worn out, leaving Ruby to play fetch alone with her furry companion. The two of us walked along the beach hand in hand, watching the busy clouds roll in. We should have felt a sense of urgency to retreat indoors before the imminent downpour, but none of us were inclined to do so. Parker took the trail to the bluff above us. I kept an eye on Ruby running along the edge of the surf.

I didn't dare to admit it, even to myself, but I'd hoped a trip to the coast would clear my thinking and help me stabilize my condition. I wanted to believe a change of scenery, a place I loved to visit for solace and peace of mind, would give me exactly that. I needed the rhythm of the tide and the fresh ocean breezes to clean out the cobwebs in my head. I'd hoped my vision would stop fading in and out, and my hearing would no longer echo.

That didn't happen.

The echoing had been constant while on the beach, as were the blurred and faded images of sand and sea. Additionally, I now had seconds that lapsed into nothingness, as if I'd been momentarily removed from time altogether. I stood at the edge of the surf and watched the waves crash onto the jagged rocks. The sun had slipped away behind the dark clouds, which were directly overhead now. Rain soon spilled from the sky and soaked us all to the bone. Ruby was oblivious to the wet and cold. She jumped and laughed and skipped her way along the heavy rain-soaked sand with Goldie at her heels. I envied their light, carefree hearts. How many more moments did I have with them?

Through the downpour I watched Parker's shadowy figure up on the bluff. Was this day a memory I could keep? I could feel warm tears running down my cheeks and mixing with the cold rain. They were tears of joy. Real or imagined, my time here with Parker and Ruby was nothing short of glorious.

I watched the ocean gobble up the shore and then release it. I watched the cold shower end and the warm sun peek out. I watched Ruby splash barefoot in the waves and heard Goldie bark with delight. I saw the wet, glistening sand sparkle in the sun where just a minute ago it had been ominous and dark. I felt the roaring wind turn into a kitten's breath and gently dry my tears.

Whether real or imagined, this whole new life of mine was divine.

VISITOR

I was sitting at my desk catching up on paperwork and trying not to let my mind wander when, quite unexpectedly, Lorelei popped her head in the door.

"Oliver?"

"Good morning, Lorelei. How did you get past my secretary?"

Lorelei shrugged. "She told me to come on in."

I laughed. "I guess since you weren't a patient or a colleague, she assumed you were a lady friend."

Lorelei slipped into the chair facing my desk. "Do you have a lot of those?"

"A lot of what?"

"Lady friends."

"No. That's why I find it so amusing. Attila the Hun couldn't get past my secretary, but she let you come right on in."

Lorelei smiled. "Why do you suppose that is, Oliver?"

"In all honesty, the thought of me having a lady friend probably pleased her."

"I'm sure everyone in this hospital wonders why you aren't married or have a girlfriend."

"I don't have time for either," I reminded her.

"Was it wrong of me to visit your office? Do you think everybody will get the wrong idea?"

"No. I'm glad you stopped by," I reassured her. I'd rather visit with you than sign all these papers, and I don't care what anyone thinks."

"You won't like what I came to tell you."

"Is it about Katya?"

"It's more about Miles."

"Now what's he done?"

"You won't believe it."

I watched her stare at the grove of oak trees outside my office window and thought she looked thinner than I'd remembered. Maybe it was the black leggings. She had her hair all pulled up in a messy bun, which was an attractive look for her.

"Did you come here from an exercise class?" I asked, because I'd never seen her look so casual.

"Yes. I've started doing yoga again." She glanced at me and those blue eyes of hers matched the shirt she wore. It made me wonder again why she wasn't married.

Lorelei stood up and began to pace on the well-worn maroon carpet. "The classes are helping me hold on to my sanity."

"Is your work that stressful?"

"Yes, but Katy not waking up is what really has me rattled. I barely sleep at night. And then when you factor in Miles, and how he couldn't seem to care less about her, it makes me livid." She stopped in front of my bookshelf and a title caught her eye. Lorelei pulled the book out and paged through it. "Have you read this?" she asked.

I could tell by the cover it was one of my books on coma patients. "Yes, every word."

"I suppose nothing in here helped."

"I've read everything there is to read about comas. I think at this point our answers lie within Katya herself."

Lorelei closed the book and looked at me. "What does that mean, exactly?"

"It means there doesn't appear to be any physical reason for her to still be asleep."

Lorelei put it back on the shelf and sat in my leather chair again. "Miles was in Katy's room recently and said a lot of threatening things to her."

"Were you there?"

"No, but I am there a lot. I can't sleep anyway, so why not watch Katy dream? I only wish I were *in* her dream, instead of here."

I ignored her abuse of the after-hours visitor pass. I could only hope if I were in a coma someone would spend that much time with me. "How do you know Miles was there?"

"Meghan was at Angele with a friend, and I overheard them talking." Lorelei glanced at my painting on the wall. It was a dense stand of evergreens and reminded me of where I liked to fish in Alaska. I'm not sure Lorelei really saw it. It was more like she was looking right through the painting and into the past. By the tension in her face, I could only assume she was reliving Meghan's unwelcome visit to Angele.

"Does she know you manage the place?" I asked.

"Probably not."

"I don't understand why she didn't recognize you," I said, perplexed.

"She was seated at the table next to me, but I had my back to her. I was staring out the window at the river, drinking a gin and tonic and stewing about Katy. I could feel my blood pressure rise when I heard Meghan's voice. If the woman has any credibility, and I'm not sure she does, Miles said things to Katy we can only hope Katy didn't hear."

"Like what?" I asked. Just the thought of Miles trying to threaten someone in a coma made me angry.

"According to Meghan, Miles had a bit of a breakdown and took it out on Katy. He laughed about it when he told Meghan. She and her friend also thought it was funny, Miles yelling at someone who was probably no more coherent than a vegetable . . . in their opinion. It was all I could do not to turn around and throw my drink on them."

"I'm glad you didn't. Katya wouldn't want you losing your job over Meghan. She's hardly worth it."

"I wouldn't put it past Meghan to be scheming with Miles about how to end Katy's life so they can inherit her property on First Street."

"Did she say something to indicate that?"

Lorelei shrugged. "Not specifically. Meghan rambled on to her friend about how Miles scolded Katy for falling in the first place, that if she'd listened to him, she wouldn't have been on that ladder again."

"She was on the ladder more than once? That's news."

"I suppose. Who knows how many times Katy felt the need to cry over infant wear she'd never get to use."

"What else did you hear?"

Lorelei slid out of the chair and began to pace again. "Meghan told her friend how much Miles is looking forward to inheriting Genevieve, only she didn't refer to the home that way, of course. She just said the property on First Street."

"Is that all?"

Lorelei sighed. "No. She rambled on about how Miles had drawn up the will and estate planning he and Katy had discussed."

"Damn him. He forged those documents."

Lorelei sat back down. "Unfortunately, we can't prove it."

"I'm going to talk to the Director of Patient Care Services about this. She's a hospital administrator here and a friend. She'll know if we have any recourse."

"That's a good idea." Lorelei nodded approval. "I've practically gone mad since Katy's fall. I worry day and night that Miles will suffocate her when no one's looking."

"You've been watching too many movies. I don't think Miles will try to hurt Katya himself, physically. He's an attorney. Miles will try to use his forged legal papers to end her coma state."

"He could do that?" Lorelei began chewing on a nicely polished fingernail.

"No, because we are going to find a way to prove her advanced directive was forged."

"We are?"

"I hope so. That's why I'm going to see Margo. Meanwhile, you need to stop worrying about what Miles is doing, or Meghan. They don't seem like the murdering type to me." I smiled.

"It's not funny, Oliver."

"No," I admitted, "it isn't. But you really will lose your mind if you don't get a better perspective on this," I scolded. "Men like Miles are not cold-blooded killers. He will let his falsified papers do his dirty work for him, and we are going to find a way to block that."

"If you say so, but I wouldn't put it past Miles to do something unforgivable. Have you ever looked into his eyes? They betray his cold and unfeeling heart." Lorelei rose to leave. "Please let me know what Margo has to say."

"I will."

She left as stealthily as she'd come in, with those fluid movements that defined her. A faint lilac scent always lingered in her wake. It was beyond me why I didn't snatch her up myself. It seemed ironic to me that the most prevalent thing we had in common was our obsession with Katya. In fact, we were both a nervous wreck over this tiny wisp of a woman in a coma. So many lives had been affected by Katya's fall, not the least of which was Katya herself. Who knew if she'd ever return to us? The main thing, as I saw it, was to make sure no one impeded her chance to fully awaken and recover. This is all I could think about while waiting to see Margo. I stared at the nameplate on her office door, which read *Margo Bastille, Director of Patient Care Services*. I honestly didn't know what exactly her job entailed. I hoped if she couldn't help me herself, she'd know who I needed to speak with.

"Good morning, Oliver. What brings you to my office?" Margo stood up and shook my hand. I was once again taken aback by her striking eyes, the shape of almonds and color of chestnuts. Margo's skin was a dark shade of honey, and just as smooth. I, however, found her intellect to be even more impressive than her appearance. Margo always had a warm smile and professional demeanor about her, as she did now. The combination made you feel welcome but not overly comfortable. Despite the air of authority that clung to her fashionable business attire, I had no fear of Margo. I had too often witnessed the heart of gold she hid from mere acquaintances. After settling into a chair across from her massive desk, I wondered where to begin.

"Do you remember the coma patient I told you about?"

"Yes. Over coffee in the cafeteria at midnight, as I remember."

"Why are you here at midnight?" I asked. "Most administrators keep decent hours." We both laughed. Margo and I had become friends mainly because she visited the cafeteria late at night. She took her rather overwhelming job very seriously and I loved that about her.

"What's the issue with your patient?"

"Katya Harrington's husband has written an advance directive for her and falsely signed it."

Margo raised one of her perfectly arched eyebrows. It matched her dark hair, pulled into some sort of twisted knot.

"He's an attorney," I added.

"How did you find this out?"

"Miles came to me recently and said his wife has an advance directive, which he plans to use in order to end her coma state." I got angry just thinking about it and had to pause there to collect my thoughts. Margo waited for me to continue.

"He plans to use it if she remains unresponsive, or if her vital signs begin to decline. He claims she wouldn't want to live in a vegetative state or wake up permanently compromised and without quality life."

"What makes you think the directive is false?"

"Someone overheard a conversation about it, a Miss Lorelei De Luca, who is the only visitor our patient has had. I'm sure she'd be willing to pass on what she heard, to you or anyone else. Of course, it's still just her word against his."

"How could someone overhear? Surely, he didn't say all this in front of a witness?"

"Lorelei overheard his girlfriend discussing it with a friend."

"He has a girlfriend?"

"Yes."

"I see. Well, that would certainly give him a motive for not wanting his wife to recover."

We were both quiet for a minute, absorbed in our own thoughts. I had no doubt Margo was wondering how to approach the situation without proof. I was trying to talk myself out of confronting Miles.

"Oliver, I will look at the advance directive we have on file for Katya Harrington and make sure it appears legitimate. If I can't find any incriminating evidence regarding the document being forged, then I'll consult with a few colleagues and the proper authorities for advice."

"You mean the hospital attorneys?"

Margo nodded her head. "Meanwhile, I suggest you cool off a bit. I am sensing you are too emotionally involved in this case. I'd hate to have to assign a different doctor to Katya Harrington, because you are by far the best neurosurgeon we have. She deserves your talent and skill."

I took a deep breath before responding. The last thing I wanted was to be removed from Katya's care. Everything inside of me screamed that Margo was correct in her assessment. My emotions were beyond all reason and accountability when it came to Katya Harrington. Nevertheless, I couldn't admit this.

"Margo, I can assure you, my care and concern for this patient is no different than for any of my patients. It is morally wrong and a despicable act on the part of her husband to forge an advance directive."

"I completely agree, but you must restrain yourself. I wouldn't want your righteous indignation to land you in court." Margo shot me a no-nonsense look. She stood up to see me out and I felt better knowing she'd be on my side in a fight to choose life over death for Katya. Regardless, I left not feeling much better about the situation. Miles was a slithering serpent, and I had a strong desire to crush him beneath my feet. Then he could do no harm to anyone, especially Katya. It was an unsettling way to feel about a patient's husband, especially when considering my underlying motive for wanting to be rid of him.

NIGHTMARE

The ride home from the coast was quite subdued. Ruby had worn herself out and slept most of the way, with Goldie snoring beside her. I stared out the window at Oregon's thickly forested terrain and contemplated my physical instabilities. I thought of going in for tests to see if my condition could be treated. Perhaps I suffered more than a concussion when falling from the roof or maybe my symptoms weren't rooted in anything physical at all. Maybe I was mentally unstable, a condition caused by some past trauma that Parker and Lorelei didn't want me to revisit. Lorelei's words at the Studio Café kept haunting me. *Don't you remember anything about what happened, anything at all?*

"Parker, is someone managing my micro farm in Napa?" I couldn't believe I had completely forgotten about it until now. Fat, juicy heirloom tomatoes glistening in the morning dew flashed through my mind. I could almost smell the aromatic pots of herbs I had lovingly tended. I longed to see my baskets of root vegetables in their rainbow of muted colors. The micro farm had taken my mind off not conceiving a child. How could I have so easily dismissed it? I recalled all the time I had spent tilling the earth, weeding and watering, harvesting the crops. Parker was speaking to me, and I barely heard him.

"Rosy?"

"I'm sorry. What were you saying?"

"I was telling you about the roses."

"Roses?"

"Yes. Once we moved to Oregon you decided to plant a rose garden where your micro farm had been."

"I did?"

"You did. And I must say it has finally come into its own. There can't be a more impressive rose garden anywhere in the world. You have such a gift with growing things."

"Why haven't I sketched the rose garden?" I asked. "There aren't any silk screens or etchings of it at Desert Sky, or Studio Café."

"I think you have, Rosy, only just recently. I don't think any of the rose garden art was ready for public viewing yet. You weren't really inspired until this last visit to Napa. All your time before that was spent fussing over the roses, not drawing them."

I didn't say anything. What was there to say? I had evidently planted a rose garden I had no recollection of, and then recently was inspired to draw the roses. According to Parker I also produced etchings and silk screens of roses, but where were they? I'd been through all the art against the walls in my studio. No roses.

The minute we got home, after waking Ruby up and helping Parker unpack the car, I went straight to my studio. Standing inside the door I studied the room, wondering where sketches and etchings and silk screens of roses might be. Then I saw a door I hadn't noticed before. It was tucked away in a corner and looked more like the entrance to a crawl space. The door wasn't normal height. It was only about half that size. I turned the knob and instantly thought of the last time I'd opened an odd door in an unconventional place. That had gotten me tossed into all of this, whatever *this* was.

The door opened easily and was indeed a sort of crawl space, but I had stuffed it with canvases. I pulled one out and discovered a silk screen of roses with non-definitive lines and bleeding different shades of reds. I found a couple etchings incredibly detailed down to the last thorn. Parker, as usual, was right. I must have wanted to surprise someone with these. Why else were they packed away out of sight? Maybe Ruby would know the reason for my secrecy.

As if to answer my question, Rubes appeared in the doorway. Her cheeks were flushed from running up the studio steps. "Hey sweetie, are you hungry?" I asked, not waiting for an answer. I'd already found a box of Goldfish crackers in the cabinet and placed some in a bowl. She scooted onto a chair at the table and began lining fish up, with their smiles facing the same direction. I set a glass of milk in front of her. "Ruby, do you have any idea why all these pieces of art were in the closet?" I pointed to the canvases spread across the floor. Ruby studied the art for a minute, while stuffing three goldfish in her mouth.

"Mommy, those are your rose pictures."

"I know, honey. I just don't understand why they were in the closet."

"So Auntie Lori wouldn't see."

"Auntie Lori? Do you mean Lorelei?"

Ruby nodded her head up and down emphatically. I didn't know who came up with "Auntie Lori," but it made me smile. We spent the next few hours drawing together. I drew sharp-edged rock formations being pummeled by the sea while Ruby drew smiling seagulls on the beach in the sun. Everything associated with Ruby was like a bright light bursting through dark shadows. If only I could relive the years with Ruby I had lost. As it was, I didn't know how much time I had left in the present. Fragmented moments of nothingness were growing more frequent. It was as if I were short circuiting, like a computer with bad reception.

That night I tossed and turned, unable to sleep, until finally crawling from the bed to lie on the sofa in Parker's den, so as not to disturb him. I curled up in the afghan we'd made love on not that long ago. It was cozy and warm and smelled of Parker. I wanted to live in that afghan, safe and secure, and reminiscent of lovemaking with the man of my dreams. *Truly my dreams* because what else could this be? Of course, it did have its nightmarish aspects. I decided it couldn't be heaven. God would never make heaven more stressful than earth. Would He?

Somewhere around eleven o'clock I had a nightmare. I had walked off a cloud full of red-headed angels. When I landed, I was at the bottom of a deep abyss, where all I could see was a pair of angry eyes staring at me. There was water dripping from somewhere above. The more I listened to the drip, drip, drip of the water, the harder I stared into the angry eyes. It soon occurred to me the eyes were familiar. I knew who these icy blue pools belonged to, and it gave me the chills. My teeth chattered and my fingers grew numb. The dripping sound became louder just as Miles began talking.

I can't believe you Katya. Of all the ridiculous stunts a wife could pull, here you are incapacitated and leaving me with no recourse other than to find a way to end your misery, and mine. You see I can't marry Meghan until you are out of the picture, and I certainly can't divorce someone in a coma. You leave me no choice but to find another way to rid myself of this dilemma.

I listened to Miles lecturing me from a cold dark space that I couldn't define and didn't recognize. It might have been an arctic cave, with icicles dripping above me. I couldn't be sure. Every drip was louder and slower until each drop endlessly echoed, as if in slow motion. Miles, however, came through loud and clear.

I can't believe you got pregnant with another man's child, Katya. Were you going to push that kid off as mine? Well at least now I know what you were doing all those afternoons supposedly spent drawing in a vineyard. You were off with your lover, whoever it was. All I feel for you is contempt. I'm not going to let you lie there and ruin my life. I have found a way to put you out of your misery and that's what I intend to do.

The dripping icicles in the arctic cave stopped echoing. Miles's voice became so loud and yet so distant, I thought perhaps he was a flea sitting inside my ear, shouting into the dark hollow of it, dark and hollow like this cave that held me hostage.

You wouldn't have fallen off that ladder in the first place if you'd listened to me. But then you never did listen to me. All I can say is that I am looking forward to inheriting your Napa house. It's worth a small fortune, and so of course I've made sure the will and estate planning we'd always meant to do . . . got done.

I took a deep breath through my mouth, as if surfacing from beneath a pool of freezing water. Then I sat upright and screamed. Before I opened my eyes, Parker was in the den with me. He took me into his arms. "Rosy, what happened?" I fell into him like a wilted flower, shriveled and spent. I couldn't speak. The eerie dream sat inside my head and refused to leave. "It must have been a nightmare, Rosy. You had been tossing and turning, but then I fell asleep until I heard you screaming. I woke up and you were gone."

"I'm sorry. I left because I didn't want to disturb you." My voice was barely audible, buried in his chest. I couldn't get those angry eyes from the nightmare out of my head, or the angry voice. Even more disturbing was knowing who the eyes and the voice belonged to.

Miles.

MARCUS

Now that Katya wasn't getting any better and there was less and less hope that she ever would, I felt compelled to make another trip to Three Gates Winery. All night I had wrestled with my conscience regarding what I should have done the last time I was there. I made myself a strong pot of coffee and took a brisk shower. It was my day off and I couldn't think of anything I'd rather do than take a drive through wine country. Granted, the leaves were shriveled on the vines by November, but the drive was inspiring in any season. Besides, I might never sleep again if I didn't make the trip. Bringing Katya's Parker to her might be the last chance I'd have to awaken our sleeping beauty.

I barely saw the lush scenery. There were too many things on my mind, like the upcoming holidays, which were fast approaching. I'd already decided I wouldn't go on my usual Alaskan fishing trip. I couldn't abandon Katya. Lorelei had offered to serve me Thanksgiving dinner at Angele. She said she'd join me, and we could get drunk on wine to forget our misery. The tasting room looked nearly deserted when I arrived. Of course, it was barely noon on a Thursday and far from the height of the season. I sat exactly where I had the first time I'd been there, but the young woman with a dark brown ponytail and green eyes was nowhere to be seen. This time I was waited on by a man who had a striking resemblance to Parker.

"Would you like a full flight?" he asked.

"Yes, please," I replied. "You wouldn't happen to be related to Parker Mancini?"

"I'm his older brother, Marcus."

We shook hands and Marcus asked how it was that I knew his brother.

"We met when I was here last, but I must confess I don't really know him. I just thought he was quite pleasant, and we had a nice conversation."

"I see. Parker is quite charming, when he's here."

"That sounds like he isn't around." I tried to ignore a sinking feeling in the pit of my stomach.

"No. He's off traveling somewhere."

I wanted to ask where he was and when he'd be back, but I didn't have a good reason to pry, so instead I took a sip of the first wine Marcus poured.

"This has sweet notes of pear and perhaps a hint of cinnamon," I commented, while swirling it around in the stemmed glass and wondering where Parker had run off to.

"Yes, it's quite pleasing to the palate, isn't it? We're especially proud of this particular pinot gris." Marcus smiled broadly and it was obvious how passionate he was about the vineyard and the wine. I hadn't detected that same over-the-top love for the family business in Parker. I tried to think of a legitimate reason to inquire about his whereabouts while Marcus poured the next wine, and then I remembered Parker had mentioned he wrote articles for a living.

"Marcus, is there a way I can be in touch with your brother? I need a couple articles written. I'm a neurosurgeon, you see, over at the hospital in Napa and I need a good writer to work up some case studies for me. It's for the journal our hospital distributes at the national neurosurgeon's conference."

"Normally I could tell you exactly where he is and have him get in touch with you, but he isn't answering my texts or emails. I wouldn't feel right sending him a client under the circumstances." Marcus didn't look up while saying this. He was focused on arranging the wines behind the bar and I interpreted that to mean he was a bit concerned about his brother. Finally, he stood tall and we made eye contact. "This is our chardonnay. You won't find it to be big and buttery. It's on the dry side and has accents of lemon with a hint of pineapple."

I downed the tasting and complimented Marcus on the unique flavor, which was quite enjoyable. I wasn't into buttery chardonnays, so this was a nice diversion from that. "I hope everything is okay with Parker."

Marcus shrugged. "I'm sure he's fine. It's just some sort of girl trouble. I think he might have run off with one, not that he has indicated as much. Parker can go off the grid from time to time. I respect that and I just let him be."

This, of course, took me by surprise. "Has your brother ever been married?" I asked, knowing damn well it was none of my business.

"Yes, once, but it didn't last long. He's been in love forever with some girl he met back in college but that didn't work out either. I don't know if he's found someone new to help drown his sorrows in or not, but I hope so, for his sake. He was moping around here looking miserable these last couple weeks, until he took off."

"What makes you think he's left with a woman?" I tried not to show how nervous this whole conversation was making me. Katya's only hope for waking up might have moved on and was nowhere to be found.

"Some pretty girl came in every day and flirted with him shamelessly. I honestly don't know if they're together or not, but a new relationship might do him a lot of good."

"You're probably right," I agreed, but my stomach was churning as I said it. I pretended to hang on every word about the remaining tastings, but in truth I didn't hear anything Marcus said. All I could think about was how I'd had an opportunity to connect Katya and Parker, and then blew it because of my own selfishness. Now Parker was off somewhere and probably with another woman. Meanwhile Katya was looking less and less likely to come back to us without a huge incentive. I wanted to believe hearing Parker's voice, feeling his touch, and having his scent nearby would awaken something in her. Maybe I'd read too many fairytales as a child.

On the drive back I got a call from Margo. I hoped she'd confirm Miles had forged Katya's advance directive, but I doubted that's why she called. Attorneys thrive on making the unscrupulous seem impeccable.

"Hello Margo. What can I do for you?"

"I wish there was something *I* could do for *you*, and more specifically, for your patient. Our attorneys can't find anything out of order with Katya Harrington's advance directive."

"I didn't think they would. Miles strikes me as the type who excels at deceptiveness."

"Oliver, how well do you know this man?"

"Katya has been in a coma for almost four weeks now. I've seen more than enough of him."

"Does he visit her often?"

I evaded answering her question because I rarely saw Miles at the hospital. I mostly saw him outside of it, which wouldn't make me look very objective as Katya's doctor. "Is there any valid reason we could give, Margo, for not accepting his document?"

Margo didn't answer right away. She must have been mulling that over. When she finally spoke, her answer was no, there wasn't any acceptable reason for not honoring what should have been the patient's wishes. Unfortunately, in this case it had nothing to do with the patient's wishes and everything to do with her greedy, heartless husband. I was careful not to point that out again, lest I sound too emotionally involved. Margo encouraged me to keep my eyes and ears peeled for anything Miles might say or do that would give us reason to question the document. We finished the call by discussing a few other patient issues and Margo subtly warned me again about not becoming too involved in Katya's case.

I spent the rest of the drive berating myself for not telling Parker everything when I was at Three Gates the first time. It was sadly ironic how none of my skills as a doctor could save Katya from a premature death, but if I'd broken my own rules, I might have saved her and Parker both from the tragic loss of each other.

It annoyed me to picture them together, but it also raised my guilt level knowing I had stood between them. I was all for fate and true love, but more than anything I wanted a shot with Katya myself. How insane was that? My decision not to tell Parker about Katya went beyond professional ethics, which had merely been a convenient excuse. I glanced at the endless rows of winter vines along the side of the road, cold and barren in the late fall chill, not unlike my heart had been until Katya came along. Without knowing it she awakened something in me I hadn't felt in a long time. She was like a rose in a glass case. Just looking at her could melt your heart. She was so fragile and yet had endured a horrific fall. Now if she would just wake up before her petals withered on the floor.

Pulling into my driveway I stared at the setting sun. I was deranged to be thinking this way. How could I undo this insanity? Maybe I needed a therapist. All I knew for certain is that I couldn't quit trying to save Katya until either God or fate took her from me, and Miles would have no hand in it. I would see to that.

PACKING

Lorelei showed up at my studio with two large cups of coffee. She handed me one and said it was a cinnamon dolce latte, my favorite. I had to take her word for that, but after my first sip I completely agreed. "Look at what I found in the crawl space," I said between sips. Lorelei studied the new artwork, which I'd propped against a wall.

"Wow, Katy, these are amazing." She soon became lost in the rose garden art, setting her own latte on the windowsill so she could pick each one up and admire it more closely. "The method you use to create silk screens and etchings on canvas is impressive. Why haven't I seen this series before?" Lorelei looked up from the art and studied me.

I shrugged. "I'm not sure why I haven't shared them with you. Ruby said I wanted these pieces to be a surprise."

We looked at one another as if pondering this mystery, until Lorelei finally spoke. "I bet you were saving this new work for the grand opening of the downtown gallery. They wanted something entirely different than what I have at my café."

I sighed. "I wish I could remember that, but my mind is still a blank slate regarding the past seven years."

"That's so odd, Katy. Why seven years? That's exactly how long you and Parker have been together." Lorelei picked her coffee drink back up and wandered over to the drawings Ruby and I had done when returning from the coast. "This sketch has a very different feel to it than all your other work."

"Does it?" I said, suspecting it was darker than any of my other work. It looked as if the storm within me had spilled onto the paper.

Lorelei studied me again over her venti cup. "I was hoping you'd let me steal Ruby for a couple days. She's so wonderful with the twins, and it would give you and Parker some time alone."

I didn't know what to say. Every minute with Ruby was precious to me. Lorelei could see my hesitation.

"I think you should take the horses and camp by the river like you usually do in the fall. If anything is going to jog your memory, Katy, maybe that will do it."

"Living in this house should have sparked a million and one memories, but it hasn't." I sat down at the table by the window, frustrated.

Lorelei sat across from me. "Fresh air. A running river. Peace and quiet. Nature. Always better for the soul than anything else." She reached across the table and put her hand on top of mine.

"Maybe you're right. Maybe I could get some perspective being out in nature for a few days. God knows I haven't felt inspired to be creative since the fall."

"Your memory loss seems to be wearing on Parker as much as you," Lorelei shared.

"Parker has been stressed?" I suddenly felt terrible for not noticing. Obviously, I had become too caught up in my own frustrations.

Lorelei patted my hand. "He's been venting to Zac. It's hard for him, Katy. He loves you so much, and all your memories with him are gone. It really hurt when you thought you were still married to Miles, after you regained consciousness from the fall. And nothing has come back to you since then. In your head you're stuck in Napa, but your life here on Desert Sky is the dream you both worked so hard for. It's why you finally became motivated to sell your art, so you could help buy the ranch and build this life with Parker."

I let everything Lorelei said sink in. I'd been so consumed by my own confusion I hadn't considered how difficult all of this was for Parker. "You're right, of course. We need to get away, just the two of us, and do something we've always loved doing together. What would I do without you, Lorelei? Your perspective is just what I needed."

"I can't tell you how many times your insight has helped me, Katy. That's what friends do for each other." Lorelei smiled. It was the first time I had seen her smile today, evidence that her mom's death was heavy on her heart. "The twins and I are going to have a great time with Ruby."

"I'm sure Ruby will be over the moon. She adores Kooper and Ryker. How are you doing otherwise?" I asked.

"I'm fine. You are my main focus now, you and Parker. You both mean the world to me and Zac. Go fish and camp. Get some perspective on your challenging situation."

We stood up and hugged tightly, then we threw our empty cups away in the trash under the sink. "I'm going to grab Ruby and the twins and head out, Katy. Maybe Parker can drop a suitcase by for her later? I promised Kooper and Ryker we'd bring Ruby with us to lunch."

Together we walked out to the meadow where I hugged Ruby goodbye. Lorelei had already discussed everything with Parker, including Goldie coming along. It was hard letting Ruby go for a couple days but I needed to focus on

Parker for once. He deserved that. It had been all about me for four weeks now. I hugged Ruby one last time and waved as they sped away. Standing on the front porch I could hear the horses whinny. It occurred to me I didn't know their names. Parker soon emerged from the house and put his arms around me. "Our camping trip will be fun, you'll see."

"Parker, what are the horses' names?"

"You named your quarter horse Finnegan, after the James Joyce book, *Finnegan's Wake*, but you call him Finn. You thoroughly enjoyed the book, apparently, although you've never said why." Parker smiled.

I didn't share how the book was written as part reality and part dream, but now I found it more than a little ironic, since I couldn't decide if I was living in a dream or reality myself. "And what about your black beauty over there?"

Parker laughed. "My faithful steed goes by Rocco, because I was a big fan of the Rocky films and that was Rocky's nickname."

I felt a pang of sadness. "I'm sorry I don't remember your favorite movies or actors or anything at all about you, Parker. It must be hard, having to fill in all the blanks for me."

"Sometimes. But it's also fun having you get to know me all over again."

I looked at him skeptically, especially after what Lorelei had just said.

"Okay," he admitted. "It has been hard knowing your life with Miles is the only one you remember, but every day we make new memories here at Desert Sky."

"How am I at fly fishing?" I asked.

"You're pretty good with a fly rod, almost as good as me."

"Almost?" I playfully pushed him, but Parker grabbed me for a long and passionate kiss. When we finally tore ourselves apart, we headed back to the house. I started packing our clothes while Parker finished his work in the den. It was warm for November which meant we wouldn't freeze to death in our tent beside the river. I wondered if I'd remember how to ride a horse. I decided it wasn't a big concern since I'd been riding my whole life. Surely it would instinctively come back to me, just like wake surfing had on Lake Billy.

I walked out to the pasture when I finished packing and perched on the fence by the horses. There was a scent of pine needles in the air, and fresh hay. It was peaceful watching their tails switch and listening to them whinny. My fear and anxiety about the trip melted away and was replaced with anticipation. I hadn't sat on the fence long when Finn came over to greet me. I petted his nose and spoke softly to him, mostly asking for his patience during our trail ride tomorrow. Then it occurred to me I still needed to pack our food. I didn't know what we'd taken on these trips in the past. I didn't know what Parker's favorite foods were in general, let alone when camping. Nonetheless, I wanted to please him. Since PB&J with wild honey seemed to be a staple at our house, I decided it must be favored over anything else for sustenance, so I made peanut butter sandwiches and added an extra dollop of honey for good measure.

We'd have no refrigeration and little storage space, but I was up for the challenge of coordinating yummy meals. In the cupboard I found a package of instant potatoes that only needed water to hydrate. I also packed a can of baby sweet peas and white meat chicken, just in case we didn't catch any trout for our dinner. Next, I whipped up some dense, chewy brownies, one of the few things I knew Parker loved besides peanut butter and honey. When he joined me in the kitchen after finishing his articles, I was still involved with food prep.

"How did you know everything you've packed is what we like to take camping?" he asked, while rummaging through the leather saddlebags on the counter.

"I don't know," I said, while placing flour tortillas in the pouch beside a can of spicy black beans. It was an honest answer.

Parker leaned against the counter, grinning. "So, it looks like we've packed all the usual meals, but you can't explain it?"

I stopped what I was doing and looked at him, at this man who had to be every bit as confused as I was. "I can't explain it. That's just it. I can't explain anything except that you are more real to me than I am to myself. Whenever everything becomes sketchy, like bad internet reception in my head, you are still there. Bigger than life. Solid. My rock and my anchor."

"I'm glad to hear that, Rosy, because it frightens me sometimes, how you seem to only recall your life *before me*."

"It frightens me too," I confessed. "Especially since *you are* my life. Without you, nothing matters."

Parker held his arms outstretched and I slid into them, burying my head in his expansive chest. "You'd be fine without me Rosy. You'd have Ruby, and you're so much stronger than you think." He stroked my hair gently, smoothing down the blond waves, which bounced back up when he ran his hands beneath them. Then he lifted my face to his for another long, intense kiss, only this time one thing led to another until Parker picked me up in his strong arms and carried me to the master suite. After some slow, thoughtful lovemaking, we climbed into the hot tub and watched the sun set behind the mountains. Soon we were blanketed in darkness. Stars popped out above us. Coyotes howled in the distance, which was a familiar sound from my childhood. Everything about Desert Sky took me back to my childhood.

Was this all just a dream based on things I clearly knew? Was I pulling from memories of the past? My father and I rode horses and fished the river. Every spring and fall we'd spend a night in the woods. Mother relished the alone time. With no one to care for she'd sit on the porch and drink martinis. Funny how I never liked them. Having a daughter of my own made me want to know my own mother better, despite our differences.

CAMPING

The next morning there was not a cloud in the sky. It was perfect for a trail ride. The brisk morning air would soon warm up as the sun rose higher. Finn and Rocco were full of good spirits and seemed excited to take off. Parker had fly rods, a tackle box, and a lightweight two-person tent on the back of his saddle. I had the leather bags full of food and a few utensils for cooking and eating. We both had canteens of water and bedrolls with an extra woolen blanket. It was the first of November. Night and early morning would be chilly along the river.

For the better part of the morning, I followed Parker down a trail he must have known by heart. It led to the Metolius, where we stopped to eat lunch and do some fly fishing. I laid out sandwiches, dried fruit, nuts, and brownies while Parker assembled the fly rods. Together we sat on an old log beside the rushing river and ate our sandwiches. Occasionally a fish would jump up as if to say hello. At one point we craned our necks to see an eagle flying high above us, no doubt eyeing the lunch spread out on the log.

I put the food away when we finished our humble feast. It was time to fish. I was amazed at how easily I attached a fly to my line, and how I somehow knew which flies to use for this time of day, and time of year. Fly-fishing must have been something we did frequently, but I chose not to ask Parker about it. The sanctuary of this scenic place encouraged a need in me to be still and listen.

Regardless that conversation was scarce, the connection between Parker and I had never been stronger than it was there among the beauty of nature. Every tree was filled with chirping birds. Trout nearly jumped onto the flies at the end of our poles. Busy chipmunks scampered about, occasionally glancing our way to see if we'd caught anything yet. I wondered how many days like this were lost to me, but instead of dwelling on it, I was determined to make new memories.

We spent a couple of hours trying to out-fish one another. Parker caught more, but mine were larger. He said it was my patience that reeled in the big fish. He would cast and release twice as often. He loved the art of it. I preferred to drag my line along the current, reeling in slowly.

By mid-afternoon we'd loaded up the horses and were heading back down the trail toward our favorite camping spot along a bend in the river. Parker was excited for me to see it, no doubt hoping it might spark a memory. On our way to the campsite, we came upon an open field speckled with late fall flowers.

Everywhere you looked there were clusters of burnt orange or baby blue. Snow covered mountains framed the picture. It was like trotting through a postcard. An excerpt from *Alice's Adventures in Wonderland* flashed through my head.

"How long is forever?"
"Sometimes just one second."
"If you knew Time as well as I do," said the Hatter, "you wouldn't talk about wasting it."

Feeling overwhelmingly happy in the moment, I broke into a canter. Parker kept up just beside me. It felt as if we were flying through time and space, and maybe we were. Then everything went blank. No flowers, field, or majestic mountains. There was only the sensation of falling, of slipping from the saddle into nothingness.

CRISES

Lorelei shut the Lewis Carroll book just as I walked into Katya's room.

"It's over, Oliver."

"What's over?" I asked.

"*Alice's Adventures in Wonderland.* I've finished it." A tear trickled down Lorelei's cheek. She wiped it away and looked up at me. "Katy should be awake by now."

I wanted to say something positive or at least comforting, but as I struggled to come up with a response Miles stepped into the room. Lorelei and I both stared at him as if he were an unwelcome intruder. Even the Gucci suit suddenly looked sinister.

"Do either of you ever leave this room?" he asked, rather cynically.

"Is there something we can do for you, Miles, or are you here to visit Katya?" I stopped short of adding *for once.*

Miles ignored my question.

"You know, I was here the other night and Katya opened her eyes. She had no idea who I was. It was quite creepy, I can tell you. The woman is a vegetable. We need to remove that feeding tube and let her go."

Lorelei and I looked at one another and then at Miles. We were stunned by what he said. "Are you sure?" I asked.

"Quite sure. But she obviously didn't comprehend a thing I said. I doubt she opened her eyes by choice. I don't think she's able to do anything by choice at this point. Her body is reacting, but her mind is gone."

"That's not true, Miles. Her brain waves have been quite active, more so than expected in a coma state. This is good news, about her eyes opening. It means she is waking up."

Lorelei's breath caught in her throat. "You mean she is finally coming back to us?"

"I think so," I said, more confidently than I felt.

"Why hasn't she opened her eyes for me?" Lorelei sat down beside the bed. She kissed Katya lightly on the cheek, and then gently stroked her hair.

"If I had to guess, I would say Miles's voice was a strong stimulus. Perhaps just his tone, which she hadn't heard in some time." We both looked at him disgustedly. "Or maybe it was what he said that caused her to react." We continued to stare at Miles, as if demanding an explanation for what, exactly, he had said to Katya. In truth we already knew, based on what Lorelei overheard between Meghan and her friend at Angele.

"I don't remember what I said." Miles rolled his eyes.

I couldn't stand there another minute conversing with him. "I need to make my rounds," I announced. Before leaving I examined Katya, looking for any sign whatsoever that she was indeed awakening. Nothing appeared different in her condition. Fortunately, it didn't look like Lorelei was leaving anytime soon, which was a relief, since I didn't trust Miles to be alone with Katya.

After seeing two patients on a different floor, I was paged over the intercom. I recognized the room number immediately. It was Katya's. When I arrived her heart monitor was going off and the Code Blue team was there. Katya had gone into respiratory arrest. Lorelei was leaning against the window, white as a sheet. Miles stood right beside her. I sent Miles and Lorelei to the hallway while the Code Blue team intubated her. We moved Katya to the ICU where we put her on a ventilator. Miles followed us there, verbally protesting the whole way. I paid little attention to him. I was focused on being sure Katya was out of danger.

"Katya has an advance directive not to resuscitate! Why is she intubated and on this ventilator?" Miles shouted. "Katya didn't want to live without quality of life. I'm getting a different doctor and I'm suing you. You'll never practice medicine again!"

Lorelei had wiggled past Miles, who was throwing his arms around and spewing threats at me. She slipped into a chair beside the bed and grabbed Katya's hand, while talking to our sleeping beauty nonstop. "Katy, sweetie, wake up! Come back to us! We are here waiting for you." Then she ran her other hand through Katya's hair, and I wished I could do the same.

If Miles didn't quit his ranting and raving, I was going to punch him in the stomach. To avoid punching him, which would not turn out well for me professionally, I got right up into his face. We were nearly eye to eye, which caused him to finally shut up. "Miles, there is no indication your wife will be a vegetable. She might still wake up and live a long, healthy life."

"I think not," Miles answered, and then he stomped out of the room.

No doubt he was headed to Margo's office. I didn't care. I only hoped she would continue to support me and not assign someone else to Katya. Thank God I didn't blow up as I had wanted to and punched Miles, or even shouted at him. The nurses would be my witnesses, and Lorelei of course. If it appeared at all that

I was emotionally involved or defiant of Katya's advance directive, then I would be removed as her doctor.

The hospital would side with the legal document because we had no proof it was fake. I didn't know if what Lorelei overheard would matter. In my world attorneys were mortal enemies of doctors. They mixed as well as oil and water. Both had a completely different agenda. Doctors only wanted to save lives but occasionally succumbed to human error, at which time attorneys rushed in to extract absorbent amounts of money for the victim, and possibly end the doctor's career.

Whether or not I would be reprimanded for saving Katya's life didn't matter to me in the least. All I presently cared about was her well-being. "Oliver, what's happening? Are we losing her?" Lorelei peered up at me with incredibly sad eyes and I feared I might choke on my answer.

"Not necessarily. Only time will tell. Keep talking to her, patting her hand, stroking her hair," I said, envious that I couldn't do these things. "Maybe play her favorite music," I suggested. "Have you done that yet?"

"No. I've only been singing to her, as you know. She listens to piano music when creating art."

"All right then, play piano music. Doctor's orders." I smiled to reassure her, but it was difficult.

Lorelei didn't smile back. She still looked quite somber. "Miles is going to get a different doctor. Is there any way we can stop him?"

I shrugged. "I don't know what Margo will decide. The most important thing right now is that we focus on trying to awaken Katya."

Lorelei nodded, and shifted her attention to our patient, who appeared whiter and more ghostlike than ever. The color in her lips had drained and I thought we were indeed losing her. I had no time to ponder this, because I was being summoned via intercom to see Ms. Bastille.

Margo was waiting when I arrived. Her secretary ushered me right in.

"Oliver, I just got Mr. Harrington out of here. I thought he'd never leave."

"What did he want?" I asked, knowing full well what he wanted.

"He was quite agitated, actually. He wants you removed from his wife's care."

"What is he basing that on? Saving her life?"

"Basically, yes. You know his wife has an advance directive. I realize you don't think it's legitimate, but we have no proof it isn't. The hospital could pay dearly for this, Oliver. You know that."

"And so . . . are you removing me from her case?"

Margo went silent. She stared at her desk while tapping a pen on it. Finally, she looked up at me and sighed. "No. I told him we have no other attending physician available, and that no one else was as qualified as you to provide her with the most expert care. As for a lawsuit, I think we can justify that Mrs. Harrington still has a shot at quality life. Is that correct?"

"Absolutely." I didn't hesitate to sound firm about it, although I knew this was more of a lie than the truth. "I need to run a few tests and then I can tell you precisely what her odds are for full recovery, given this setback. Let me add that I have read numerous cases where this has happened, and the patient fully recovered."

"I trust you, Oliver. My only hesitation is that you might be too involved in this case, which I have mentioned before."

"Again, I care about all my patients, Margo. You know that. Mrs. Harrington's case is unique. You know that, too. It's important for me to follow it closely and learn from the outcomes, in order to help other coma patients if, God forbid, we should have any."

"I understand. You have my full support." Margo stood up and I did as well., feeling quite relieved.

"Thank you. You won't regret it." With that, I left her office, and prayed that I was right. Prayer had never entered my life until Katya, and if she died, so would my attempt to believe in God.

I didn't hesitate to run a few tests that afternoon and what I discovered was exactly what I suspected might be the outcome of her scan. Her brain waves were weakening. We were losing her. It nearly broke me to admit Miles might have the most merciful solution after all. But how could I ever let her go?

FLICKERING

It felt as if I had fallen into a dark tunnel where voices echoed everywhere, yet there was no one to see. Every person who mattered in my small world, except for Ruby, seemed to be speaking all at once. I heard Miles and Lorelei, and Parker, and a few voices I didn't recognize. Why all these people would be in a space that sounded like an echo chamber I had no idea, but when I opened my eyes, it was Parker that I saw. Or almost saw. He was out of focus.

"Rose. I thought I'd lost you for a moment."

"I'm sorry. Everything just went black and then I was falling. Is Finn okay?"

"Yes, Rosy. The horses are fine. It's you I'm worried about."

I sat up and stared at the sky behind Parker. It appeared to be more vivid than he, as if the sky were real but Parker merely an illusion. It was the first time Parker wasn't sharp and clear during these episodes. "I just got the wind knocked out of me. No big deal," I said, as convincingly as I could.

"Thank God, Rosy. You gave me quite a scare." Parker helped me up and gently pulled me into his arms. "Are you sure you're okay?"

"Yes. I promise. I'm embarrassed, mainly. I've been nothing but a burden for the past month, ever since my bright idea to paint the barn roof."

"It was a great idea. Not such a good idea to have fallen, though."

We both laughed.

The horses were grazing nearby, unconcerned about my tumble from the saddle. "Let's get to camp," I said, emphatically, then I reached up and kissed him on the cheek.

"Are you sure you don't want to head home?"

"No." I shook my head. "I'm looking forward to our evening by the river. I'll try not to slip off Finn again." I smiled, hoping Parker would see how I was truly fine.

Whether thoroughly convinced or not, he agreed to keep going, so we mounted our horses and rode the rest of the way to where we had planned to camp. Everything was still fading in and out, but I was determined to stay on Finn and not slip from the saddle again. Finn followed Parker and Rocco without hesitation, or we never would have made it to the campsite. Between my blurry vision and split-second blackouts, I felt like a flickering lightbulb near the end of its life, until it abruptly goes out.

I tried not to let my worsening condition affect our lovely evening. We set the tent up beside the river and then fished for our dinner. It was nearly dusk, and so the fish were biting. It was fun catching and releasing them, except for the two we kept, to fry in our pan over the open fire. I boiled water to hydrate the potatoes to go with it and we feasted on the meal while watching stars pop out one by one, until whole masses of them hung overhead. The rushing river flowed busily in front of us as we sat on a log facing the Metolius.

Parker and I were mostly quiet, enjoying the nature that surrounded us. We had leaned against each other on the hollow log that was our dinner table. Staring at the half moon above us was like staring at half my life. Napa seemed to have fallen into darkness, much like half the moon. This glowing fairytale side was no doubt temporary. I couldn't seem to keep it firmly in my grip.

We snuggled together in each other's arms all night, in our cozy tent on the riverbank. I had never felt closer to Parker than I did sleeping there beside him, my limbs entangled with his, breathing in unison beside the rushing water and under the millions of stars. In the morning I awoke to the strong smell of coffee and when I exited the tent it was clear Parker had been up long before me. There was not only hot coffee but pancakes rising in a pan over an open fire. Parker handed me a cup of coffee in a lightweight tin mug. "I couldn't sleep," he said cheerfully, but his eyes were far from cheerful. "How do you feel this morning?" he asked.

"I feel good, especially being beside this river I have known my whole life. The Metolius was such a large part of my childhood, and now here I am with you. I couldn't have dreamed a better dream." I didn't mention my fear that this *was* only a dream.

"What about Napa, Rose? Is half of your heart still in wine country?"

I shrugged. "I did love spending time with Grandma Rose as a child and then living in her home after she passed. Napa itself is a very special place to me. The earth begs to be tilled and what grows there is some of God's most luscious bounty. Micro farming was addictive in that magical place."

Parker refilled my cup and our eyes met, although I saw him through blurred vision. Everything was blurry for that matter. "And then of course, there was you," I went on. "Your vineyard. All the sketching I did on the hill beside the sprawling oak. The day we tasted wine. The night we made love under the stars."

Parker smiled and this time his eyes smiled too.

"Otherwise, Napa was a lonely place for me, stuck in a dismal marriage and not able to have children. How foolish of me to think giving birth would improve my relationship with Miles."

"Forget about Miles. We have each other now, Rosy. And we have Ruby. Those years are behind you. It's too bad they aren't the ones you've forgotten." Parker's tone took on a slight annoyance with that last statement. He handed me a plate of pancakes covered in maple syrup. We sat on our log side by side, facing the river to eat our breakfast.

"I wish our years together were the ones I remembered, too, Parker." I looked at him, admiring his profile. "With all my heart," I added. He looked at me then, and I couldn't be sure because my vision was sketchy, but he seemed to be looking for answers neither of us had about my odd memory loss, and what must have been lingering symptoms of my head trauma.

"It's not your fault, Rosy. You just had an unfortunate accident. We need to deal with it the best we can."

I didn't say anything, not wishing to further worry him about exactly how messed up my head really was. I decided right then and there I would see Ellis when we returned and have some tests run. It was obvious I suffered from more than a concussion and it was no longer enough to simply be mesmerized by my amazing life here. I needed answers. I needed a way to try and hang on to this "wonderland," rather than let it slip away from me into nothingness.

Parker and I broke camp after breakfast and headed back to Desert Sky. It was a tedious trip. My blurry world was not unlike riding a horse beneath a river. Finn seemed not to notice that I couldn't see clearly. I gave him rein to maneuver as he saw best and that is exactly what he did. It was exhausting from my perspective, viewing the world as if underwater. Vertigo had set in as well and I could not have been more tense by the time we stopped for lunch halfway home.

It was my personal mission for Parker not to know any of this and so I faked normalcy while pulling lunch items from the saddlebags. Parker built a fire to heat our spicy black beans and tortillas while I watched. It helped me to relax, and I could even smile by the time we sat down on a massive tree stump to eat. It was just chilly enough to appreciate the warmth from the fire before putting it out and finishing our trail ride home.

Once we'd made it back, we took care of the horses and unpacked everything. Both of us were eager to sit on the porch and wait for Ruby. It was late afternoon by then and the mid-November sun was at quite a dramatic angle. I could barely see my best friend's vehicle pulling up the driveway, between the glare and my blurred vision. Goldie exited first and came running, barking a greeting all the way. Ruby wasn't far behind, and I nearly burst into tears seeing her again. At this point I had no idea when this surreal dream world I was dimly hanging on to would be snuffed out for good.

"Mommy, Daddy! We had so much fun!" Ruby had barely gotten the words out and she was in my lap, hugging me. Lorelei brought her suitcase up to the porch and said the twins needed a nap, so she couldn't stay. After assuring her our camping trip was rejuvenating, she left, promising to stop by soon for wine, brie, and details right here on the porch. Once her car had left the long driveway, I ran my fingers through Ruby's red hair and realized her face looking up at me was sharp and clear. I glanced at Parker, who was also in focus. I barely heard what Ruby was saying. All I could think about was my clear vision. Hearing had also improved. Ruby's voice didn't sound like it was echoing in a tunnel.

"Rosy? What do you think? Our daughter is sad she didn't get to go fishing and camping. Any idea what we could do about that?" Parker winked at me as Ruby scrambled off my lap and crawled into his.

"Did you miss us, or did you only wish you could have come?" I asked, laughing, genuinely happy that my senses had returned to normal, at least for now.

"It was fun at Auntie Lori's, but I want to go fishing and sleep in a tent." Ruby stared up at Parker. "Please, Daddy? Can we?"

"I suppose we could camp at Three Creek Lake this weekend, if your mom says okay and this wonderful fall weather holds."

"I guess it's settled then," I said, pleased we were going camping again, only this time we'd take the Land Rover. Three Creek Lake was less than an hour away, and great for fishing. Parker and I had been so in-sync on our Metolius trip, I had a feeling he wanted to repeat that experience as much as I did. Except for my slip from the saddle, and consequent blackout, it had been a wonderful outing. I only hoped my hearing and vision would stay sharp, and there wouldn't be any seconds of nothingness. It wasn't occasionally slipping into nothingness for a few seconds that concerned me the most, it was knowing at some point I might not return at all.

CADENCE

I had decided it might be a good idea for me to visit my personal attorney for some sage advice. Miles was no one to mess around with in the legal arena. My hands were clammy when I arrived at her office and I attributed this to possibly losing Katya, either to death or another doctor. I did not wish to succumb to defeat on either front, but it was getting harder by the day.

Cadence James and I had met at a bar in Napa, and might have dated, except she was in a relationship at the time, and I was avoiding complications in my life. We did however become good friends and occasionally got drinks together. She was the only attorney I had met that didn't rub me the wrong way in every regard. CJ packed a powerful mind in her petite Asian body. She'd won every legal case for me in which somebody wasn't happy with a medical outcome. However, this visit wasn't about anything I had done, it was about what I wouldn't do.

"Oliver, every good attorney needs a worthy challenge occasionally, and you are definitely mine."

I laughed, despite my grim mood. "Well, at least my legal worries are always because I've gone the extra mile and not because I fell short of it."

"That's one way to look at it. I must say, you aren't the type that botches your work. Quite the opposite, you only get in trouble for overachieving."

"Well then, you might call this my classic case," I admitted.

"Why don't you tell me about it?"

We both sat comfortably in her state-of-the-art office chairs, with CJ behind the expensive teakwood desk and me in front of it. "I have a patient who has been in a coma for over a month now." I paused there, not sure what to say next. I could have thrown my heart out on the tasteful Persian rug beneath my chair and confessed an irrational infatuation with my patient, but that didn't seem appropriate.

"Go on, Oliver. What about her? Does she have a name?" CJ's dark eyes twinkled, as if she already knew I'd fallen in love with my patient. She smoothed a jet-black hair off her shoulder and stared at me. I wondered again briefly if I had lost my sanity and needed therapy more than an attorney.

"Her name is Katya Harrington."

"Is she Russian?"

"I believe her maternal grandmother was."

"I see."

"Her husband has forged an advance directive and estate documents, in order to end her coma state and inherit her property in Old Town Napa," I said, realizing all the questions this single sentence would raise. "Katya's best friend overheard his secretary say these things to a friend." I cleared my throat, feeling as if in the middle of a bad *B* movie.

"How does your livelihood factor into this?"

"The fabricated directive states no resuscitation unless quality life would once again be possible."

"And you resuscitated her?"

"Yes."

"Does she have a shot at waking up and having a quality life?"

"It's complicated. I would say yes, except after doing more tests it is clear her odds are deteriorating."

"It sounds like you didn't know that at the time of resuscitation."

"No. I keep expecting her to wake up any minute, and after some therapy, return to a normal life."

CJ stared at me, as if reading my thoughts, or at least trying to. I could almost see her razor-sharp mind determining how to approach this case, should it turn into one, which it would if Miles sued me. But I had a distinct feeling there was more going on in her head than merely the developing case.

"Did you know this Katya before her coma?"

"No."

"Why do I get the impression she is more to you than just a patient?"

Now it was I who stared at CJ, wondering how to respond. Unfortunately, I found myself tongue-tied. I had an overwhelming urge to come clean with her and say everything I would spill to a therapist, if I had one.

"Oliver, I fear you might be in a bigger mess here than you are indicating."

"How so?"

"I don't sense that you can be objective with this patient. You might be too emotionally involved in her case. Have you lost someone close to you from this same condition maybe?" CJ leaned forward and thoughtfully studied me. "Why are the emotional stakes so high for you that they may be impairing your judgment?"

"That's a very good question, Cadence. I don't have a rational answer for you. Katya does look a great deal like a woman I once loved, still love if I'm being truthful, but she got away. It was my own fault." I shrugged and leaned back in my chair. "There's more to it though. Katya has a great deal to live for. She's a gifted artist, for one thing."

I stood up and began pacing back and forth across CJ's plush, neutral-colored carpet. "And then there's her micro farm."

"That's right. You love to garden. I'd almost forgotten."

"Yes, well, Katya's micro farm is behind her Napa property in Old Town and being there at her home, seeing her impeccable gardens, I've gotten a good feel for who she is as a person." I stopped pacing and stared out CJ's window. "There is also her despicable husband, who makes me want to protect Katya all the more."

"Thanks for the clear picture of how you slid down this slippery slope. And it is a slippery slope, Oliver. You could end up losing your medical license if you resuscitate a patient with a signed directive not to."

I glanced at CJ and then focused again on the parking lot outside her window. For someone with such a classy, upscale office, her view was not great. I liked mine better. "Honestly, I feel like I've already fallen off the only slippery slope I presently care about. I can't find a way to unlock Katya's coma, so we may lose her anyway, which is exactly what her greedy husband wants, and furthermore, I'll never get a chance to meet this woman who has touched me to my very core."

"You're basing your emotions on who you perceive her to be, not who she actually is." CJ said this with such a kind voice I had to turn and look at her.

I sighed. "That's true. Exactly why I think I need help. I don't trust my own judgment anymore, and if I don't trust my judgment, how can I perform surgery on people that are literally entrusting their lives to my good judgment?"

"I tend to agree with you. I think you need a therapist more than you need an attorney. But Oliver, you're not crazy. There's nothing wrong with being moved by a particular person, or their situation. Your compassion for people who need healing is why you're so good at your profession."

I sat back down in front of her desk. "Thanks for the pep talk, but I don't believe a word of it. My feelings for this patient are ridiculously inappropriate and outside any *normal* range."

"Couldn't you assign a different physician to her case?"

"I don't want to do that."

We were both silent for a minute, a very long minute. Finally, she spoke. "I have no other advice for you my friend, except to be sure and contact your malpractice insurance agent, just in case. I must say this Katya is a very lucky woman to have you in her corner."

"Is she? Would you want your doctor to be obsessed with you while in a coma?"

CJ laughed, which lightened the heaviness of this visit. "If his obsession kept my creep of a husband from killing me, I would be fine with it."

"And what if my obsession causes me to make wrong decisions because I am desperate for her to live? What if I keep her alive until she wakes up only to find out she is too damaged to appreciate it? Then I would be a monster. How do I live with myself if that happens?"

CJ, of course, had no answer for me, except to say that in her estimation my instincts had always proven to be reliable. She reminded me that my reputation was impeccable. Her flattery was not reassuring. Regardless of my judgment being on point in the past, my present judgment did not feel the least bit reliable. All of this weighed heavily on me as I returned to the hospital and completed my rounds. When finished I entered Katya's room for the third time that day, obsessively checking on her. Not surprisingly, Lorelei was there on my last visit. It would be after work hours for her by now. I scratched my head while glancing about the room.

"Where did all these flowers come from?"

Before moving to ICU, Katya had only one vase of fresh flowers, which Lorelei changed weekly. The flowers always caught my attention because they were stunning. I was usually too wrapped up in my workload to notice flowers in patient rooms, but the arrangements Lorelei provided were exceptional. She had also brought some of Katya's favorite comfort things—a hand-made quilt, a few hard-back books which had obviously been read more than once, judging by the way their bindings were broken in. There was a silver-framed photo of her Grandma Rose and another one of her father. They were the only non-hospital amenities in the otherwise drab room. It gave the space a homey feel, which might be one reason I frequented it so often. Lorelei had already brought everything to ICU. I wondered how she got away with that, and why all these flowers were here considering it was against ICU policy. There was even a small basket overflowing with cards.

"I took the liberty of letting her clients and neighbors know about her condition," Lorelei shared, "and why Katya won't be taking or delivering produce orders until further notice." She looked up at me from the chair beside the bed. I couldn't begin to count the number of hours Lorelei had sat beside Katya, hoping for her to wake up. "I finally realized you and I can't run her business forever." Tears formed in Lorelei's brilliant blue eyes.

I had to look away.

"Have you chosen another book to read?" I asked, thinking a subject change might help us both hold it together.

"I've been reading the cards as they come in, and talking to her about who sent the flowers, and how that person is doing."

"How did you get around ICU policy with all of this?" I asked, feeling amused.

Lorelei shrugged. "Everyone here is rooting for her. They've decided all of this might help her wake up. Coma patients are rare in this little hospital. Katya is somewhat famous."

"I am glad you aren't giving up on her," I said. "She still might pull through this." I was hoping to convince myself as much as Lorelei.

"I could never give up on my sweet Katy, not until she takes her last breath, which might be a blessing. Wherever she is and whatever she's doing, I can only believe she doesn't wish to come back to us.

"So, you think mind over matter is keeping our sleeping beauty in a dreamworld?"

"It's as good a theory as any, since you have no medical explanation."

Whether to a dreamworld or death, it did feel as if we were losing her. "I guess time will tell," I said, and then I left the room. I couldn't stand there another minute facing a truth I didn't want to accept.

HAUNTED

In anticipation of our weekend at Three Creek Lake I planned to bake cookies with Ruby and have her help me in general with food preparation. Nothing was a chore when Ruby helped. Everything became a fun adventure. Instead, I spent a good deal of the next day in bed. My body was weak and lethargic, and my head hurt. I did manage to make an appearance at mealtime. After dinner, which Parker had prepared, he and I lingered at the table.

"Rosy, do you think you might have another concussion from falling off Finn?"

"No. I've had hearing and vision problems ever since my fall a month ago. This lethargy is new, but in general my health seems to be deteriorating." I didn't mention the horrific headache that ibuprofen didn't seem to touch.

"I'm going to try and move up your appointment with Ellis. Maybe we should postpone our weekend."

I glanced at Ruby out the window, playing with Goldie. "No. I'm well enough to go. Our sweet girl would be so disappointed if we canceled."

"Okay then, we'll keep your appointment for next week."

Parker and I had agreed with Ellis that running a few tests might be prudent, but in my heart, I didn't believe anything would help. I didn't fully believe I was here to begin with. In a way, I still felt married to Miles. Being with Parker felt more like cheating than having been married to him for the past seven years. Life couldn't have gotten more confusing, or at least I didn't think so, until Parker and I went to bed. Sleep would not come, and no matter how hard I tried, I could not get Lorelei's voice out of my head. She was chatting away about my Napa clients and neighbors, but I couldn't *see* her.

It wasn't a dream. It was only her voice, clear as a bell, and because my clients and neighbors were scattered throughout Old Town Napa, all those places came rushing back to me. It was very odd. It was also odd that I'd barely given Miles a second thought until now. Certainly, guilt had not been there before. Now the life I left behind in Napa was literally haunting me. I almost wished I'd asked Lorelei to fill in the blanks regarding my divorce, the why and how of it, but I'd had no desire to hear the details. Now it felt as if everything was catching up with me. Reality was shattering my dream world.

I woke up restless and agitated, but at least I wasn't lethargic. I had a strong desire to sketch, so I threw on my sweats and went straight to my studio. I left a note by Parker's phone so he would know where I was. By noon I still hadn't eaten anything or changed out of my sweats. There was a coffee pot in the studio and the only break I took was to make a full pot, which I finished while reviewing my work.

There were sketches everywhere. I had drawn vivid memories of Napa. Most of them were spread across the art table in the middle of the room. It was where I'd eventually transform them into etchings or silk screens, God willing. Once that area was filled, however, I placed the drawings on the counter, and then began to lay them on the floor. The sketches were 24 inches by 36 inches, and I had been using a variety of soft, hard, light, and dark pencils.

One drawing was of Genevieve's front porch with the flowerpots that held colorful blooms. I'd carefully added the rattan furniture and orange pillows scattered about. Next, I'd sketched Oxbow Public Market across the street from Genevieve, replicating every detail of the brick building, including its outdoor seating where umbrellas gave customers welcomed shade. Standing there looking at the drawing brought all the sights and scents of the vendors rushing back to me. My mouth watered for fresh oysters at the oyster bar and a frothy latte from the coffee corner. Although rustic and without frills, the indoor market was made warm and inviting by the friendly businesses and their happy customers, which included tourists from all over the world. I missed it and decided in a perfect world I could have both my Genevieve in Napa and Desert Sky in Central Oregon.

Where had the time gone? By one o'clock I'd collapsed into a chair at the table by the window. My back hurt from standing at the easel for hours. It was a very satisfying feeling, the ache of achievement. I often believed that pouring myself into my art was the only reason I had never gone mad. Whether sitting on the fence sketching horses as a child or sketching a vineyard from under an oak tree, it was a necessary stress reliever. Sometimes my need to sketch felt like a dark secret, like a ploy to hide my madness. It had occurred to me more than once since my fall that all of this was just my madness run amuck. But as I sat beneath the window and stared at my work scattered everywhere, I realized I never felt more alive. Napa seemed far away, as if living there had been the dream and this was my reality all along.

Just when I thought I might head back to the main house Ruby came bouncing in the door. She stopped dead in her tracks and quietly studied my sketches everywhere. "Oh Mommy, these are so pretty!" Ruby stared the longest at my sketching of the boardwalk by the river, with its old-fashioned streetlights and clustered kayaks beside the dock. She also enjoyed the sketch of Angele, having seen photos of it at Lorelei's Studio Café. We returned to the house hand and hand, where I made us both a bowl of ramen. It sufficed as both my breakfast and lunch, and a mid-afternoon snack for Ruby.

After slurping down her last spicy noodle, Rubes helped me pack the cooler and food box. It was going to be a hotdogs and hamburgers kind of weekend, with pancakes and bacon for breakfast. Peanut butter and honey, of course, would be packed for sandwiches at lunch, which Ruby loved to help make. Licking honey off the knife was her favorite part of helping, but who could object to such an adorable helper? We planned to leave in the morning. I fervently hoped our weekend by the lake would create new memories to cherish, ones I could recall as an old woman in a rocking chair, right here on our Desert Sky porch.

HIATUS

When I entered Katya's room after my rounds, the first thing I observed was a smile on Lorelei's face. That was something I rarely saw in this hospital where her best friend lay still as a corpse. My first thought was that Katya must be sporadically opening her eyes, just as Miles had said. It goes without saying I wanted Katya to wake up and be everything she ever had been. On the other hand, in the past four weeks (and a few days) these two women had become fixtures in my life. They were, in a way, my new normal and I wasn't looking forward to that changing. It was a crazy, unpredictable response that helped further my self-evaluation as being hopelessly disturbed.

"Oliver, Katy has been opening her eyes! She isn't really responding to me at all, but she is definitely waking up!" Lorelei looked jubilant. Silently, I observed Katya and then checked all her vital signs, pupils, reflexes, etc. Lorelei watched me, without comment, as if our quiet reverence would make a difference. Perhaps she was only respecting my somber diligence regarding this evolving situation of our patient finally coming around. I had no sooner finished examining the not-quite sleeping beauty when she did indeed open her eyes and stare up at me. I couldn't help but stare back, while a chill raced through my body. Of all the medical scenarios that could have been occupying my mind, none were. My only thought was about the unusual gray color of Katya Harrington's eyes. I also had not anticipated them being so stunning, with a hint of lavender in the iris.

"Oliver? What's happening? Is she waking up?"

I looked at Lorelei but said nothing. I had no medical words of wisdom or even a prediction of what might happen next. I wasn't worried or anxious about how events would now unfold. In fact, I couldn't remember when my mind had ever been this blank, or at peace with the world. Seeing Katya Harrington open her eyes was a miracle I needed a minute to appreciate. Eventually I came to my senses, asking Lorelei to stand over her best friend and speak to her as if she'd never been in a coma. Lorelei dutifully took Katya's hand and chattered away about nothing in particular. She stroked her face and kissed her cheek. She asked her questions and stayed upbeat, jovial even, but nothing brought a reaction from Katya. Finally, her eyes closed again, and Lorelei gently laid her head on our sleeping beauty's chest.

Tears ran silently down Lorelei's face and onto the hospital blanket while I took Katya's vitals again, which indicated our patient had not been at all stimulated by the opening of her eyes. This of course meant it was probably not a voluntary decision but merely a physical reaction. Nonetheless, it did tell me her brain was ready to wake up, and her subconscious mind was somehow trying to communicate that to the rest of her body. It would only be a matter of time until every part of her brain remembered how to work together as one unit.

The only question now was, how much function of her mind and body would she regain? That was the unknown for any doctor. You can predict, research, jostle odds, and even tear your hair out wondering if your efforts have been appropriate, and enough, but in the end, it is anyone's guess. It is a game of wait and see. In the past I had never tortured myself over the odds. I always confidently knew I had done everything in my power to heal a patient and the rest was up to fate, or God, or whatever chance element we mortals have no control over. That was not true this time.

I wanted to sit by Katya's bed and pray to a God I wasn't sure existed, and somehow convince said God that I never doubted Him for a minute if he would only heal Katya. Instead, I left the room with instructions for Lorelei to have me paged should there be any change in our patient. It took all my will power to play the role of a cool, calm, in-charge physician. Fortunately, a stack of paperwork on my desk helped take my mind off Katya, at least intermittently. Nothing, however, could void my head of the numerous what-ifs that kept circling there.

What if Katya Harrington never fully recovered and instead suffered severe physical and mental limitations, much like Miles had been predicting for weeks now? What if, in my irrational quest to meet this woman, I had used poor judgment in reviving her? What if an angry God punished me by causing Katya to be incapacitated, because I took matters into my own hands instead of letting her transition into whatever happens next? Heaven was a place I could not visualize or understand, yet something compelled me to beg God's forgiveness for interfering, for preventing Katya's perfectly timed entrance, if that is what I'd done.

I was aware I had worked up a sweat over my tortured thoughts, which no matter how hard I tried, I could not push to the back of my mind. I barely read any of the papers I'd been signing and would need to revisit every one of them in a more rational moment. Setting the pen down I realized what a futile effort it was to try and accomplish anything right now. I contemplated heading to the cafeteria for a cup of coffee when Miles burst into my office. He had barely shown his face at the door before engaging me in a confrontational conversation.

"I went to visit my wife just now and Lorelei tells me she is waking up. Is that true?"

"Yes, she does appear to be coming out of her coma."

"I am telling you there will no longer be a practicing Dr. Oliver Easton if she has no quality of life to wake up to, which I absolutely believe she will not."

"There is every chance for her to completely recover, Miles. I have told you this, many times." I couldn't bring myself to look at him, at this man who had no business being married to Katya. Nor did I gesture for him to leave the doorway and come sit down.

"If she is waking up then she no longer needs a ventilator or to be intubated."

Miles, although uninvited, helped himself to the chair in front of my desk. He left the door open, and I wondered why my secretary hadn't interceded and asked what he was doing here without an appointment.

"When she is fully awake, we will remove everything."

"Maybe you should be doing that now, so she doesn't wake up. Do you want to see her as a vegetable? Are you looking forward to that, to spite me?"

"Don't be ridiculous, Miles. You're talking nonsense." I stood up. My hands were shaking with anger. "Get out of my office," I shouted, in a growly voice I barely recognized.

Miles stood and stared at me while I considered jumping over the desk and wrestling him to the ground. His expression was quite emotionless. "I think you're scared, Dr. Easton. Why else would you be so angry? You're mortified at the thought of me being right, and that Katya will never be the person she once was."

I didn't say anything for fear I might say things I would regret, like suggesting his concerns had nothing at all to do with anyone's quality of life except his own. We continued to stare at one another until Miles turned to leave. He looked at me one more time from the doorway before exiting. "You will regret this decision to keep my wife alive, consequently subjecting her to a lifetime of mental and physical impairment. I will see to it that you never practice medicine again." With that said, he left.

I remained standing for a long time, staring at the doorway, worrying whether he was indeed correct. I didn't care a fig about his lawsuit threats, but I shared his concerns for Katya, and they were decimating my ability to think clearly. When Margo appeared at my office door, I thought surely this was all a nightmare and I would soon wake up. As she entered, I sat down in what felt like submissive defeat.

"Oliver, several people, including myself, heard a lot of shouting going on in here a few minutes ago. Are you okay?"

Margo was looking at me inquisitively. "Yes," I said without conviction. I suddenly regretted renting space in the old wing of the hospital, not far from where Margo's office was.

She slid into the chair across from me. "Was that Miles Harrington I saw storming out of here?"

"Yes," I repeated.

"I have also heard about your coma patient waking up. Is that true?"

"It is true."

"What on earth were the two of you shouting about?"

I stared at the papers on my desk, all too aware that I lacked the courage to look at Margo. "He is concerned that his wife will be a vegetable and he is angry that we are doing everything possible to keep her alive."

"That's not a typical request from a husband, is it?" Margo looked confused.

"Of course not. Most husbands love their wives and want them to recover." I tried not to sound as hateful toward Miles as I felt.

"I think we need to take you off this case, Oliver. Your entire medical practice could be at stake. I think a different physician could be more objective at this point."

"No." I said this so vehemently it was clear to both of us that Margo was right.

"No?" Margo looked surprised by my emotional response.

"I mean, we can't give in to him. I agree it would be prudent to get a second opinion. I'm okay with that. However, it's not in the best interest of the patient to have an entirely new doctor take over her care this late in the game."

"I don't know, Oliver. It's my job to keep these situations from escalating, and in your case it already has. I feel remiss in not having already removed you from this case."

"I am humbly requesting you not do so, Margo, especially now that our coma patient is waking up."

Margo stared at me while contemplating what to do. I forced myself to smile slightly, just enough to indicate I was not demon possessed or poised to sprint out the door and murder Miles with my bare hands.

"Okay." Margo stood up. "Just promise me you will avoid any further altercations with Mr. Harrington."

"Of course." I also stood, and this time I genuinely smiled. "Thank you, Margo."

After she left, I shut the door, wishing it had a lock on it. I couldn't put two thoughts together to save my life, and I regretted not having a bottle of Jack Daniels at my disposal. When I finally emerged from my office it was to find more suitable sustenance. Thankfully, I didn't see anyone who would feel the need to speak to me on the way to the cafeteria, where I ate a club sandwich on rye and drank several cups of coffee.

When finished eating I was tempted to check on Katya and Lorelei, but a bigger part of me wasn't ready to face the music yet. With no other patients for the day, I decided to go home, take a hot shower, and catch up on some much-needed sleep. There hadn't been any substantial changes in Katya's condition, because if there had been, the hospital would have alerted me. This was why I found it permissible to let everything go for a while, to clear my head, to make room for the optimism and confidence I hoped would soon resurface.

THREE CREEK LAKE

The drive to Three Creek Lake was quite memorable. Aside from the breathtaking scenery, it felt as if we were a real family. Not a mirage, or a dream, or a figment of my imagination. As I watched tall, endless stands of Douglas Fir roll past my window, tears pooled in my eyes. One blink would spill them over, so I didn't blink. My tears would only worry Parker, who glanced at me frequently, as if I might suddenly vanish when he wasn't looking. Although tears were pooling in my eyes, a smile never left my face. If Ruby said something especially comical or Goldie barked at something out the window, my smile would instantly turn into a grin. I felt dizzily happy staring at the creek gushing busily by on one side of the road. I was mesmerized by the sparks of sunlight reflecting off the water.

"When will we be there Daddy?"

I glanced at Ruby fidgeting in the back seat. "Soon. You'll be putting wiggly worms on a hook before you know it, so you can catch our dinner."

Parker laughed.

"Yuck!" Ruby kicked her feet and made a face.

I winked at her. "I thought playing with worms was the best part of fishing at your age."

"Apparently you never caught any fish," Parker chimed in. He glanced at Ruby in the rearview mirror. "We won't have that problem, munchkin."

As if by magic the lake appeared directly in front of us, and everyone forgot about worms. Parker stopped along the road for a better look. It was breathtakingly blue and surrounded by tall fir trees. Mountains jutted up from the far sides of the lake, jagged and snow covered.

"It's spectacular, Parker." The tears I'd been holding at bay spilled over.

"Didn't you tell me once your dad used to bring you fishing here?"

"Yes, but I forgot how special the lake is."

"Did you catch big fish when you were my age, Mommy?" Ruby spread her hands out as wide as they would go.

"Maybe not that big, sweetie."

We couldn't resist climbing out of the car for a closer look. Goldie ran along the shore of the lake and Ruby picked a few late blooming wildflowers. Parker and I sat on a log near the water's edge and quietly admired the view. I had not been affected by any recurring symptoms on this glorious fall day. My vision was good, and my head didn't hurt. I wasn't lethargic. There were no split-second flashes of nothingness. I had no idea why I felt so completely *present*. Maybe I was suddenly healed, or maybe I had willed this weekend camping trip with Ruby to be perfect.

"We had better find a place to set up camp." Parker stood and extended his hand to me. We returned to the Land Rover while coaxing Ruby and Goldie to join us. It took a lot of shouting to get their full attention, but eventually we had Rubes secured in her car seat with Goldie sprawled out beside her.

Not a lot of people were hardy enough to brave camping in November, but it was only the first week and we'd had unseasonably warm weather. The site where we chose to set up camp had a perfect view of the lake. Parker and Ruby wasted no time setting up folding chairs at the water's edge, where they sat and held fishing poles baited with fat worms. Parker had attached the wiggly critters to the hooks while Ruby cringed. I watched them amusedly while making sandwiches with the egg salad I had prepared at home and put in the cooler. Nothing had nibbled on their lines yet when I joined them for lunch. After we'd finished eating Parker did some fly fishing while Ruby impatiently bobbed her pole up and down in the water, hoping to attract a fish. Luckily Parker's expert casting and handmade flies lured in several big rainbow trout for dinner.

Ruby was disappointed she didn't catch anything. "Why didn't they want my worms, Mommy?" She sat at the picnic table and stared at the wiggly creatures while holding the bait container in her lap.

"I don't know, sweetie. Maybe tomorrow the fish will be in the mood for worms."

"Put the lid back on, Ruby, or you won't have any worms whether the fish want them or not," Parker scolded.

Ruby begrudgingly did as her father asked and then helped me prepare dinner while he put up the tent. Rubes stuffed hotdogs onto sticks for us to cook over the fire while I made mac & cheese from a box mix. After dinner we roasted marshmallows and stuck them between graham crackers with a piece of chocolate. The sun had set by now and a full moon appeared above us. It glowed so brightly in the clear night sky we didn't need our lanterns.

"Look, Mommy! I see the moon and the moon sees me, God bless the moon and God bless me." Ruby grinned ear to ear, delighted by the big yellow ball looming over us protectively.

"You remembered that verse from our bedtime stories! That's wonderful, Rubes." Parker reached over and mussed her hair in a loving gesture. As if on cue Ruby ran to get the bedtime book from her backpack in the tent. Parker read to her while I tidied up our makeshift camp kitchen. After brushing her teeth with a glass of water to swoosh the brush in, Ruby nestled into her sleeping bag covered in Disney princesses. I personally cherished her princess phase. I could only hope I'd be around long enough to help her learn that princesses make their own way in the world. They don't actively seek a prince to rely on, although true love is a very special thing if you can find it and hold on to it.

Parker and I sat by the fire for a bit and silently enjoyed the endless stars shining brightly above us, along with that glorious moon. The perfect day ended abruptly once we doused the fire out with a bucket of water. After brushing our teeth, we huddled together in the double sleeping bag, both of us weary from the long day. Oddly, the minute I closed my eyes I saw dozens of flowers, not wildflowers growing in a meadow, but clusters of flowers in vases.

They were everywhere.

One vase was an arrangement of sunflowers that reminded me of the full moon Parker and I had admired all evening. I could clearly see red alstroemeria and blue iris sprinkled in the arrangement. There were vases of roses and daisies, lilies and mums. The sweet scents mingling together were nearly suffocating, but then I forgot all about the flowers when I saw Lorelei, staring down at me. *Was I in a casket? Was this my funeral and these flower arrangements had been sent out of sympathy?*

Next, I saw the face of Miles, who didn't look a bit sorry I had died. His icy blue eyes appeared colder than usual and there was no sorrow in them. The face of a strange man I had never met appeared. It was quite a handsome face, full of warmth and compassion. It was not a face I would have forgotten, so I was sure we hadn't met. This made it hard for me to understand the sadness in his eyes.

I woke up from the nightmare sweating and could barely catch my breath. As quietly as possible I snuck out of the tent and walked down to the water's edge. I had grabbed my coat and a lantern as I exited the tent, but I didn't need the lantern. The moon was still shining brightly, although it had lowered quite a bit in the sky. I sat on a log and stared at the ripples in the water, which glistened in the moon glow. I couldn't get that nightmare out of my head. Why were Lorelei and Miles peering down at me? Why were flower arrangements scattered everywhere? *Why would I dream about my death?*

What was most ponderous was the face of the handsome stranger. I fully believed we would meet. Whether I was living or dead, or somewhere in-between, I had absolutely no doubt there was a strong connection between us.

EYES WIDE OPEN

The next morning when entering Katya's room, I became instantly overwhelmed by the scent of flowers. It was not the subtle fragrance one anticipates when seeing a bouquet, no, this was too many arrangements in too small a space. I nearly choked on the heavy scents all mingling together. Lorelei entered the ICU room right after me and her eyes widened. We looked at one another and didn't need to say a word about the obvious.

"Let's distribute these among other patients on the floor," I said, and then left to retrieve a cart from the nurse's station. Together we loaded the flower arrangements. Placing them on the cart caused me to realize how lovely they each were individually. "Lorelei, I was under the impression Katya barely spoke to a living soul. Who are these people that send such gorgeous arrangements?"

"Everybody in Napa loves Katy. She is always so kind and generous to everyone, giving neighbors free produce from her micro farm and delivering overflowing boxes of whatever her clients order." Lorelei was silent for a few seconds and then she added, "Katya is such a good listener, too. People are drawn to her quiet, non-judgmental spirit. They pour their hearts out to her, saying things they'd never share with anyone else. I've watched all of this happen many times from afar."

"From afar?" I asked.

Lorelei tiptoed into a room and left an especially cheerful vase of yellow and white daisies. She answered me as we pushed the cart down the hall again. "Katy and I used to walk along the river during my lunch break. We could never get through our whole walk without running into one of Katy's clients, who would thank her for the extra radishes or kale, or whatever they had ordered. Then they'd share the outcome of some situation I was not privy to. The same thing would happen with neighbors whenever we walked down to the section of river by Genevieve."

"And all this time I thought she was mainly a recluse," I commented, while handing Lorelei another floral arrangement to deliver. "Why has no one sent flowers or come to visit until this past week?" I asked, puzzled. Lorelei gave me a guilty glance before ducking into a patient's room with blue chrysanthemums. When she returned, the look in her eyes could only be described as vulnerable.

"It's my fault no one knew she was here." She paused there to swipe at a tear which seemed to have sprung from nowhere. "I couldn't find the words to tell anyone about her condition. Besides, I thought it might hurt her produce business. Who would blame her clients if they looked elsewhere for their specialty vegetables, not knowing how reliable her deliveries would be under the circumstances?"

We rolled the cart in silence down to the next room. Lorelei grabbed an especially large arrangement of white lilies and looked me right in the eye. "If you must know, I was also having a hard time accepting her diagnosis. I felt confident Katy would wake up any minute and return to her normal life. Telling others that she was in a coma would have made it more real than I could handle at the time."

"I understand, Lorelei. Really. No judgment here." I hoped that might ease her guilt. We finished distributing flowers in silence and I returned the cart to the nurse's station. Lorelei left for Angele, and I impulsively drove to Katya's house. My afternoon surgery had been canceled, and Lorelei had shared that Miles was in the Bay Area for a few days. She had said it to ease my mind about any potential visits from him over the next forty-eight hours. Just having her mention his absence somehow made me long to see the house again, and Katya's art. I could inspect the now dormant gardens and make sure they were ready for winter. Maybe if I was lucky Crow would be around. I was all too aware of how insane it was needing to visit her place of residence, as if it were some sort of shrine. Somehow it seemed the perfect place to reflect and pray for her.

I opened the gate with the key Lorelei had made for me and parked in the back of the house. It was necessary for me to have a gate key if I was going to harvest, load, and deliver produce for Katya, not to mention caring for the crops. Much to my amusement Crow was seated in his usual place on the fence between the gardens and the alleyway. He greeted me boisterously and I felt honored, since according to Lorelei he only spoke to Katya. Slowly I approached him, speaking softly. I shared how much everyone else missed Katya, too. Oddly, he let me approach him until we were literally face to face. I looked into his eyes and somehow I knew he'd let me touch him. Crow purred loudly while I gently petted his sleek black fur. He rubbed his face against my jacket and when he'd had enough, he jumped down and sprinted across the alley. I watched him until he'd run out of sight and then I trotted up the back steps to the house, using the door key under the matt to enter.

Once inside I felt strangely at home, not a bit guilty for breaking and entering. The home was too cozy and charming to feel anything other than welcome. While standing in the kitchen I couldn't help but look up at the insanely high cabinets and think about Katya falling off the ladder. How different would her life be right now if that hadn't happened? Maybe she and Parker would be together, anticipating the birth of their child. Maybe Miles would be gone forever, having moved on with Meghan or some other secretary who was a sucker for Gucci suits.

I quit pondering what might have been and slipped into Katya's studio to admire her art. I had thought about her work often, and longed to see it again, which is partly why I'd taken this opportunity to stop by. It was just as vivid as I had remembered. The silk screens bled purple and green grapes in lush sun-filled vineyards. The etchings were delicate and detailed in a mesmerizing way. I could have stared at her work for hours, but I didn't want to overstay my welcome, although Genevieve hadn't dropped anything on me and there were no spiders lurking about. The spirit of Katya's Grandma Rose seemed to be smiling upon me, more so than she had Miles and Meghan, at least.

I paused to admire Katya's book collection again on my way to the front porch. A cinnamon-scented candle on the bookshelf explained why the whole house smelled like hot cinnamon candies, which I used to eat as a child. I pulled a book from the shelf with an especially worn binding and decided it must be one of Katya's favorites. It was a book of poems by Emily Dickinson. I brought it with me to the front porch. Maybe reading poetry would give me a momentary reprieve from the harsh realities looming over me. I settled into a rattan chair, with book in hand, and stared at Oxbow Public Market across the street. I recalled having oysters there with Lorelei, which reminded me of the first time we'd shared wine and cheese on this porch. I didn't know if I would ever get to meet Katya, especially now that we seemed to be losing her, and yet I had memories accumulating on her front porch.

Once I'd nourished my soul with some of Emily's poems, I set the book down, closed my eyes, and silently pleaded with God to awaken Katya. The noonday sun on my face was glorious. I must have dozed off while praying, which was not surprising, since I hadn't been sleeping well. When I awoke the sun had nearly set. I locked everything up and headed back to the hospital. Margo called while on my way and wanted me to stop by her office. As I suspected, her summons had to do with the malicious Miles Harrington and his demand for us to remove everything stabilizing Katya's condition. The rest of the drive to the hospital was a blur. I had expected this, and I didn't honestly disapprove, but it was blindingly difficult nonetheless to face Katya's deteriorating condition.

I soon found myself in Margo's office doorway, not sure how I got there. My feet refused to cross the threshold, and so I simply stared at her from the open door. She told me I must remove Katya from everything, except her IV, since not providing necessary liquids to the body would be considered inhumane. "Mr. Harrington has all but a restraining order against you at this point, Oliver. After today visit Ms. Harrington at your own risk. You will no longer be in charge of her care. I have assigned Dr. Martinez to her case."

I continued to stare at Margo. I knew I should respond, but nothing came out of my mouth, which suddenly felt dry and incapable of speech. I liked Anthony Martinez. He was a good doctor. It was a relief to know Katya would be in good hands.

"I'm sorry, Oliver. I truly am. But my superiors have cautioned me at this point. Harrington is a very good attorney, and they are worried about an expensive lawsuit. The last thing we want is to go to court on this one. It could be disastrous for you, I'm afraid."

"Do you think I give a damn about the lawsuit?" I said, angrily.

"Well, I guess you have found your voice."

I didn't apologize for my anger. At this point nothing mattered to me except Katya's well-being. "I will do as you say, Margo, and if my patient does not survive the night, then God help us all. We will have murdered Ms. Harrington because of a forged document."

If Margo had a response for that, I didn't wait to hear it. Letting Katya go once every shred of hope had been exhausted was one thing, having the process sped up to accommodate her self-serving husband was another. I knew if I refused to accommodate his request, Anthony Martinez would do it. I immediately arranged for everything except an IV to be removed from Katya and had her moved to a private room down the hall. Then I stood at the foot of her bed for at least an hour. That time seemed to have passed in a single heartbeat. During my inevitable self-reflection, I realized no longer being Katya's doctor might be a blessing. If by some miracle she did wake up, I was free to be her friend and help her maneuver the arduous road to full recovery.

"Oliver, what happened? Why have you removed everything? I had to ask the nurses where they'd taken Katya. It gave me quite a scare." I turned to look at Lorelei standing in the doorway. Her expression was somewhere between fear and relief.

"Miles finally got his way, but she is doing just fine on her own, for now at least."

"What is it?" I shouted.

"It's the biggest pinecone I ever saw." Ruby picked it up just as we approached her.

"It's from a sugar pine," Parker told her. We all looked above us, and sure enough, we were standing right below a sugar pine tree.

"Can I keep it?" Ruby asked, making it hard to ignore the hope in her eyes.

"Will it fit in your backpack?" Parker chided. We all stared at the huge pinecone. It was at least eight inches long and nearly as big around as a pineapple.

"No." Ruby sounded quite dismayed.

"Well, sweetie, what are the rules of the trail again?" Parker asked.

"Okay, Daddy." Ruby carefully set the pinecone down and skipped along the trail again. Goldie doubled back and barked at her to stop dawdling.

By lunchtime my joy began to wane. The on again, off again headache I'd experienced since my fall had come back with a vengeance. I smiled through the pain and pretended nothing was wrong. We ate our sandwiches while skipping stones across the lake. Parker, of course, was much more adept at it than me and Ruby. We did improve a little from his expert instruction.

On the hike back after lunch we saw an eagle overhead and stopped to stare in awe. He swooped into a tree far up the trail and we soon realized he was guarding a nest.

"Is it way up high to keep the babies safe?" Ruby asked.

Parker told her that having the nest high up in the tree couldn't guarantee those baby eagles would be safe. He explained to her how foraging animals climb trees, and there are predatory birds that might swoop in unannounced. It reminded me that none of us are safe from life unfolding in a way we can't predict. All we can do is live each day to the fullest and prepare for tomorrow as best we can. I suspected my tomorrows here were ending. My father always said if something seems too good to be true, it probably is.

When we finally returned to camp, Ruby collapsed onto a blanket I had spread beneath the trees and fell asleep while paging through her books. Goldie was soon napping at her feet. Parker and I stood at the water's edge and admired how blue the lake was. It could have been a postcard with the snow-covered mountains surrounding it. My life felt like a postcard at the moment, a perfect vacation. But vacations always end and then you have your memories. I wondered if I would have mine.

"Parker, if anything ever happens to me, you must fall in love again and remarry. Ruby will need a mother."

"What about me? Won't I need this woman as well, to keep me warm at night?" Parker grinned ear to ear, not taking me seriously at all.

"No, I mean it, Parker," I said, and then I gently kissed him on the lips.

His response was to kiss me back and I reveled in the scent of him, hinting of pine needles and trail dust. I slowly ran my hands up his strong arms and thought about how much I would miss the feel of him, the sound of his deep, raspy voice which could arouse me with one breathy word. I pulled away from our embrace and ran my fingertips along the curve of his cheek, and then up into his raven hair. I thought about how much I adored the dark and brooding look of his deep-set eyes.

"Rosy, what's wrong? You're crying." Parker gently wiped away my tears.

"Nothing, and everything."

"I'm not following you, sweetie."

"This day is perfect. This life. You and Ruby. But it's only on loan. My gut is screaming that it's almost over, wherever, whatever this is. I can't stay and time is running out."

"You're not making sense, Rose. What's going on in that brain of yours?" Parker looked suddenly frightened, as if a bear had ambled near and was eyeing us up for dinner.

"The truth I think, finally. The reason why my head throbs from time to time and my vision fades, why my reality is occasionally like a blinking light that comes and goes. And then there are the echoing voices, the nightmares that seem so real."

Parker put his arms around me. "Maybe you need to see a psychologist to really heal from that barn roof fall."

"If only that would change what I know, in my heart," I answered, in a muffled whisper, just as Ruby awoke from her nap.

"Daddy, can we fish now?" She rubbed her eyes and stared in our direction.

"Yes, Rubes. Go get your worms." Parker kissed the top of my head. "You're going to be fine, Rosy. I'll ask Ellis for the name of a good psychologist when we see him next week. I promise we'll get to the bottom of this."

"I love you," was all I could manage to say. Then I kissed my one true love on the cheek and went to help Ruby find her carton of worms.

Parker gathered up the fishing poles and tackle box. We set our camp chairs by the water's edge, which lapped at our feet while Ruby attempted to bait her own hook. After a lot of squeals, she managed to get the job done with Parker's guidance.

Lorelei and Dr. Easton glanced at one another. "I'll have someone at the nurses station call him." Dr. Easton had barely said this when Miles walked into the room. He stared at me as if a ghost and did not look pleased.

"I see that our patient is awake, finally."

It was odd to have Miles stare at me and say this to no one in particular. He truly appeared to be more annoyed about my recovery than relieved.

"I would like some alone time with my wife." He looked directly at Dr. Easton, who glanced at Lorelei. The doctor and my best friend stared wordlessly at one another for several seconds.

"I can give you a few minutes, Miles, but then Katya will need a full evaluation." Dr. Easton said this with disdain, and it was clear Miles had not endeared himself to the good doctor. He and Lorelei slowly made their way to the door where Lorelei glanced back at me and blew a kiss my way. Her eyes were misty and soft again.

Once they'd exited the room Miles stepped closer and stared at me from the foot of the bed. "Katya, can you speak?" he asked, looking dismayed. I couldn't tell if he was upset that I might speak, or that I might not. Although I knew I *could* speak, I had no desire to. Certainly, anything I had to say I did not wish to say to Miles.

"Do you remember what happened, Katya?" Miles asked, assuming I could indeed speak. After a slight pause I responded.

"I . . . fell."

"What about before you fell? Do you remember cheating on me and getting pregnant?" Miles said this somewhat angrily. His icy blue eyes had a fire in them I'd never seen before.

"Answer me, Katya. You've conveniently slept away the entire month and left me wondering who fathered the child you lost!"

"Lost?" It was coming back to me . . . the vineyard . . . Parker . . . making love under the stars. Miles and Meghan.

"Yes, you lost the baby in the fall from the ladder. Imagine my shock when I was told my wife lost *our baby*. A baby I can't have, Katya, because I am sterile and have been ever since coming down with the mumps as a teenager."

Hot tears flooded my cheeks. I didn't know where they came from because I only felt numb, and honestly, I had felt numb ever since waking up, which could have been five minutes or five hours ago. I had no perspective on it.

Miles had begun to pace from my bed to the window and back, with his hands folded tightly together in front of him. It was a common gesture of his when frustrated. His dark, pristine Gucci suit looked the same as all of them he'd ever worn in the life we'd lived so long ago, or at least *felt* so long ago. Coming to stand directly over me, he uttered under his breath, "Katya, are you listening to me? Do you hear what I am saying? Whose child were you carrying?"

Looking into his cold eyes I felt a chill, despite the warm tears on my cheeks.

"You . . . can't have children?" It was impossible to believe, but then the trying and trying and trying came back to me. Always trying. The occasional hope and constant disappointment.

"No, I'm sterile. I didn't think you'd marry me if you knew, and I believed you'd give up wanting a child eventually."

I didn't respond. It didn't matter anymore. Nothing mattered anymore, especially not Miles. Only the dream mattered, and it was gone. Everywhere I looked there were bright lights and sharp edges, but my thinking was foggy. It was just the opposite of my dream, where thoughts and feelings were so intense, but the environment around me was seldom clear and usually blurry. The dream had been like a translucent silk screen. This awakening was more like a hardline etching.

"I want a divorce, Katya. I am done being married to a woman cheating on me. No doubt you would have expected me to believe the child you carried was mine. You'd have expected me to raise it. How deceitful is that, and how desperate, that you would sleep with another man just to have a baby?" Miles was pacing from the foot of the bed to the window and back while ranting about wanting a divorce. He hadn't looked me in the eye once since entering the room. It was as if he couldn't fathom why I was alive, as if it was a problem he hadn't anticipated.

"I wish you and Meghan well," I managed to say, with no sincerity and despite my dry, raw throat. Flashes of Miles with his secretary in the tasting room of Three Gates Winery crept into my head and wouldn't leave. It was the same day Parker and I had reunited. I suddenly wanted to thank Miles for that day. If I hadn't noticed how seductive they were with one another while standing at the wine bar, I might never have spent the night making love to Parker under the stars.

A flood of new tears washed over me while sliding a hand down to my barren tummy. Miles finally stood still and looked at me, his lips slightly parted as if he wanted to say something, but instead of speaking, he abruptly left the room. I stared at the ceiling and wished this day would fade into nothingness, that I would wake up in my dream and realize this had only been a nightmare.

Shortly after Miles left, Dr. Easton returned. "Where's Lorelei?" I asked, with my hoarse voice, while wiping tears away.

"She'll be back tomorrow. I told her you'd need undisturbed rest to regain your strength." He paused there and then added, "It appears your husband has upset you, Katya. I can prevent him from visiting. It is of utmost importance we focus on your full recovery, which means we can't have Miles or anyone else upsetting you."

"I lost my baby," I whispered. Dr. Easton pulled up the chair beside the bed and sat quite close to me.

"Katya, I am deeply sorry about the loss of your baby. I cannot pretend to know how you feel, but I will get you whatever help you need to cope with your loss. We have wonderful professionals on staff here. Perhaps you'd like to speak with someone?"

"Miles was not the father," I said. My voice was barely audible.

"Would you like us to contact the father?"

"No," I answered, a little too quickly. Perhaps the reality of Parker felt ominous, after creating an entire dream world in which he could not have been more perfect.

"I am no longer your physician, Katya. But your new doctor will have several specialists visiting over the next day or so, to evaluate your complete mental and physical health. Then we can schedule whatever therapy you may need to regain your strength and resume your life."

"I have no life to resume," I said in earnest. The good doctor's expression was one of concern mixed with compassion.

"Katya, your friend Lorelei has told me how full your life was before this tragic accident, and it will be again, I'm sure of it. She, by the way, almost never left your side except to eat, sleep, and work, and not even to eat or sleep half the time."

"Why are you leaving me, Dr. Easton?" I asked with what little voice I had left.

"Please, call me Oliver." He hesitated then and I could clearly see that he wanted to form his words carefully. "What you will need going forward are other specialists, not a neurosurgeon. You, my dear, are no longer in crisis mode. Thank God." He smiled brightly, and it was my only light on this dark day. I wanted to thank him for his care of me, but the words weren't forming. My mind was still thick with dark clouds of nothingness. Only my dream was clear to me, and my regret at waking up.

Oliver stood and examined my pupils. He had me track his finger left and right and then he said, "I can still visit if you wish. Check in to see how you're doing?"

"I'd like that," I whispered. A nurse brought a plastic bottle filled with ice water just then and Oliver handed it to me.

"This will soothe your throat," he said. "Sip on it as much as you can and try to eat everything served to you. It will mostly be easily digestible items like soft-cooked eggs, soups, and puddings at first. I'll stop by a couple times a day to see how you're doing." He paused and then added, "Life appears to be giving you a second chance, Katya. I want you to rest now, and dream about all the possibilities. Try not to dwell on the past. Look forward, not back."

These words echoed over and over in my head as I watched him leave the room. How could I possibly look forward when everything that mattered was behind me? I clutched my tummy and thought about Ruby, which caused me to sob uncontrollably. A nurse came and put something in my IV that made me fall into a dreamless sleep, dark and meaningless, exactly as I envisioned my future to be.

AWAKE

The next morning, I awoke to my new doctor, who told me exactly who would be visiting to determine how much I had regained of all my faculties. He then gave me a thorough examination and asked a lot of questions about how I was feeling. My answers were short. My voice was much better this morning, but I was very weak. I couldn't get out of bed without assistance. A nurse helped me shower and wash my hair. I sat in a shower chair while she did most of the work. I discovered that's why I'd need physical therapy. Mentally I was depressed. I had no desire to live in this world. I wanted my make-believe world back, with my living, breathing baby girl and the one true love of my life. Dr. Martinez was a pleasant man, but certainly no Oliver, which made me sad to have a new physician.

Lorelei came after Dr. Martinez left and brought me a bouquet of blood-red roses, which she placed in a vase already there. I hadn't noticed it, but then, I hadn't studied my surroundings in the least. If my eyes were open, they were staring blankly out the window and missing the aspen trees at Desert Sky. My best friend swooped into a chair beside the bed and took a close look at me. I could feel her pretty blue eyes penetrating my thoughts. "Katy, it's wonderful to see you nearly sitting up in bed and fully awake. The nurses tell me you had a very restless night, however. How are you feeling this morning?"

"A bit foggy," I replied. "Why was this empty vase here for my flowers?" I asked, suspecting Lorelei brought me fresh flowers the whole time I was in a coma.

"There were lots of vases," she answered. "Clients, friends, and neighbors sent so many well wishes we had to distribute them to other patients."

"I'm glad you did," I replied. "That was very nice of you. This vase is yours, though, isn't it? You've kept it filled with fresh flowers the whole time I was in a coma, haven't you?"

"Yes, I wanted you to have something colorful to look at if you woke up and I wasn't here." Lorelei smiled, but then her look became quite serious, and she changed the subject. "What did Miles have to say?"

"Miles is in love with his secretary," I said. "I never loved Miles. I don't blame him for moving on."

Lorelei seemed to be at a loss for words, so she took my hand into hers and just held it. After a minute or so she changed the subject again. "Katy, I can't tell you how happy I am you're going to be fine. I've missed you more than I ever thought possible."

I smiled at her. It was the first time I'd smiled since waking up. It was the first minute my heart wasn't overwhelmed with grief. "You're like the sister I never had," I replied, and I meant it.

"You'll get through this, Katy. I know you will."

I looked at the flowers she set on the table by my bedside. "They're my favorites you know, blood-red roses and baby's breath."

"Which represent romance and ever-lasting love," Lorelei added.

I felt a tear on my cheek and said nothing. Lorelei quickly changed the subject. "Have you been out of bed at all?"

"Yes, a nurse helped me shower."

"Of course, your IV is gone." Lorelei looked up where it should have been. "No wonder you're such a vision this morning. You're wearing the silk nightie I brought when they first admitted you, and I'd almost forgotten what a golden cloud of puffy curls your hair could be." Lorelei shook her head. "No one would ever know you've been in a coma for a month, except that your skin is deathly pale and you're much too thin." Lorelei glanced at the breakfast tray sitting on the rollaway table. "You didn't eat a thing."

"No. I haven't any appetite."

"You have to eat, Katy. How else do you expect to get strong again so you can leave here?"

This made me think of Genevieve. "I don't think I can face seeing Miles every day until the divorce is final."

"He's moved out. I've been watering your plants and feeding Crow. I fed him this morning and Miles was stuffing personal belongings into his BMW."

"How is Crow?" I asked.

"He's fine. Crow obviously misses you, but he still perches on the fence and comes to eat his tuna, no doubt hoping you'll return one day."

I thought about the dream, about Crow letting us pet him, and then more tears fell down my cheeks and onto the pale-yellow nightie.

Lorelei grabbed a tissue from the nightstand and handed it to me. "Katy, why all these tears? Why are you so distraught? It can't be over Miles. He isn't worth it."

"No," I agreed. I couldn't find the words to share about the baby I'd lost, so I didn't say anything at all.

"Now that Miles has left, you can find someone who truly loves you." Lorelei squeezed my hand. "I have to leave for work now, but I'll be back at noon, and I plan to bring you some of Chef Rosemary's homemade soup. We need to get you strong enough to go home." Lorelei studied me carefully while I willed the tears to stop so she could leave. "Katy, I know your life looks challenging right now, but honestly, I think having Miles gone is very good news. You can have a fresh start. A new beginning." She kissed my forehead and reminded me she'd be back at noon. I stared at the door when she left and could have sworn the light in the room was dimmer without her.

Later that morning Oliver stopped by. He silently observed me before speaking. It didn't feel at all awkward. It was more like I'd known him forever and we'd been telecommunicating since the beginning of time. His eyes brushed over my weak body as if he were an angelic sentinel sending special healing powers. There was a hint of more than healing thoughts in his eyes. I wouldn't call it lust, which would have felt uncomfortable. It was more like he loved me, down to my very soul. But how could that be? We'd just met.

"How do you feel today, Katya?" His voice had a soothing tone to it, which I'd noticed the first time he spoke, right after I woke up from the coma. It wasn't a low semi-whisper like Parker's, but more of a middle tone, and smooth as silk.

"I feel awake," I answered, but fell short of saying *unfortunately*.

Oliver chuckled. "Well, that's one way to describe your condition, which is exactly what I put on my last medical report about you." He sat next to me and smiled. "I'm sure waking up after a month is a bit strange."

"My physical therapy begins after lunch," I offered up, not wanting to delve into the misery of being awake.

"I see on your chart Dr. Martinez has been here."

"Yes. He is very nice."

"Anthony is a good man. He'll take excellent care of you, but you'll never get your strength back if you don't eat, Katya. The nurses tell me you didn't touch your breakfast."

"I have no appetite," I replied, which was true. Indeed, I had no appetite for this world in general. It couldn't nourish me in any way I needed. Only my dream world could feed my soul, but it had vanished.

"The sooner you regain your strength, the sooner you can go home. I can't think of a better reason to nourish your body."

"Lorelei said she'd bring soup from Angele."

"You are lucky to have a friend like Lorelei. She's a lovely person. I've enjoyed getting to know her while we waited for you to rejoin us."

"If only I hadn't," I said, and then an onslaught of tears consumed me.

Oliver reached over and gently placed his hand on mine. "I'm so sorry, Katya. I know the loss of your child is painful but believe me when I say it will get better. Lorelei mentioned your marriage is dissolving. Maybe that's for the better? You'll have a whole new life to look forward to, a new beginning in which to meet someone special and start a family."

If only I could have believed him. If only that were true, but I knew it wasn't. I would never be married to Parker because I hadn't reached out to him when I should have and now, surely, he had once again moved on. And of course, Ruby would never be born, because I lost our baby in the fall. She had only lived in my dream, along with Desert Sky and Goldie and Finnegan, and everything that mattered, or ever would, or ever could.

RABBIT HOLE

True to her word, Lorelei returned at noon with chicken soup made by Chef Rosemary, who also sent her blessings for a speedy recovery.

"Maybe I could eat a little," I said, and then proceeded to eat the whole bowl while Lorelei caught me up on Angele news. Once I'd finished, she cleared everything away and sat beside me again.

"What happened with the micro farm," I asked, fearing Miles had completely neglected it.

"Oliver helped me, and we managed to keep it afloat, at least until your last fall crop was delivered."

"Oliver helped?" I asked, wondering why a doctor, and a stranger at that, would do this.

"Yes. He loves gardening. Oliver is your neighbor, Katy. He just lives around the corner. He reached out to help keep the micro farm afloat."

"That was nice of him," I said, thankful he lived just around the corner and somehow connected with Lorelei. It felt good to know clients received their orders.

"He plans to help with your recovery when you're released from the hospital." Lorelei smiled. "He's a really great guy."

I looked at Lorelei, really looked at her for the first time since she'd brought lunch. "Is there something between you?" I asked, realizing there must be more to the story, considering her almost giddiness about him.

"We're just good friends. He really has been wonderfully supportive during this past month. You have no idea how difficult it has been for me, seeing you here in a coma and helpless to do anything about it." Lorelei teared up and this time, it was I who handed *her* a tissue.

"I'm so sorry, Lorelei. I can't imagine if it had been you lying here."

"I read to you every day, until the book was finished, and then I just sat here and prayed, nonstop."

"What did you read?" I asked, touched that she would read me a book and then pray for my recovery.

"*Alice's Adventures in Wonderland.*"

"The Lewis Carroll book?"

"Yes."

"I read it as a child." I paused for a few seconds and then quoted, "Imagination is the only weapon in the war against reality."

"You remember that from reading it as a child?"

"It's my favorite quote from the book," I said, "but there were other quotes I remember from the coma. Quotes I hadn't memorized as a child."

"Really? You were absorbing what I read. How interesting."

"Some of it at least." I recited another quote that had been in my dream. "I almost wish I hadn't gone down that rabbit hole . . . and yet . . . it's rather curious, you know."

Lorelei looked amazed. I couldn't help but consider the truth in the quote. Recalling the dream was my only joy, but it also hurt, knowing none of it was real. I couldn't decide whether I was grateful for the dream or wished I hadn't dreamt it, because it made me numbingly sad to live here instead of there.

"Do you remember anything else while in a coma?"

I thought about the long hours she'd spent in that chair by my side while I was completely unaware of her dedication. "I dreamed about Parker."

"Really?"

"Yes. We were married and had a child." My eyes teared up instantly and I couldn't go on.

"Katy, it's okay not to talk about it. Whatever you dreamt was simply that, a dream. It's time to *actually live* your life. No more escaping reality while sketching in a vineyard or tilling the earth. You must put yourself out there. Sell your art. Fall in love. Have those babies you want."

I knew she was right, but I couldn't imagine living outside the dream. I had convinced myself this was all a nightmare, and I would wake up back at Desert Sky. Perhaps I was crazy to believe this, but I didn't care. *Have I gone mad? I'm afraid so, but let me tell you something, the best people usually are.*

After Lorelei left, I dozed for a bit until the physical therapist arrived. He encouraged me to move up and down the halls with a walker. My second day of doing this I couldn't resist visiting with an elderly lady in a room nearby. Through her open doorway she looked lonely, so I knocked gently and asked if she minded a visitor. Her name was Tilly and she reminded me of Grandma Rose, tiny and fair skinned.

"Was your hair red before it turned this lovely, pure white?" I had asked.

Tilly answered that indeed it had been. "How did you know?" she'd inquired. I told her the fair skin and fading freckles were a dead giveaway, and how my Grandma Rose's hair had also turned white as snow.

The visit helped me forget about my own misery, but it was exhausting, nonetheless. I slept until Lorelei arrived after work. She brought more soup from Chef Rosemary. It was delicious and I was starving, having barely touched the hospital food. Lorelei left when Oliver came, and I couldn't help but wonder if they'd planned to tag team one another. He sat beside the bed and smiled his beautiful smile, which was quickly becoming one of the few things I looked forward to.

"Lorelei tells me you like to garden," I said, hoping to keep the focus off me. Especially since my life was a pointless subject filled with nothing but regret. More than anything I regretted not telling Parker about our child, when discovering I was pregnant. Now here I was months later with nothing to look forward to except reminiscing about an imaginary life in a dream world.

"You might say gardening is my hobby. Most doctors play golf, but I prefer growing things."

"There's something magical about it, isn't there?"

"Yes, there is, especially in *your* garden, Katya. I've never seen such luscious produce. What's your secret?"

"I sing them lullabies by the light of the moon," I teased.

Oliver laughed. "That's one thing I haven't tried."

"Thank you, for helping Lorelei harvest and distribute my produce. It was very sweet of you."

"It was my pleasure. I have to confess Lorelei brought me inside and showed me your intriguing artwork."

"Intriguing?"

"Yes. There's nothing ordinary about your work."

"Thank you, Oliver."

"I must say I've grown attached to Crow. He's quite a handsome boy."

"You've met him?"

"On my last visit, he let me pet him."

I studied Oliver's face to be sure he wasn't teasing me, and it was quite a lovely face. His large hazel eyes had a calming effect. Oliver had soft brown hair that made you want to run your fingers through it, maybe smooth back those few locks that always seemed out of place. I guessed him to be in his late thirties, and although he had a few lines here and there, they only added to his charm. He wasn't especially tall, but certainly not short. Nothing about Oliver was particularly outstanding, but all together he was very appealing. He had a way of making me feel better about anything and everything. "It's funny you should say that, because while in a coma I dreamed Crow let others pet him."

"You dreamed, and remember what you dreamt?" Oliver asked, looking surprised.

"Yes," I answered, but I didn't elaborate.

Oliver raised an eyebrow. "That's interesting."

I had no comment.

"Whatever you dreamed, it is part of who you are, and will always be with you, Katya. Just know you can still attain those dreams. You have your whole life ahead of you to marry again and have children."

I was silent. Words would not come. What could I have said anyway? No one could possibly understand the depth of my anguish and grief, and the hopelessness of knowing I'd made up the world I wanted to live in, but that world had now disappeared. Before he left, Oliver assured me he'd stop by after his rounds in the morning. I watched him leave, staring blankly at the open doorway until I must have dozed off again, with a Lewis Carroll quote floating around in my head: *I wonder if the snow loves the trees and fields, that it kisses them so gently? And then it covers them up snug, you know, with a white quilt; and perhaps it says, "Go to sleep darlings, till the summer comes again."*

JOY

Lorelei brought breakfast every morning before work. She would swing by Genevieve to feed Crow and then stop by Model Bakery for coffee and muffins. The muffins would still be warm when she swept into my hospital room and cheerfully handed me one. Sometimes she brought scones instead, or fresh danish. Whatever had just come out of the oven was generally her choice. She popped in again at lunch and dinner with something from Angele. With Lorelei and Chef Rosemary fussing over me I was gaining back the weight I'd lost, which, according to Oliver, I could ill afford to lose in the first place.

Oliver would stop by after Lorelei left. Every morning he brought me a fresh flower, which I suspected he charmed out of patients with recent deliveries. Lorelei would share the latest Napa news, fresh from Angele patrons, whereas Oliver focused on my health. How was physical therapy going? Did I still become overwhelmed by grief? His visits were short and sweet, whereas Lorelei stayed longer, but never long enough to be tiring. I slept a lot and didn't have any other visitors, at my request. Waking up in a world I didn't want to be in would have made me terrible company for any well-wishers.

There was just one other person I visited with, and that was Tilly. She was, I had found out, recovering from surgery. I'd never asked what the surgery was for, and she never said. Tilly was that special kind of person who focused so intensely on others, you never had a chance to inquire about her own life. Maybe that's why I felt so compelled to see her. I desperately needed to talk with someone who didn't care about me the way Lorelei and Oliver did.

Lorelei wouldn't understand why I hadn't shared with her about Parker and my pregnancy, and the last thing I wanted was to hurt her feelings. As for Oliver, it felt as if his visits were a pleasant escape for him, a few minutes to unwind from the ongoing stress of his occupation. I didn't want to contribute to his stress, rather than relieve it. Tilly was the perfect stranger I could share the burdens of my heart with. I'd gotten into the habit of bringing her the flower Oliver gave me each morning. It always made her smile. Her face would light up and she'd look almost young and vibrant again. I could clearly see the woman she'd been many years ago, with shocking red hair and bright green eyes, like my Ruby. Tilly was especially cheerful this morning when I entered her room.

"Ah, Katya dear. Where do you get these lovely flowers from?"

"Dr. Easton brings me one each morning."

"Does he now? What a nice doctor."

"Yes, he is. It feels as if I've known him all my life, but of course I haven't."

"He took care of you during your coma, my dear. Maybe your subconscious has bonded with him. How are you feeling today?"

"Every day I'm stronger physically, but mentally I have lost any desire to live."

"Now, now, my dear, don't talk like that. God has a way of healing broken hearts. You'll see. It just takes time. One day you'll feel joy again, I'm sure of it."

"I don't think so, Tilly."

Each day I told her more about my coma dream, and she looked forward to hearing the ongoing saga as much as I looked forward to sharing it. When I came to Tilly's room on the seventh day after I'd awakened from my coma, the bed was empty. I thought it odd, since she hadn't mentioned being released. I asked a nurse about her and was told Tilly had passed. Stunned, I didn't know what to say. I had so many questions, but I hadn't pried about her life or her condition. It seemed that she wanted it that way. Finally, I asked the nurse, "What did she die of?"

"Oh sweety, Tilly had terminal cancer and her surgery wasn't as successful as they'd hoped. Fortunately, she passed in her sleep before what would have been a slow, painful death. God was merciful."

I didn't leave my hospital room the rest of the day. I'd lost any incentive to get out of bed. No tears would come for Tilly, because it had been clear to me all along that she was ready to leave this earth. I had been a welcome distraction while waiting for her exit slip. She had been a distraction for me as well. It was the one hour of the day where I could live once again in my make-believe world. The memories of Parker and Ruby and Desert Sky would come alive and be vivid, filling that empty space in my mind and heart that nothing else could ever fill.

The next day I was released from the hospital. It was decided that going home might help with my depression. Besides, I'd regained whatever weight and strength I'd lost. There was no reason to keep me there. *Get back into the rhythm of life*, Dr. Martinez had said. *It will be the best medicine.*

Lorelei drove me to Genevieve. The ride there was quiet, each of us lost in our own thoughts. When we pulled up in front I sat and stared at the house for a few minutes. Lorelei patiently watched me stare. "Why did you park in front?" I asked.

"I thought you might like to see it. The house is charming to look at, isn't it? The fresh coat of white paint from last summer has made it gleam, and I love the unexpected tropical look of your front porch. I have so many great memories of drinking wine with you on that porch."

I looked at Lorelei and had no idea what to say. Her cheeriness was not helping in the least.

"Katy, the house has missed you. I think your grandmother's spirit has been sad while you were away."

"Maybe now that Miles is gone and I've returned she'll be happier than ever," I said.

We both laughed.

It was the first time I had laughed since waking up. Hesitantly I stepped out of the car and slowly walked up the front steps, with Lorelei right beside me. We stood at the rail for a minute and observed First Street. It was almost as if I'd never left. I heard all the familiar sounds of home: a car door opening and closing, someone honking at someone else, the laughter and footsteps of tourists. I could smell pizza dough from the bistro two doors down. This must have been how Dorothy felt in The Wizard of Oz when she at last returned to Kansas. I could now relate to what a rush of joy that was for her. Of course, Dorothy's family was there when she woke up. Waking up for me meant the opposite. I decided not to dwell on that. Instead, I reached over and squeezed Lorelei's hand, eternally grateful for her friendship.

As much as I loved being home, I hated how standing on the porch made the coma dream less real. I couldn't accept not being married to Parker or giving birth to Ruby. I couldn't let go of my dreamt-up time at Desert Sky. I wanted to fall again, fall back into the dream, not walk back into Genevieve, and live as if none of it ever happened.

"Let's go inside, Katy." Lorelei unlocked the door and motioned for me to follow her. I hesitated but she took my hand and coaxed me. Lorelei chattered away, about what I didn't know because I wasn't listening. I couldn't hear anything at all except my own heart beating in my throat and wishing it would stop beating altogether. I smiled to reassure her I wasn't going to bolt back out the door and jump over the railing, which wasn't high enough to do any bodily harm. Otherwise, I might have considered it.

Satisfied everything was as it should be, Lorelei rushed back out the door to retrieve groceries from her SUV. I lingered in the front room, observing not a book or candle to be out of place. Lorelei must have tidied everything up after

Miles moved out. Meandering into my art studio I stared at the canvases leaning against the wall. They reminded me of Three Gates Winery where I'd done the original sketches. Flashes of Parker and lovemaking under the stars made a tear roll down my cheek. If only my dream with Parker and Ruby had been true. Lorelei stuck her head into my studio, and I quickly wiped away the tear.

"Oliver is coming to dinner, Katy, if that's okay with you?"

"That sounds nice. What can I do to help?"

"Nothing. This is your homecoming dinner. It's a celebration. You just relax and enjoy it." Lorelei planned to stay a few nights, until I was settled in. I had no doubt her main concern was my mental state. I tried to hide my depression, but she was my best friend. It was obvious to her I had no desire to live. Maybe she thought she could help me find a reason to wake up each day. I loved her even more for believing she could help fix my broken life. I didn't have the heart to tell her that wasn't possible.

Hesitantly I walked into the master suite, relieved to find not one shred of evidence Miles had ever been there. All his things were gone—clothes, toiletries, everything that belonged to him. I collapsed onto the bed and must have fallen asleep the minute my eyes closed. When I awoke, I could hear voices coming from the kitchen. It was Lorelei and Oliver, busy preparing dinner. I freshened up and joined them, standing in the doorway for a minute before they noticed me.

"Katya! Did you rest well?" Oliver poured me a glass of red wine and I immediately thought of that day long ago in the tasting room with Parker, when we first met again, exactly ten years after our college encounter.

"Yes. Thank you." I studied him as he handed me the wine and Oliver seemed to be studying me as well. He was smiling and appeared to be savoring the moment, as if he never truly believed I would wake up, or maybe he thought I would and had anticipated this celebration.

"Katy, we're having chicken parmesan with fettuccine, one of your favorite dishes." Lorelei was literally beaming when she said this. "Oliver has made your favorite dessert, which I told him was bread pudding with caramel sauce."

"Are you both still conspiring to fatten me up?" I asked, touched that they had planned a celebratory meal for me.

"It couldn't hurt to put more meat on your bones," Lorelei teased.

Oliver laughed and suggested we have a toast. "Here's to our sleeping beauty waking up."

"That's what we affectionately called you, Katy," Lorelei explained.

We clinked our glasses together and I saw flashes of me and Parker in the cellar at Desert Sky, naked and intertwined on the red couch, having a toast to *us*.

"Thank you both for taking such good care of me, while asleep," I offered up, wishing I was still in my dream, back on that red couch. "I'll set the table," I said, as cheerfully as I could muster.

"It's already done," Oliver informed me. "I just need to light the candles."

I peeked around the kitchen doorway and saw three places set with my Grandma Rose's china. There were cloth napkins and crystal goblets filled with ice water. A forest-green candle sat in the center of the table, next to a small vase of peach roses. The pine scent from the candle mingled pleasantly with the sweet aroma of the fresh cut flowers. Lorelei and Oliver insisted I sit at the head of the table. Oliver lit the candle and poured us each more wine, while Lorelei brought in steaming plates of chicken parmesan with fettuccine. They sat on either side of me and had another toast to friendship and good health. I suddenly felt terrible for wishing I was still asleep and living in a fantasy world. It was as if my eyes had opened for the first time since being awake and I could clearly see that my wish was both selfish and ungrateful.

Lorelei's dinner was divine, as was Oliver's desert. I was grateful they had conspired to make the most deliciously fattening meal possible. After dinner, in which I was not allowed to lift a finger cleaning up, we sat in the living room where Oliver had built a fire. It was too chilly to sit on the porch, even with a blanket for our laps. Thanksgiving was only a week away and I hadn't given it a single thought until Lorelei brought it up.

"Katy, Oliver and I are bringing you to Angele for Thanksgiving."

"I didn't think you were open on holidays," I said, surprised.

"We aren't, but Chef Rosemary has agreed to prepare a feast for a few of our dearest neighbors. She wanted this to be a celebration of your recovery."

"That's very sweet of you, Lorelei." I smiled and looked at Oliver. "You're the newest neighbor in our fold," I said, grinning.

"It's a privilege to be in *your fold*," Oliver shared. The expression on his face was so tender it moved me to my core. We studied one another for a second longer than perhaps we should have, being new friends and nothing more. Then he added, "After Lorelei returns home, I'll stop by evenings to check on you, if you'd like."

"I'd like that very much," I said. Seeing Oliver was something I had come to look forward to. I felt guilty about it, knowing I had abandoned Parker and Ruby, even though I had made them up, which caused my guilt to make no sense.

Maybe it was sadness I felt more than guilt, because Parker was probably not the man I dreamed him to be, and Ruby never had a chance to show us who she might have been.

REVELATION

Lorelei and I ruminated over the pointlessness of my marriage to Miles during the few days she stayed with me. If I hadn't been so depressed, I would have shared about meeting Parker in the vineyard and getting pregnant before my fall from the ladder. I felt guilty for keeping it from my best friend all this time, but I seemed to be crawling beneath a thick fog and couldn't find my way to the light. My only goal in those first weeks after waking up was to hold on to my sanity.

I was careful not to speak of the dream I'd had while in a coma, or mention how real it felt, for fear Lorelei would insist I seek professional help. The last thing I wanted was to relive it all with a therapist. It was too painful to speak of. I was grieving, and in mourning. Not only had I lost the love of my life, but I had also lost our child, who had been so vibrant and real in the dream.

Lorelei and I sat on the front porch during the warmest part of the day, drinking herbal tea together on the rattan loveseat. We draped Grandma Rose's quilt across our laps and watched all the tourists on First Street heading into Oxbow or a wine bar. I was sullen and not very talkative, so Lorelei did her best to carry the conversation. Her last night there we baked chocolate chip cookies, after consuming a bottle of wine. The project involved a lot of remeasuring, sweeping up spills, and laughter. I can't remember what we found so funny about our disastrous attempt to bake cookies but laughing with abandon began to heal the edges of my broken heart. I couldn't remember the last time I had laughed with abandon.

I felt chilled to the bone when sitting on the porch after Lorelei left. I shivered even while basking in the sunlight and tucked under Grandma Rose's quilt. I knew I should be taking walks, preparing the soil for spring planting, or mustering up the courage to create art in my studio. Instead, I spent all my time recalling the dream and wishing I were still in it. I couldn't move forward until I made peace with the past, and that was a struggle. Falling through the back of the cupboard had felt so real, whereas falling forward off a ladder had never entered my mind as even a vague possibility.

I was becoming consumed with how and where I fell, so I mustered up enough energy to retrieve the ladder from Genevieve's cellar. I needed to see if the doorknob in the back of the cabinet was really there. So many things rushed through my mind as I placed the ladder against the wall beside the cupboard. I recalled the onesies I'd placed there originally, and my disappointment at not being pregnant with Miles's baby. I had flashes of Parker and our night together and how I was truly pregnant the second time I climbed this ladder. I remembered how grateful and excited I had been and overwhelmed at the prospect of telling Miles. I suddenly felt foolish for fearing he would think the baby his. Not only would he know the child was someone else's, he would not have wanted to raise it, which had been my biggest fear: Miles wanting anything to do with the child.

I opened the cabinet door and saw the baby clothes right where I'd left them. Picking up a onesie I examined it as if fine art, running a finger across each stitch in the soft yellow fabric. I thought about Ruby, and never seeing her in these onesies. I thought about how real Ruby felt to me. Even now, after waking up and realizing it was all a dream, I knew she existed. She was my red-headed rosy cheeked daughter, and although I had been cut off from her, Ruby lived and thrived somewhere in the universe. I had no tears this time, only faith that one day I would see Ruby again.

I returned the onesie and looked past the pile of baby clothes to the tiny round doorknob in the back of the cupboard. Reaching for it nearly lifted me off the ladder. I froze, with my hand on the doorknob, wondering if I would fall through time and space, and back into my dream world. To be honest, I wanted that more than anything.

The door in the back of the cupboard opened after one good tug and several papers fell out. Disappointed, I retrieved the papers from the floor of the cabinet and closed the door to the shallow space where they'd been kept. After one last glance at the baby clothes, I swung the outer door shut and put the ladder away. Then I returned to the front porch and curled up in the rattan chair again, to soak in the last remaining sunlight. Staring at the papers clutched in my hand, I realized without a shadow of doubt I had fallen from the ladder that day, not out the back of the cupboard. The doorknob to the false back was tiny and not easily seen, especially if inconsequential things were stacked in front of it. Grandma Rose must have put these papers there for safe keeping.

I carefully examined the paper on top. It was a birth certificate for Rosemary Genevieve Delaney. I was positively grinning now. Grandma Rose's middle name was Genevieve! When I named the spirit in this house, Genevieve came to me as if from thin air. I didn't realize it was my grandmother's middle name. I looked at the next paper and it was my great grandmother's birth certificate. Her name had been Genevieve Rose. I must have been named after both grandmothers. Rose was my middle name. Katya, of course, had been my grandmother's name on my mother's side. They were from St. Petersburg, Russia. The Delaney's were from Dublin, Ireland, which would explain Grandma Rose's red hair.

I looked at the final two papers. They were Grandpa Delaney's birth certificate and a letter from his commanding officer during WWII. I never met my grandpa. He died in the war. The letter was handwritten and quite a tribute to what a hero he'd been. I wish I could have known him. Grandma Rose's eyes always lit up when she mentioned his name. I decided I would frame all these historical family documents in some sort of collage and hang them in Genevieve. I wondered what might have happened to this home if I'd never awakened. I shuddered at the thought of Miles living here with Meghan. Lorelei had mentioned Miles forging a will and estate plan in my name.

It was getting dark, and too cold to remain on the porch. I gathered up the quilt and while folding it, Crow jumped onto the side rail. I'd barely seen him since coming home from the hospital. Every morning I opened a can of tuna and left it at the entrance to the cellar, but Crow had come to eat when I was no longer there. Now here he was on the porch rail. I'd never known him to come to the front porch. Slowly I walked over to the side rail, talking to him gently the whole way. "I've missed you, Crow. How have you been? Lorelei tells me she took care of you."

Crow just sat there, purring. He was not the least bit spooked by my stepping nearer and nearer. Finally, I was looking right into his large amber eyes. I remembered Oliver saying he petted Crow, but I thought it would be a violation of our trust if I reached out to touch him. I stood there quietly admiring his presence, but then he butted his shiny black head up against my sweater and purred louder. He was giving me permission. I carefully reached up and petted his silky black fur. It was like a reward for all I'd been through. After a few minutes he jumped down and was gone in a flash, like my dream world.

I took a long nap after that, and by the time Oliver arrived with dinner I was eager for the company. He brought a chicken pot pie. We put it in the oven and made a salad together while it baked. It didn't feel strange to have him there, even though it was our first time alone together in the house. Oliver felt more like an old friend than a new one. Maybe in a way he was an old friend, since he had cared for me while in a coma.

"I didn't know you cooked," I commented, while tearing off pieces of romaine and placing them in a bowl.

"I do, especially when it involves vegetables from my garden. There's not much growing out there right now though, except for the carrots and potatoes in the pot pie, and a few salad greens."

I thought about my micro farm and how the fall vegetables would have been lost without Lorelei and Oliver. "I can't thank you enough for your help with my garden."

"It was my pleasure." Oliver looked at me and our eyes met. We were standing close together at the counter, slicing and chopping veggies for the salad. Our prolonged eye contact would have been intimidating, except he was such an open book. His whole demeanor was gracious and kind. He was very different from Parker, who's mysterious qualities were always lurking about in an enticing way.

"Are you walking every day, Katya?" he asked.

"Lorelei and I took a few walks down by the river."

"It's important you walk every day to rebuild your strength."

"Yes, doctor." I laughed, and then set the dining room table for two. Oliver opened the pinot gris he'd brought and poured it into the stemware I'd set out, while I lit the candle from my first night home. Lorelei and I had lit the candle every night she stayed with me. I admired how it built up walls of sculptured wax, each layer adding another memory of sharing a meal with a friend or neighbor. Visions of lovemaking by candlelight with Parker flashed through my mind.

During dinner Oliver told me about his childhood and I told him about mine. After dinner we cleaned up the kitchen and built a fire. A neighbor dropped off a box of chocolates as a get-well gift and we tasted a few with the rest of the pinot. It was a lovely evening, cuddled up on the sofa by the warm fire eating chocolates and drinking wine.

"Have you been depressed at all?" Oliver asked, when our wine glasses were empty, and I'd closed the chocolate box.

"Perhaps a little," I admitted.

He put another log on the fire and sat down beside me again. "I know how hard it was for you to lose the baby you were carrying, and of course, divorce is never easy. Add to that losing a month of your life and basically needing to rebuild it, both physically and mentally. It's easy to see why you'd be depressed."

I didn't know how to respond. I still felt underwater most of the time, and in a way I was grateful. Not thinking too much made it easier not to feel too much. "The father of the baby I lost was someone I met in college. We hadn't seen one another for ten years, almost to the day," I shared. "Then suddenly there he was, at the vineyard where I would often go to sketch."

"Parker Mancini?"

"How did you know?"

"Lorelei told me about your brief college encounter with him, and how you always sketched at the vineyard you thought was owned by his family."

"Does she know about our reunion, or the baby?" I could never think of Ruby without tears forming. Oliver handed me a tissue from the box nearby.

"Even if I'd wanted to, as your doctor it would have been unethical for me to reveal such privileged information."

"I never mentioned my reunion with Parker because I could barely believe what had happened myself, seeing him again after all those years. I was curious about his family's vineyard. I can't deny there has always been a part of me that couldn't let the hope of him go."

"The hope?"

"Of true love. That it exists. I felt something with Parker that I have never felt with anyone else." I wanted to add how the dream had been all about a life with Parker, a life I didn't want to wake up from.

"I understand," Oliver said. "I've had that feeling with someone before."

"That day when Parker and I ran into each other on the vineyard grounds is the same day I realized Miles had been cheating on me. I saw him with his secretary in the tasting room and it was obvious how they felt about one another. It was that night Parker and I slept together. He only wanted to comfort me, but then the chemistry between us took over."

Oliver smiled. "I'm glad you had your night with Parker. I'm just sorry it has turned out so bittersweet for you."

"I should have gone to Parker and told him about our baby. Now it's too late."

"I would encourage you to go to him now, Katya, and see if there is any hope for the two of you, except that . . ." Oliver didn't finish his sentence.

"Except what?" I asked.

"Except that I went to see Parker, based on what Lorelei told me about the two of you. I thought there might be a chance you had indeed run into him at the vineyard and that he was the father of your baby. It was worth a shot, because I needed someone to talk to you, a voice you might respond to."

"Was he there? Did you speak to him?" I asked, holding my breath.

"I did speak to him, but not about you. I should have, but at the last minute I couldn't bring myself to do it, because it felt more like interfering in your life than helping you recover."

"How was he?"

"Parker seemed like a fine person, smart and accomplished. He was quite friendly. I went back a second time, when at my wits end with how to awaken you. But he was gone."

"Gone?"

"Yes. His brother said he'd taken off quite suddenly to work remotely again with his article writing, and he didn't know where."

I was literally speechless. All I could do was stare at Oliver, at his kind hazel eyes, momentarily filled with sadness for me. My breathing felt labored, and I could have sworn there was a ton of bricks pressing against my chest.

"There is more, Katya, and I hesitate to tell you this, but I feel I must be completely honest with you."

"What then," I asked, with no real desire to know.

"His brother thought he hadn't left alone. He suspected Parker met someone, a woman who'd frequented the tasting room while you were in a coma."

I nodded my head up and down slowly. I don't remember what we said or did after that, or Oliver leaving. I went to bed engulfed by a thick black cloud. When I awoke the next morning all I could think about was coffee—black, strong, refillable. It was something to get me through another day of shattered dreams, surrounding me like shards of broken glass. I had to ward off a desire to cut myself and bleed to death.

THANKSGIVING

I'd spent the morning the same way I'd spent every morning lately, drinking gallons of coffee and working on etchings and silk screens in my makeshift bedroom studio. The coffee was to keep me from curling up in a fetal position on my bed, which is what every fiber of my being wanted to do. Lorelei somehow understood my longing to shrivel up and float away into nothingness, so she popped in every morning at seven o'clock to keep me grounded. She'd storm through the front door balancing a tiny white bag with blueberry muffins and two venti coffees.

I'd nibble on the warm blueberry muffin while she chattered away about Angele's daily specials or my new artwork. It was always a one-way conversation in which I watched her flutter from room to room straightening a book or fluffing a couch pillow. She somehow knew how miserable I was in my own skin regardless of how well I hid it. This realization seemed to make her nervous for both of us, but I had no idea how to fix that, or me. It was quite a helpless feeling to watch your best friend try so hard to cheer you up, when nothing could possibly lift the veil of darkness clinging to your body. Some days were worse than others. On the worst days it felt as if that veil had tentacles slithering around inside my brain. I couldn't do art on those days.

This day, however, was different. Oliver was picking me up at two o'clock to join Lorelei at Angele for a Thanksgiving feast. While waiting for Oliver I scrutinized my etching of Ruby. I had remembered every detail about her face, from the light dusting of freckles across her rosy cheeks to her signature impish smile. Lorelei had hesitated to inquire about the portrait when first seeing it. *Do you know this adorable child?* she'd asked, finally. *This was my daughter in the coma dream,* I'd replied.

My entire world from that dream was tumbling onto etching plates and silk screens. There were several etchings of Finnegan and Rocco, and a couple silk screens of mountain and meadow views from Desert Sky. My new work was different than the obsessive vineyard art of my precoma days. I had no desire to return to that topic, or the vineyard for that matter. Even gardening did not appeal to me. I felt too dead inside to try and grow things.

Oliver knocked on the door and all my thoughts of the dream disappeared. They were replaced with fear and dread. I didn't want to leave Genevieve and attend a feast at Angele. I only wished I'd begged Lorelei and Oliver to bake a turkey right here in my oven, for just the three of us.

"Happy Thanksgiving!" I said cheerfully, while standing in the doorway and not feeling cheerful. I hoped I had disguised my feelings well.

Oliver broke into a wide grin. "Katya . . . I don't believe I've ever seen you dressed up." He didn't move for a few seconds, and I must confess I didn't either. All I could think about was how nice he looked in his khakis and navy sweater. He usually stopped by each evening after work in a white button-down shirt and suit pants. Just when I thought he was frozen to the front porch he handed me a bouquet of sunflowers. It made me smile.

"Oliver, this arrangement is beautiful. How sweet of you to bring me these." The flowers made me forget about my stressful morning, fretting over the feast at Angele.

"You're quite a vision yourself, Katya." I glanced at my white blouse and denim skirt. After weeks of wearing nothing but yoga pants, these clothes felt foreign. My knee-high leather boots were stiff and awkward, which is how I felt in general.

"I guess I haven't been anywhere except down to the river," I confessed.

"No one would expect you to be out and about yet, Katya. Your recovery is going to be slow and steady."

I hoped he was right. To me, my recovery seemed more than slow. It seemed impossible "Let me put these flowers in water and grab my coat," I said. "Please, make yourself at home."

Oliver did exactly that. He wandered from the bookshelf in the front room, where he'd examined a few titles, to my artwork in the studio. That's where I found him after grabbing my coat and examining myself in the mirror one last time. I was so pale I put on lipstick to not look like the walking dead. It didn't help that my white blouse and golden hair could have doubled for an angel sporting a puffy, shimmering halo.

"I'm ready," I said, while not feeling ready at all to face the outside world.

"This new work of yours is stunning." Oliver tore his gaze away from the portrait of Ruby and looked at me. "And so are you."

"I don't look like the walking dead?" I asked.

"Not at all. You look like an angel visiting straight from heaven."

"That was my second fear," I confessed.

Oliver laughed. "There are worse things to look like than an angel."

It took determination to grab the pumpkin pie I'd baked and walk out the door, instead of locking myself in the bedroom and crawling under the covers. We decided to walk to Angele since it was a lovely brisk fall day. Oliver asked to carry the pie and I was grateful, because walking in heeled boots after living in sneakers proved to be challenging. I tried not to think about seeing other people, even knowing they were friends and neighbors. I should have been excited to reunite with them. Guilt welled up inside me. How could I be so ungrateful? Why did I dread this second chance God had given me? I needed to snap out of it. Parker, afterall, had moved on. It was time I did the same.

Lorelei greeted us at the back door of the restaurant and took the pie from Oliver. I was pleased to see it was indeed a small gathering of our friends from the neighborhood. Chef Rosemary's husband and their two half-grown boys were also there, looking very dapper, with freshly combed hair and button-down shirts. Oliver had invited a few nurses who otherwise would have been alone. I was touched that he included them. Nurses, I had discovered, were the true angels, not caricatures dressed in white with puffy hair-halos over their heads.

Conversations revolved around memories of past Thanksgivings, which led to inquiries about everyone's family in a different state and at a different gathering. It was all typical holiday talk, and I was grateful for the light heartedness of it. No one asked about my coma, and I was relieved, because this is what I had feared the most. It was, however, clearly on everyone's mind. This gathering had been a way of thanking God for my recovery. A special thanksgiving, yet no one dared ask about the accident or coma. I could see the curiosity in their eyes when they looked at me, along with relief that I had made it through.

Wine, beer, and cocktails flowed generously and went down smoothly with the mouthwatering appetizers Chef Rosemary had served. Oliver handed me a glass of red wine and hovered near as if he were my older brother protecting me from a gang of ruffians. We nibbled on stuffed mushrooms and bacon-wrapped dates, candied nuts, and a variety of cheeses. There were clumps of purple grapes and several creamy dips served with bowls of salty chips. I didn't think I'd have room for turkey and dressing. I shared my concern about it with Oliver who laughed heartily. "Well, that's the whole idea, Katya, to stuff yourself before the stuffing is served."

I felt completely relaxed after a second glass of wine and managed to have conversations with every guest before sitting down to a scrumptious feast. Along with the turkey and dressing we had candied yams with a caramel glaze and creamy mashed potatoes. There were several green vegetables sautéed to perfection. Cranberry relish was served alongside baskets of warm rolls fresh from the oven and accompanied with herb butter. After everyone had filled their plates, Lorelei suggested we hold hands and name one thing we were thankful for. She started by offering thanks for everyone there, who were like family to her. I fretted and worried about what I would say until it was Oliver's turn to speak. He looked at me specifically and said he was thankful for patients he'd been able to heal this past year.

Then it was my turn. "I'm grateful to have a second chance at life," I said, "and that's because of the good doctor seated beside me, and my best friend who almost never left my side while in a coma. I am not just thankful but indebted to both Lorelei and Oliver." Everyone applauded and cheered. A few eyes became moist. Someone shouted *praise God.*

And just like that, the elephant in the room was vanquished.

SHOPPING

Every morning at six o'clock I had fallen into the routine of brushing my teeth and throwing on sweatpants with a warm shirt. Next, I would tightly lace my sneakers and smash my hair into a ballcap before heading out the front door, down the porch steps, and along First Street for my daily run. It was a comforting ritual. I'd loop around the riverfront shops and back home again, just in time to greet Lorelei with her blueberry muffins and venti coffees.

The rest of the day was spent in my art studio, where I pushed away any thoughts of it one day being a nursery. Instead, I focused on turning my coma dream into etchings and silk screens. This obsession with "The Dream Art" kept me from succumbing to a deep depression, which nonetheless licked at the corners of my mind like a hungry monster.

Today was different because it was nearly Christmas. Instead of waiting on the porch after my run for Lorelei to appear with muffins and coffee, I entered Oxbow Public Market across the street. The kiosk stores were just beginning to unlock wire gates and freshen up displays. I wanted to buy a few gifts for Oliver and Lorelei, whom I'd invited over for Christmas Day. Lorelei was having us to her home Christmas Eve, after church, which was a new activity for Oliver. I'm not sure if it was God that got him in the door or Lorelei and I badgering him to come with us.

We'd become quite a threesome, although I mostly saw them separately because they were still playing tag team with my care. Lorelei came before work every morning and again at lunchtime. Oliver stopped by most evenings if not overwhelmed at the hospital with new patients or emergency surgeries. Every Friday night Lorelei and I shared a bottle of wine on the front porch, like we had done before my fall from the ladder. It was especially nice not having Miles there, who always seemed to be bothered by our ritual.

Truthfully, everything bothered Miles. He was an unhappy man who judged the world and everyone in it through a cynical eye. Miles perpetually claimed himself a victim when even the slightest thing went wrong at work. It was always someone else's fault, but he alone had to deal with the consequences. Now his wrath was aimed at me. It was my fault he had to divorce me. If I'd loved him properly, he wouldn't have wandered. Again, he was a victim. He must have forgotten we frequently made love because I wanted a baby and thought he did too. I suppose it was my fault for not knowing he was sterile, and someone else's fault for the fact that he was.

Oliver had encouraged me not to think about Miles. He thought the stress was counterproductive to my healing. My divorce attorney was someone Oliver had highly recommended, and as my new confidant, Oliver was handling most of the correspondence between my attorney and Miles.

Saturday evenings had become a night out for Oliver and me. He'd insisted I quit cooking for him and wanted to take me to restaurants. He said he hated eating alone and I was doing him a favor, because there was no better cuisine than the downtown Napa fare and therefore, we should partake of it. He was right of course. We were blessed with an excellent diversity of options.

I'd told Lorelei she needn't stop by this morning after my run, but she insisted on dropping off my muffin and coffee anyway. It would be there waiting for me after my shopping spree. By the time I'd finished exploring all the kiosks my hands were full of packages. I'd bought cheeses and chocolates, aged wines and reserved whiskey, a ceramic vase in earth tones for Oliver and a few scented candles for Lorelei. They were her favorite scents, sandalwood and lavender. I bought a few for Genevieve too, wild honey and apple butter.

I hid the packages in the closet and made clam chowder for lunch, using fresh clams I'd just purchased at the fish market in Oxbow. I'd bought a baguette from the bakery to go with it. Since Lorelei insisted on coming to lunch every day to check up on me, I'd decided the least I could do is prepare it. Chef Rosemary had been beyond generous with feeding me when first waking up from the coma.

Lorelei swooped in the back door at half past noon, and we sat on the front porch to eat our lunch. It was an exceptionally warm December day. The sun poked through the railing and our heavy sweaters were all we needed to feel cozy.

"This chowder is excellent, Katy. I'd forgotten what a good cook you are, which is surprising since it looks as if you never eat."

"I'm not sure if I should thank you or apologize for my heritage."

We both laughed, knowing my grandmother Rose had also been a tiny woman. If only I'd gotten her luscious red locks. I could never think about Grandma Rose these days without Ruby's face haunting me. It was time to come clean with Lorelei about Parker and my pregnancy. No more excuses, and we had time since Lorelei wasn't returning to work this afternoon. She was taking it off to do a little shopping herself.

"I never shared very much with you about my dream while in a coma," I said, looking Lorelei square in the eye.

She reached across the porch table and patted my hand resting there. "I knew you'd share when ready."

"It's more about what happened before the dream that needs to be said."

"I'm listening."

"I ran into Parker at the vineyard, a couple months before I fell from the ladder. I never had a chance to tell you because we were both so busy with harvest."

"Katy, I had no idea." Lorelei looked genuinely surprised.

"There's more. The same day I ran into Parker, I saw Miles in the tasting room, with Meghan."

"You're kidding?" Lorelei put her chowder spoon down and gave me her full attention.

"It all made sense then, his evasiveness and constant trips to the Bay Area." I put down the piece of bread I'd been nibbling on and stared at the empty street, momentarily devoid of bustling tourist traffic. "I was so angry I let myself get carried away with my feelings for Parker."

"What happened, Katy?" After a moment of tongue-tied silence, I confessed we made love under the stars that night in the vineyard.

"I think that's completely understandable." Lorelei sounded pleased. "You've been in love with Parker ever since I've known you, and Miles certainly never deserved you."

"I got pregnant that night, Lorelei. And I lost the baby when I fell from the ladder. I didn't know until I woke up from the coma."

"Oh no. Katy, no."

"I'm sorry I never shared that with you, until now."

Lorelei began to tear up, which made me tear up.

"And Oliver knows, doesn't he?" Lorelei asked.

"Yes, and he knows Parker is the father. I just told him a few days ago."

"And Miles? Does Miles know?"

"Yes. I hadn't said anything about Parker or that I was pregnant, but Oliver told Miles I lost the baby I was carrying when I fell from the ladder."

"Did Miles think the baby was his? Was he angry that you lost the child?" Lorelei looked as if she'd seen a ghost and I realized just how overwhelming all this new information must be.

"Miles can't have children," I answered, "because he had the mumps as a preteen. He is sterile."

"Oh my goodness, Katy! He has lied to you throughout the whole marriage."

"At least now I know why Miles was never frustrated about my inability to get pregnant."

"I can't believe he would deceive you like that!"

"What's done is done. I was equally foolish to believe our marriage would be better once we had children."

We were both quiet for a minute, angry and sad that anyone could be so devious. Lorelei moved chowder around with her spoon and I continued to stare at the street. An elderly man and woman walked out of Oxbow Public Market and strolled hand in hand down the sidewalk. I wondered if I'd have someone to stroll hand in hand with when I was old.

"Did Parker know you were carrying his child?" Lorelei looked up at me.

"I procrastinated telling him," I answered, sounding as regretful about it as I felt. "I needed to figure out what to do about my marriage first. I didn't want anything to do with Miles after seeing him with Meghan, but I didn't want to split our assets, which might mean selling Genevieve. Miles knows how much this property is worth. His eyes lit up every time he mentioned it and he practically drooled when discussing all the things we could do with the money."

Lorelei shook her head. "I never liked that man. He was always so hard to read, like a closed book. Katya, why haven't you gone to see Parker now that you're awake and nearly back to normal?"

I shrugged my shoulders. "Oliver suspected Parker might be the father of my baby, so he went to the vineyard, but Parker's brother said he had left."

"Did he say where Parker went?"

"What he said is that Parker probably left with a woman he had met at the vineyard."

"No!" Lorelei looked as distraught as I felt. Our mutual disappointment was ironic, considering that Parker didn't owe me anything. It wasn't as if I'd notified him that he was to be a father, or that I was leaving Miles and wanted to spend eternity with him. As far as Parker knew, I had gone home and resumed my life as if nothing happened that day at Three Gates Winery.

"Some things just aren't meant to be," I said, while carrying dishes into the house. Lorelei helped me and never said another word. I think she suspected I didn't want to discuss it any further. It was too painful. She hugged me tightly and left to do her shopping.

It wasn't long until Oliver appeared. We did our leisurely river walk as usual, but tonight Oliver convinced me to get dinner with him at the bistro two doors down, even though it was only Tuesday and not our usual Saturday night. We shared a bottle of chianti and ate crusty bread with butter while waiting for our Caesar salad. I barely touched my chicken fettuccine, while Oliver managed to eat every bite of his ravioli with meat sauce.

"Katya, you need to eat more," Oliver scolded, while I slid my dinner into a Styrofoam box.

"I have so much on my mind lately, Oliver. It ties my stomach into knots."

"If you mean Miles and the divorce, just put that out of your head. My attorney will see to it that you keep your land and property."

I didn't tell Oliver it was impossible not to worry about what Miles might be up to. Having lived with him for seven years, I knew how underhanded he could be when it came to his attorney skills.

We left the bistro and decided to drop my food off at the house before taking a walk. It was such a beautiful evening I soon forgot all about Miles. We stopped at the bridge overlooking the Napa River, which looped behind Genevieve and past Angele on the Riverfront, causing the famous oxbow. It was usually a quiet river that rose and fell with the tidewaters of the Pacific, which was only an hour away as the crow flies. In the rainy season, however, it had been known to roar like a lion and threaten to swallow the entire Oxbow District.

Oliver threw a rock into the river and watched the ripples expand, then disappear. In the summer months there would be live music on the patio at the culinary institute across the street from the bridge. The food they served on the patio was farm to table cuisine, stocked by their own gardens, which were as picturesque as they were plentiful. Being mid-December, the garden was mostly bare, but twinkle lights were strung from the trees and Poinsettias lined the patio, which made everything look quite festive.

I pulled my collar up around my neck and tried not to shiver.

"Are you cold, Katya?"

"A little," I admitted.

Oliver pulled me into his arms and rested his chin on my head. "Maybe we should head back."

"But it's so beautiful here," I protested. "The moon shimmers on the water like dancing stars." I looked up at him and smiled.

"It also shimmers in your eyes," he said, and reached down to kiss me. It was such a surprise I nearly panicked. Oliver must have sensed my discomfort, because he kissed the top of my head instead of my lips. I didn't know if I was disappointed or relieved. Dr. Oliver Easton had become a good friend, and I cared about him a great deal, but I hadn't let myself consider anything more than friendship. I wasn't sure if it was possible for me to love another as I had loved Parker.

THE STREET LAMP

Christmas Eve was a quiet affair. Lorelei, Oliver, and I went to dinner at Basalt on the riverfront, just down the street from Angele. After dinner we went to church. The choir had been so moving there was not a dry eye among the parishioners. Afterward we hung out at Lorelei's home, which sat on the edge of a vineyard across town. Everything in her house was elegant, just as she was. Even her tree had a touch of class that set it apart from most. We drank too many salted caramel martinis and ate too many frosted sugar cookies. We laughed with abandon while playing games. Oliver brought me home at midnight.

The next day we celebrated Christmas at my house. We opened gifts and had prime rib, which Oliver brought and prepared himself. Lorelei and I sauteed French beans with slivered almonds and whipped potatoes into fluffy mounds. For dessert we had apple pie, compliments of Chef Rosemary, who'd sent it home with Lorelei on Christmas Eve. After dinner we watched old movies until Lorelei could no longer keep her eyes open. She was exhausted from a busy week of family gatherings at Angele.

Once we'd hugged goodbye and sent her home with a bag of leftovers, Oliver and I bundled up for a walk down to the waterfront. Darkness had just blanketed the dock and stars were emerging above us. There was a magical feel to the air, almost like Santa would appear with his sleigh on the rooftops across the river. But that had happened the night before. Oliver and I decided next year we'd come down to the dock on Christmas Eve and wait for Santa to show up. Then we both laughed and walked in silence for a while along the boardwalk. Christmas lights sprinkled in the trees shimmered brightly. A festive wreath hung at each streetlamp.

I couldn't help but wonder what the new year would bring. I had grown accustomed to Oliver and Lorelei tag teaming their care of me. Now that I was strong again, their lives would no doubt be consumed by whatever they were doing before my fall from the cupboard. I hadn't realized how lonely I was when married to Miles. He had been emotionally absent from the marriage for a long time, if indeed he had ever been emotionally present. Miles had a smooth-talking way about him that was quite instrumental in his success as an attorney. Now I believed it played a large part in securing our marriage. Miles only wanted to marry me so he could pay off his college loans and live mortgage free in Genevieve while building his career.

"Katya, what are you thinking?" Oliver asked.

"I was thinking about how nice you and Lorelei have been to take such good care of me while recovering."

"It has been our pleasure."

Oliver and I sat on a bench near the dock. Together we watched the moored boats bob up and down in the water. It was mesmerizing with the steady rhythm of the water lapping against their bows.

"I love the art you've been producing." Oliver moved closer to me, sensing I had begun to shiver in the chilly night air. "Who would have thought such beauty would pour out of you after being in a coma for so long?"

"That's just it, Oliver. Everything I dreamed while in a coma was beautiful."

"And you think you dreamed the whole time?"

"It was so real I still mourn the loss of my life there."

"That's remarkable."

"The portrait of the little redheaded girl is Ruby. I thought she was the child I'd been carrying before I fell, but obviously I lost that baby." I looked up at Oliver and our eyes met. I wondered if he thought I should see a shrink. What surprised me the most in that moment is how much I cared about what he thought. His opinion was important to me. *He* was important to me.

"Katya, there is something so pure about your approach to everything you do and how you do it. I know in your heart and mind you were truly there, living your dream."

I sighed. "Yes, it felt quite real, but maybe I just wanted it to be. If I were going to create a fantasy world, it would be the one I dreamed."

We left the bench and headed back down the boardwalk until Oliver stopped beneath a streetlight and turned toward me. "Do you have any idea what I would dream for my fantasy world if given the chance?"

I studied his face and immediately knew what he would dream. It had been so obvious ever since waking up from the coma. It was written in his eyes when he looked at me, and in his smile whenever I spoke. It was the tender way he touched me when given the chance. Oliver was in love with me. I had never said it even to myself, but I knew. "I think you would create a world in which you had someone you cared deeply about to share your life with."

"Katya, do you know who that person would be?"

I didn't answer, except maybe with my eyes, which must have told him something, because he kissed me, right there beneath the streetlamp. It was a kiss that showed his love and his longing for me, but it was more tender than forceful. Nothing about Oliver was overbearing. His gentleness did not detract from his masculinity. In fact, it made him that much more desirable.

"I would like to be more than friends, Katya," Oliver shared, when our kiss ended. "But I don't want to rush you into anything. If you tell me there is hope for us, I can wait as long as it takes for you to be ready."

I looked into his vulnerable eyes and contemplated my answer. I didn't want to hurt him, and I didn't want to lose him, either. I honestly didn't know what I wanted. "So much has happened, Oliver. It's as if I died and you brought me back to life, but not all of me is alive again yet."

"Do I see a ray of hope in there somewhere for us?" He moved a lock of hair off my cheek.

"Yes." I smiled then because it was true. His kiss left me wanting more. If only I could be brave enough to love someone again.

"May I hold your hand?" he asked.

"I'd like that," I said, and so we walked back to Genevieve hand in hand, where Oliver kissed me again, and then left for home. I sat on the top porch step after he left and stared at the stars. I thought about how I'd walked the boardwalk a hundred times alone or with Lorelei, and now with Oliver, but I had never walked the boardwalk with Parker. I had never experienced Napa with my one true love. Parker suddenly seemed like something I had made up, a pretend life we all have when we are eight years old. But Napa was real, Napa was home, and Oliver was in Napa, whereas Parker never had been. He had not come for me, or fought for me, or been a part of my life here. I only knew him in a house off campus, and at a vineyard in St. Helena, and in a dream while suffering a coma.

Perhaps it was time to let Parker go.

NEW YEAR'S EVE

The week between Christmas and New Year's was a turning point in many ways. Lorelei was busy at Angele, and I only saw her once, when we met across the street at Hog Island Oyster Bar for a late lunch. At my request she had quit dropping off a blueberry muffin and venti latte. I assured her I no longer needed the pampering and had begun to make my own muesli again. Oliver, who still dropped by every evening, was much less secretive about his feelings for me. I had to admit I was falling in love with him. Who wouldn't? He was intelligent and attractive, caring and attentive.

What I liked most about Oliver was his patience. He was careful not to rush anything between us, although we did kiss occasionally, which awakened a longing in me for intimacy. I didn't act on those feelings. It felt too soon. My head was still partially buried in the coma dream and hiding from the reality of my impending divorce. Miles had wasted no time having papers served. He was smart enough not to ask for anything, especially now that I had become so close to Oliver, who had helped me secure an attorney with a reputation for winning.

Holding Oliver's hand during our walks was not only comforting, but exciting. As the dream of my life with Parker slowly faded, so did the agony of knowing it had never been real. Even my grief for Ruby was transitioning. I didn't cry every time I thought about her, although admittedly, I still thought about her way too much. If I were to be perfectly honest, I still thought about Parker too, but my growing affection for Oliver no longer caused me to feel guilty. The New Year's Eve party at Angele would be our first opportunity to appear as a couple.

I heard a knock on the door and suddenly felt nervous. I couldn't remember the last time I had dressed up in party clothes. It felt strange to wear a glittery gold dress and high heels. The short, sleeveless gown exposed my pale, thin arms and legs, making me question if I was truly a ghost. Perhaps I had died when disappearing into the water that day with Parker and Ruby at Three Creek Lake. Maybe I was never meant to be a part of this world with Oliver. Maybe this was dreaming, and my time with Parker and Ruby had been real.

The scoop neck on my glittery dress showed the tiniest bit of cleavage, making it clear I was not a buxom blond. It was also evident my blond clouds of baby fine hair would never make a substantial braid, even if I had nothing to do but sit in a tower like Rapunzel and let it grow. Bright red lipstick diverted my attention from these self-conscious concerns, and so it was with confidence I answered the door. I instantly smiled, seeing Oliver standing there in a black tux. It looked so good on him I didn't quite know what to say.

"Oliver . . . you look quite dashing!"

"You look quite dashing yourself."

"Please . . . come inside."

Oliver stepped just inside my living room as if this was a first date. "Are you ready for this?" he asked.

"Ready for what? To have dinner with the most handsome and available bachelor in Napa?" I laughed while watching Oliver blush. He reminded me of a teenager, a bit unsure of himself.

"You think I'm handsome?"

"Of course. Hasn't anyone ever told you?"

"It's just that, well, I've met your Parker. I'm fairly certain I pale in comparison."

"Don't be silly, Oliver. And he's not my Parker. I'm not sure he ever was."

Oliver gently pulled me to him, the teenager in him gone, replaced with a man I was wanting to take to my bed this very minute. "Katya, if you need to find Parker and pursue a relationship with him, or maybe just have closure, the last thing I want to do is stand in your way."

I shrugged. "If Parker really cared about me, he'd be here. It isn't like I've been hiding under a rock. He knows where I live."

Oliver gently stroked my cheek. By the look in his eyes, I suspected he had always wanted to do that. "Parker struck me as the type of guy who wouldn't want to complicate things for you by interfering in your marriage, at least, any more than he already had."

"You're forgetting his brother said Parker left with another woman."

"He didn't know that for sure."

"Are you having second thoughts about us dating?" I asked.

Oliver pulled me even closer, and we kissed in a way that made it clear there were no second thoughts for either of us. Afterward I studied the look on his face and could see something was bothering him. "I have a confession to make, Katya. I am in love with you, and I have been ever since the ambulance brought you to the ER that night. Life stood still for a moment and has never been the same since. I wanted to make you well again more than I have ever wanted anything."

"But you didn't even know me, Oliver. I was just a damsel in distress, and you felt compelled to heal me, because you're compassionate and kind and dedicated to your profession."

"No. It was more than that. *You* were more than that, which frightened me at first. I thought perhaps I was losing it and had been alone too long. I should have made relationships more of a priority, instead of being married to my work."

I smiled at him. "That's true. Lorelei tells me you did work too hard and never took time to socialize."

Oliver kissed the top of my head. "I'm just glad you fell into my life, almost literally."

We both laughed.

"Me too," I said. "We're going to be late," I added. For a few seconds I wondered if we would go straight to the bedroom instead of exiting the house. The air held a tension that only getting naked and exploring each other on a different level could resolve, but we walked to Angele instead. The night air cooled us both off and soon we were engaged in small talk. We held hands the whole way, even boldly entering Angele hand in hand. Lorelei saw us immediately and her eyes sparkled. "It looks like you two have become more than just friends. I leave you alone for one week and look what happens!"

We each had a silly grin on our faces because we were at a loss for what to say. Lorelei ushered us to our table where we had our first romantic dinner. Lobster was a special menu item for the occasion. Oliver dipped a succulent piece into melted butter and fed it to me, so I returned the favor. We shared an excellent bottle of wine and afterward, we danced to a stringed quartet on the patio, all lit up with twinkle lights. At midnight fireworks went off in the park just a few blocks away. We could see them perfectly from Angele. The best fireworks, however, were the ones set off in me by Oliver, when we kissed at midnight. So many things went through my head, most importantly, that it was a new year with renewed hope. Suddenly the possibilities seemed endless.

ROMANCE

New Year's Day was spent playing cards at Oliver's house. He'd made a lamb stew and served it with freshly baked sourdough bread. He said the stew was his Aunt Ginni's recipe. Lorelei had especially loved it, which inspired me to make Grandma Rose's Shepherd's Pie for our lunch. It would double as dinner with Oliver. Cooking for him each night had become a fun diversion from my art obsession.

I couldn't believe how fast January sped by. Here it was one week into February, and I hadn't seen Lorelei since New Year's Day. Angele's night manager quit at the end of the year, and Lorelei hadn't found a suitable replacement. It kept her quite busy, managing both the lunch and dinner crowd. She swept in through the back door just as I took the savory pie from the oven. We hugged as if long lost relatives reuniting at a train station. Finally, Lorelei pulled back and looked into my eyes. "Where did the time go?"

"I don't know. It just got away from us, didn't it?"

"Katy, we need to get together once a week again."

"I do miss our Friday night bottle of wine," I confessed.

"I've hired a new night manager and won't need to be there on Friday evening anymore," Lorelei shared, looking perplexed. "Will that upset Oliver?"

"I think we can manage one night away from each other." I smiled and could feel my cheeks heating up. Thinking about Oliver made me blush for no reason lately.

Lorelei studied my rosy cheeked face. "Do you love him, Katy?"

I didn't answer right away. My feelings for Oliver were still unclear. With Parker I had been like a moth to the flame. Everything about him was exciting and irresistible. There had been no hesitation on my part. I loved him instantly and completely. Now, pain had taught me to think before I jump. I suspected my heart was not ready to let someone completely in.

"I'm not sure," I finally answered. "My feelings for Oliver are different than they were for Parker, but I never really knew Parker, did I? Anyone can be mesmerizing when you're just getting acquainted." What I didn't share with Lorelei was how most of what I thought I knew about Parker had come straight from my imagination while in a coma. "I don't believe in true love anymore. It was just a myth perpetuated by fairytales. Perhaps what I feel for Oliver is the real thing and what I felt for Parker was infatuation."

"Just be careful, Katy. Oliver has been in love with you since the first time he laid eyes on you in the emergency room. I'd hate to see him get hurt."

"If I didn't know better, Lorelei, I'd say you're in love with Oliver yourself." I looked her straight in the eye, hoping to see all the way to her heart, which I couldn't, no matter how hard I tried.

"Don't be silly. Oliver is just a dear friend. Nothing would make me happier than for the two people I enjoy most in the world to be a couple, that is, if you feel the same way about him as he feels about you. There's no need to rush into anything. That's all I'm saying. Take your time so you can be certain one way or the other."

"I am not rushing," I assured her. "He's been very patient with me. I feel a bit guilty about how slowly we are taking things."

"I thought as much. Oliver would never want to rush you. We both know you've been through a lot."

We changed the subject then, and I was grateful. When Oliver came by later for dinner, I told him Lorelei had been there and was worried I might hurt him.

"I'm a big boy, Katya. Lorelei needn't worry. Having you in my life has been the best thing for me lately. If you break it off, I will always be grateful for the time we had together."

"I think I'm the lucky one," I said, while clearing the dishes. Oliver was right behind me with the wine bottle. "Having you here every night has been a very different experience than living with Miles."

"I would hope so. I don't know what you ever saw in him."

"He's very charismatic and self-assured. It was appealing at the time. Besides, he was quite persistent. I know now it wasn't me he wanted so badly. It was Genevieve and the property she sits on. I also paid off his college loans with my father's estate money."

Oliver shook his head in dismay. "We should have a toast to your divorce being final."

I poured us each another glass of wine and we clinked them together before taking a sip. "I just wish he wasn't blaming me for all the things that have happened to him since I woke up," I confessed. "It makes me feel terribly uncomfortable."

"It's not your fault he's had felony charges brought against him and will no doubt be disbarred. His partners were appalled to discover he'd forged the will and estate planning so he could have your house and property."

"I know." I didn't tell Oliver how stressful all this was. First the divorce, and now I would have to appear in court to testify about the fake will and estate planning, not to mention forging an advanced directive for me. We left the kitchen and ended our unpleasant conversation about Miles. Oliver built a fire, and we watched *Casablanca*. It was our favorite Bogart movie. Old movies, we had discovered, were something else we had in common, and there wasn't much else to do until March when we could prepare the soil for our gardens. I hadn't decided yet if I wanted to continue as a micro farmer. It had lost its appeal. I still had a passion for tilling the earth and growing things, but on a much smaller scale and not as a business venture. I was ready to sell my art. At least, I had decided I would try and make a go of it. Sharing that news with Oliver cemented it in my mind.

"I think it's a great idea, Katya. I'm sure your art will sell for a good price. It's exquisite. Your new pieces, based on dreams you had while in a coma, are quite different from your earlier vineyard work, but it's all wonderful."

"Which do you like better?" I asked.

"It would be hard to choose. Every piece of your work has something intriguing about it."

"That's a very diplomatic answer," I said, and then I laughed. I was amused by his gift for diplomacy, but then my mood shifted. I thought about Ingrid Bergman in *Casablanca*, having to choose between two men she loved. I wondered who I would choose between Parker and Oliver, given the chance. I would never need to make that decision, I decided, because Parker had made it for me. According to Oliver, Parker had moved on, and I needed to as well.

"It's time for me to go." Oliver said this while looking at the clock, but he had said it rather unconvincingly. It was nearly midnight, and we were still intertwined on the sofa. He usually left around ten, but the fire was exceptionally cozy, and the movie was so thought-provoking. We lingered to discuss everything we loved about the Bogart film until Oliver grew quiet. I looked away from the fire and saw that he was studying me. He reached out and gently ran his hand through my hair, then drew me to him for a kiss. Every part of me wanted more. My feelings for Parker had been a blistering fire, whereas Oliver awoke in me a slow burning ember. I couldn't decide which was more appealing. He pulled back and looked into my eyes, sensing I was ready for more.

"Are you sure?" he asked.

I didn't answer. Instead, I pulled off my sweater. It was getting too hot in the room, and I wanted to heat things up even more. Soon our clothing was strung from the sofa to the bedroom, where we spent the night making love. We would doze for a while in each other's arms, and then our passion would rise again until by morning we were both spent, and since it was Oliver's day off, we slept until noon.

VENDETTAS

Oliver and I made love beneath the pulsating shower head when we'd finally awakened and dragged ourselves out of bed. Then we dressed and he made coffee while I threw on a jacket and ran across the street. I headed straight for the bakery and bought cranberry scones. When I returned, we ate our scones and drank our coffee on the front porch while people-watching, which was an interesting endeavor by midafternoon on First Street. When nearly finished with our little feast a man hesitated and then stopped on the sidewalk directly below us. To our amazement it was Miles. He stood across from Genevieve's small front lawn and stared up at Oliver and me. We both approached the porch rail to acknowledge his presence. At first we were both tongue-tied, but then Oliver found his voice. "Miles, what can we do for you?"

"It isn't what you can do. It's what you've done."

"Anything that has happened to you," Oliver answered, "you've done to yourself."

Miles kept staring up at us in a strange way that made me feel uncomfortable.

"I wouldn't have needed to forge those documents if Katya had listened to me when I wanted them drawn up last winter," he pointed out, in a voice I almost didn't recognize. It was scratchy, as if his throat was raw from smoking. He looked like he'd been up all-night drinking, maybe many nights, judging by the circles under his eyes.

"I'm being slapped with felony charges and no doubt will be disbarred." Miles punctuated every word as if they were a knife in his heart.

"You should have thought about that before you forged those papers." Oliver's tone was steady and calm. It didn't, however, ease the tension in the air.

"Meghan's gone. She has no use for a washed-up attorney who might go to prison." Miles glared at me. "If only you had died, Katya."

His words made me shiver. I took a step back from the railing and folded my arms tight against my chest while Oliver responded. "You would never have inherited this property, Miles. Katya wants this house and the land it sits on to stay in her family. Ideally it would have gone to your children, but then, you never intended to have children, did you, Miles?"

Miles didn't seem to be listening to what Oliver was saying. He just kept standing there on the sidewalk, staring up at us. He was unsteady and swayed slightly. Oliver and I were at a loss for what to say or do when Miles suddenly swung his arms out and said, "Poof! I have nothing and no one, and both of you to thank for it." Then he laughed. It sounded more like coughing or choking but was clearly meant to be laughter. I had never seen him in such a state. His hair was dirty and messy, not carefully gelled and combed like usual. His clothes were wrinkled as if he hadn't changed in days. The signature white shirt was half untucked. The always-present tie was missing. Who knew where he'd left his custom-tailored suit jacket?

What happened next will always be a blur to me. Everything unfolded so quickly. The testimony of tourists, who were eyewitnesses, would later help me toward filling in details about the events of that afternoon. I remember thinking what a sad state Miles was in, and how fiercely he blamed me for his condition. It never occurred to me he might not be in his right mind. I do recall a portion of the porch trim coming loose and swinging freely, precisely when Miles began rummaging through his pants pocket. The gingerbread trim had loosened during the last storm. I meant to secure it but never had. Now, as if on cue, one section had dropped down and was swinging back and forth right in front of me. Oliver's attention had been diverted to the fallen trim, which nearly hit me when coming loose. He'd reached over to stop it from swinging, which blocked my view of Miles, so I couldn't see what he pulled from his pocket.

But I heard it.

Three shots rang out and nearly pierced my ear drums. After the first shot Oliver pushed me down onto the porch, or as I now believe, he fell, and I ended up beneath him. By then a second shot had fired and just one more after that. It was all over in a matter of seconds. I remember feeling suffocated by Oliver's body, while a pool of blood oozed out around us. There was so much of it, I assumed we'd both been shot. I lay there, unable to move, and prayed Oliver would be okay. I fervently hoped with all my heart that most of the blood was my own.

Paramedics soon arrived and took us both by ambulance to the hospital, where no one would tell me about Oliver's condition. They insisted on admitting me for observation, even though as it turned out, I hadn't been shot at all. The doctors worried I might have a concussion from falling onto the porch floor beneath Oliver. He had literally been my human shield. I have no doubt he meant to fall directly on top of me, to keep me safe.

I tossed and turned all night in the hospital, plagued by the sound of those three shots ringing out. I hadn't inquired about Miles, but I hoped he was dead, and the final bullet had been for himself. I could still feel Oliver's warm blood oozing over me, his limp body nearly crushing my lungs. I remembered whispering in his ear *Oliver are you okay, my darling?* I continually heard people running and shouting as if it were all still happening. I heard sirens ringing louder and louder which caused me to bolt upright in the bed and cover my ears with my hands. A pool of blood on the porch flashed before me as I sat there staring into darkness with my hands on my ears. A nurse came and turned on the light. She gave me a pill and some water, and when I awoke, Lorelei was sitting beside me. "What happened?" I asked. "How is Oliver?"

Lorelei took my hand and looked me right in the eye. Hers were filled with tears. She couldn't speak at first, but then she whispered, "He's gone, Katy."

"What do you mean he's gone?" My head was groggy, and I couldn't absorb the meaning of her words.

"He passed away before the ambulance even got there," she explained, and then Lorelei broke down. She buried her head in my shoulder and sobbed. I gently stroked her hair with a shaky hand. Tears streamed down my face and into my hospital gown until it was soaked through from both our tears. A nurse delivered a breakfast tray and gently set it on the table beside the bed. Then she left as quietly as she had come. Once the nurse was gone Lorelei sat up and tried to pull herself together.

"Where is Miles?" I asked.

"He's dead. Shot himself in the head after shooting Oliver and attempting to shoot you, too." Lorelei stared out the window. Her eyes were angry red and still quite wet. "Oliver saved you, Katy. He's a hero."

It was all clear to me then. I think it had been clear from the minute that first shot rang out, but I didn't want to believe it. I didn't want Oliver to die for me. I especially didn't want him to be shot by Miles. I chose not to believe it. Now I had no choice. I dressed without saying a word and we exited the hospital without officially checking me out. A nurse came running down the hall after us explaining that I needed more observation and a few more tests. Neither of us turned around to address her. Slightly bent over and leaning on each other we trudged down the hall and out the door, leaving behind the stifling hospital air, filled with pain and sadness and death.

We couldn't spend another minute in a place that held so much of Oliver and was so empty without him.

Lorelei drove us to her house. I stayed for a week. We took long walks and cooked simple meals together. We sat quietly for hours on her patio and stared at the winery behind her home, with its rows and rows of dead, tangled vines. That was exactly how I felt inside, dead and tangled. It was just as well there had been no funeral service. Oliver's body had been shipped back to wherever his remaining family lived. And life went on, outside of my dead and tangled insides that could not fathom losing the only man other than Parker I had ever dared to love.

Lorelei packed enough things to stay for a week when she brought me home. She'd wanted me to stay at her house longer, but I told her it was time to face reality. Oliver was gone, along with Parker and Ruby and Grandma Rose and my father. Everyone I loved was gone except for Lorelei, of course. I told her it wasn't necessary to stay with me, but she insisted I shouldn't be alone, not yet, not after the horrible crime that had happened right in front of Genevieve. We sat in her SUV and stared at the back porch for the longest time, neither of us having the courage to exit the vehicle.

"I think Genevieve helped save me," I said, in a tired voice.

"What do you mean, Katy? How did Genevieve save you?" I looked at Lorelei for the first time since we'd left her house. She was as disheveled as I felt.

"The decorative trim on the porch fell at the exact moment Miles pulled out a gun. It was swinging in front of us when Oliver reached above me to stop it from swinging. He had almost completely blocked my body when that first shot rang out. The shot meant for me." Tears trickled down my face again and it was surprising to have any left.

Lorelei began to cry again, too.

"Am I crazy to think Genevieve saved me as much as Oliver did?"

Lorelei smiled through her tears. "It was your grandmother, Katy. I have always felt your Grandma Rose in the house. No doubt she was there, saving you from Miles. She never liked him, you know."

"That's true," I agreed. "I remember how random things always fell on his toes, and how often the doors would mysteriously stick for him."

We laughed, despite our grief, and then we hugged one another tightly. It gave us the courage to leave the vehicle and walk up the porch steps. My feet felt like heavy bricks and my hands fumbled forever with the key in the lock, until I somehow managed to open the door. Lorelei and I had the same thought and walked straight through the house to the front porch. We needed to face what we dreaded most, the scene of the crime. Only then could we truly process what happened. We already knew someone had washed all the blood from the porch and fixed the trim. When we approached the rail and looked down below, the sidewalk was also devoid of any evidence. It was almost as if it had never happened, except for the part where Oliver was dead and Miles was no doubt burning in hell, exactly where he belonged.

"I loved him, you know." Lorelei said this as if it were a known fact, and then collapsed into one of the rattan chairs.

I studied her, sitting there all crumpled in defeat, weary of living. She looked the way I felt. "Oliver?"

"Yes. I never told anyone. Not even him, especially not him. But it's true."

"I had no idea you loved him more than as a friend. I asked you once and you denied it. Now I truly feel terrible," I said, while collapsing into the other rattan chair."

"Don't. There was nothing anyone could do about it. He was crazy in love with you from the moment you entered the ER that day. He shared with me once that you reminded him of a very special someone that got away."

"If you mean Amelia, Oliver told me about her. He didn't mention that I reminded him of her. That explains a lot," I said. "How else could he have loved me from the minute he first saw me? It was because he longed for someone he couldn't have."

"No, Katy. That's not why he loved you. It was just what drew him to you in the first place. Every day after that he fell more and more in love with the real you. At first it was just the fascinating life you lived before the fall, but then later it was from spending time with you."

"That must have been so hard for you to watch." I didn't think I could feel any worse, and yet I did.

Lorelei laughed. "Life is a riddle, isn't it? If only we could solve the mysteries of the heart."

"If only," I agreed.

"It's okay, Katy. It was never meant to be, not for me and Oliver."

"Or me and Parker," I added.

We were both quiet for a minute, lost in our own thoughts, until Lorelei decided we needed wine. She went into the house and returned shortly with a vintage cabernet and basket of food we'd brought from her house. We nibbled on smoked gouda and rye crackers, fresh raspberries and dark chocolate, without tasting a thing. Neither of us said a word while observing tourists on First Street. They all seemed so happy, obviously unaware of the recent bloodbath on this porch, or the overwhelming and incomprehensible grief we felt. They couldn't know a Dr. Oliver Easton had laid down his life to save a damsel in distress, or how because of that, nothing would ever be the same.

THE FUTURE

February dragged into March and my heart felt dormant like seeds in the earth waiting for spring. The only difference was not knowing if my heart would burst forth with life again. I cried until there were no tears left. There wasn't a day I didn't walk down to the river at one end of First Street, or along the boardwalk by the docks at the other end. I threw rocks into the rising tide waters and watched the ripples grow bigger until they disappeared, just as I had done with Oliver. His smiling face would appear in the widening circles and then fade into nothingness, just as he had.

Mostly, I sat on the porch and watched people walk by. I had no desire to do art. All the vivid images in my head from the coma dream had turned into vivid images of Oliver and I lying on the porch floor in a pool of blood. Lorelei joined me on Friday nights, on this same porch where he'd lost his life and saved mine. We would drink our bottle of wine together as always, and eat the food she brought, but no longer with the appetite we used to have. We didn't talk or laugh like we had always done in the past. We simply stared at the stars in silence. When she left, we'd hug tightly as if we might never see each other again, because life was so uncertain.

Both of us seemed to have lost our compass.

I felt compelled to till the earth and plant something—what, exactly, I hadn't decided. Then one day I heard Parker's voice. *After we moved to Oregon you planted a rose garden where your micro farm had been.* That settled it. I would plant roses, just as my grandmother Rose had done.

April finally made an appearance and the world seemed to be sitting correctly on its axis again. Days were longer and flowers were blooming. Birds were building nests, and I was certain now that I was pregnant. On the night Oliver and I made love we didn't worry about me getting pregnant because my period had not returned since the coma. Besides, we had both wanted children. We hadn't talked about marriage yet. I knew it was because Oliver didn't want to rush me, but he did say that if I were to get pregnant, he'd welcome a reason to shortcut our courtship.

After his death I thought perhaps grief was adding to my lack of a period, but then I began to feel differently. My hormones were changing, so I took a test. Oliver's baby would be born in November. Ruby's birthday in the dream had been in November, and I could never figure out why, because Parker's child would have been born in late April. Now I knew. Oliver was Ruby's father, not Parker. But then again, Ruby was just a dream. Or was she?

I'd been sitting in my usual spot on the front porch watching tourists along First Street, headed to the wine bars and brew pubs, restaurants, and quaint clothing shops. I'd often frequented those shops. I bought the rose-colored dress in one of them. The same dress Parker said I wore when I entered the tasting room that day, after having disappeared for months.

On impulse I went to my closet and started rummaging through it. Something rose-colored fell off a hanger and onto the closet floor. It seemed to have fallen for no apparent reason and I couldn't help but think Grandma Rose was there, in spirit. I could almost feel her watching me. I picked the dress up and stared at it for a full minute. So much had happened since my last visit to the vineyard. I had lost Parker's baby, a month of my life, and Oliver. A single tear fell and made a wet spot on the dress, but I pulled myself together and put it on.

Looking in the mirror was still like looking at a ghost. I put on lipstick, hoping it would help. After finding suitable sandals in the back of the closet I stood in the doorway, not sure whether to exit or turn around and crawl into my bed. It seemed like a suitable place to hide from all the might-have-beens and never-will-bes threatening to consume me. However, instead of retreating under my covers, I flew out of Genevieve in a sudden burst of courage. I was determined to make one final attempt at fulfilling what I hoped was my destiny.

Crow watched approvingly from the fence as I walked boldly to the Jeep. All the way to the vineyard I kept recalling what Parker had said. *Rosy, you just showed up one day. I was pouring wine for a tasting when you stepped inside the entryway. It was a slow afternoon and the couple I poured for had been our only patrons. I stared at you, standing there in a rose-colored sundress with those blond curls hovering about your head.*

I parked the car and sat quietly looking out the window at the tasting room. My body had begun to shake, despite it being quite warm for early April. It took all the confidence I had not to drive back home. More of Parker's words came to me. It felt like he was right there, whispering them in my ear. *You looked like an angel straight from heaven . . . with the sun streaming in the window and lighting your hair on fire. I was speechless, as if watching a visitation from beyond this world.*

Maybe that's what I really was, a visitor from another world. I couldn't be sure at this point, but I was about to find out. I looked around the empty parking lot and decided there wouldn't be many people inside, which gave me courage to enter the tasting room. The minute I stepped in the doorway I saw Parker pouring wine for a couple at the bar. My heart nearly stopped, and my breath caught in my throat. Sun was streaming in the window, nearly blinding me, but I was sure it was Parker. The next thing I knew he was walking toward me, just as he had said he'd done in the dream. Watching him walk across the tasting room caused me to have an epiphany.

What I dreamed while in a coma hadn't happened yet.

"Rosy, I thought I might never see you again." Parker stared at me as if I were a ghost, and quite frankly, I felt like one. Neither of us moved, as if frozen to the entryway floor, or perhaps frozen in time.

"Why didn't you look for me?" I asked.

"You were a married woman, Rose. It wasn't my place to seek you out. I believed you'd come back to me, but you never did."

I was silent for a minute until I blurted out the truth which I'd kept from him all this time. "I was pregnant with our child, Parker. I was going to divorce Miles and come to you with the good news, but then I fell and lost the baby."

Parker looked as if suddenly in pain.

"I fell in love with the doctor who helped me recover. It is his child I'm carrying now, but his life tragically ended."

"I fell in love with someone, too," Parker confessed. "But I couldn't commit to her. I couldn't get you out of my head, Rose. You've ruined me for anyone else."

I smiled through my tears. "The doctor I loved briefly was a good man, but I couldn't quit thinking about you, either."

Parker took my hand and led me out the back door and into the vineyard, where we sat on a bench. It was just as he had described it in the dream. We studied one another as if neither of us could believe this moment was happening. Whatever we said was a blur to me, but it sounded familiar, until Parker reached up and gently touched my face. "Marry me, Rose. There is nothing I would rather do than be a father to your baby."

I didn't answer him. It was all so overwhelming. Parker reached over and kissed me, causing so many pent-up feelings to come rushing forward. I had never felt so alive as I did at that moment. We held one another as if afraid we might once again be torn apart.

"I want to raise the baby in Oregon," I said in a muffled voice, with my face buried in Parker's chest. "I want our baby to experience the mountains and rivers, and forests of my childhood." I looked up at him then, and he was beaming with joy.

"I've always dreamed of buying a ranch on the high desert where the sky is big and blue." Parker smiled and his eyes lit up. "We could call it Desert Sky."

"I hope this baby is a girl with red hair. We could call her Ruby," I said enthusiastically, knowing full well that was exactly what would happen. "Would you like that?" I asked, with tears streaming down my face.

"Rosy," Parker answered, his own eyes filled with tears. "I'd like that very much."

REFERENCES

Quotes from *Alice's Adventures in Wonderland,* by Lewis Carroll:

Page 61:
Imagination is the only weapon in the war against reality.

Page 94:
I wonder if the snow loves the trees and fields, that it kisses them so gently? And then it covers them up snug, you know, with a white quilt; and perhaps it says, 'Go to sleep darlings, till the summer comes again.'

Page 142:
"How long is forever?"
"Sometimes just one second."
"If you knew Time as well as I do," said the Hatter, "you wouldn't talk about wasting it."

Page 186:
Have I gone mad? I'm afraid so, but let me tell you something, the best people usually are.

ACKNOWLEDGEMENTS

MJ Kuhar has given me invaluable input while penning Katya. As a fellow writer herself, she has tirelessly helped me to stay inspired and on task during every phase of this book. I can't thank her enough for sticking with me throughout the entire process, during which she has become a good friend.

Shauna Berry has been a godsend with content editing for Katya. She is an insightful and thorough editor, and I am lucky to call her friend. I cannot thank Shauna enough for her much-needed encouragement. She has faithfully championed the writing of this book, which helped me persevere when having moments of doubt.

My oldest daughter, Sasha Mattingly, has once again helped me clean up whatever was overlooked regarding typos, inconsistencies, or questionable content. I am indebted to her for always finding a few problematic issues everyone else (including me) has missed.

Finally, I want to acknowledge my husband and best friend, Dennis, who has put up with my obsessed and reclusive writerly ways all these years. He has always been my biggest fan and my closest confidant. I am eternally grateful for his ongoing love and support.

ABOUT THE AUTHOR

Kat Mattingly enjoys teaching creative writing at her local college when not busy penning her own work. She has won recognition for outstanding fiction in both long and short form. Kat lives on the high desert in Central Oregon with her husband Dennis and their Maine Coon cat, Atticus. Her favorite quote is: "You know, the farthest distance in the world is between how it is and how you thought it was gonna be," from the film *The Only Living Boy in New York City*, written by American screenwriter Allan Loeb.